Winter's Tales 18

EDITED BY

A. D. MACLEAN

MACMILLAN
ST MARTIN'S PRESS

SBN boards: 333 12410 3

First published 1972 by
MACMILLAN LONDON LTD
London and Basingstoke
Associated companies in Toronto Dublin
Melbourne Johannesburg and Madras
ST MARTIN'S PRESS INC
NEW YORK

Library of Congress Catalog Card: 55–13894

Printed in Great Britain by
THE BARLEYMAN PRESS
Bristol

CONTENTS

ACKNOWLEDGEMENTS

The stories are copyright respectively:

© Brian Aldiss 1972
© Melvyn Bragg 1972
© Freda Bromhead 1972
© Manoj Das 1972
© Andrew Graham 1971
© John Haylock 1972
© Susan Hill 1972
© Roy Holland 1972
© Anne (Marriott) McLellan 1972
© Frank Tuohy 1972

Andrew Graham's *Bird of Paradise* has been published in the *Illustrated London News*

Susan Hill's *The Custodian* has been published in a limited edition by the Covent Garden Press

EDITOR'S NOTE

Winter's Tales no doubt attains some sort of legal maturity on this its eighteenth birthday. Whatever its record of credits and demerits may be, it can at least claim to have survived without the loss of a faithful caucus of readers. We can still hope that supporters of the story – short or long – will grow in numbers. Once again we offer an annual collection in which mood, length and style vary considerably, but in which, I hope readers will agree, the contributions are pretty evenly matched in terms of quality.

BRIAN ALDISS

A TRAIL of prisoners wound slowly upwards along a mountain track until it reached the outer gates of Khernabhar Prison. There it waited in bright sunshine until the gates rolled open. Goaded on by their warders, the prisoners moved into the enclosure beyond.

The gates closed behind the prisoners, and were bolted. They stood in a courtyard formed between wall and cliff, the cliff of the great Mount Khernabhar. Offices stood in the courtyard, stern but dejected, their windows blank and dusty. A trough stood in one corner of the courtyard, against the rock; the prisoners were allowed to go over to it and drink.

Axel Mathers moved over with the other prisoners. He scooped up water and poured the first handful over his face; then he drank. As he sucked the water from his hands, he stared down into the trough, where water ran clear and deep.

The interior of the trough was rough. Pebbles and small plants could be seen, lucid under the water's disturbed surface. Although sun shone full on the trough, the liquid was brilliantly cold, cutting at a man's throat as it went down. It spurted into the trough from a fissure in the rock, spurted out of Khernabhar itself, spurted from the intestines of the great mountain. Because he knew the terrible legends of Khernabhar, Mathers found himself cocking an ear towards the fissure, half-expecting to hear human cries issue from it.

He still could not believe that the sentence of the Dictator Hener's courts was to be carried out – oh, yes, the others would serve their term, but surely for him some last minute reprieve would come! For him! He found that his every gesture was heavy with deliberation and that everywhere he cast his eye in that dreary courtyard he saw beauty. The very shards of rock tumbled from the mighty rock-face were miraculously cast and coloured. Everything was rare and beautiful – the dust, even the dust, because it would never be seen again!

He looked in the girl prisoner's face, reading there the same anxiety to draw in every memory of the world of light. He knew her first name: Joanna. Like him, she was sentenced for crimes against the State. She wore a ragged skirt that stretched down to her ankles, a long-sleeved blouse, and a poncho. Her thin face, her dark hair, were streaked with the dust that had accompanied them from the last ugly village on the plain. Yet she was attractive, the line of her nose, the line between her nose and mouth, the line of her mouth, possessing a mysterious and painful logic which was beyond words. It was easier to look at the trough, the dust, the stones, than at her face.

The party – it comprised twenty-one prisoners – was allowed to sit in the dirt and wait. Every minute spent here in the sunlight was precious. Mathers sat next to the girl while the guards who had made the trek up from the plain argued with the guards of the prison. Poor oafs – each side envied the other its job! The guards from the plain had brought drink to sell to the prison guards; the prison guards complained that the prices were too high. Slowly, cretinously, they bandied their dreary small change of language – and a minor language at that, hardly spoken outside the boundaries of the nation, not even universally spoken inside! Yet were the guards not to be envied? Would they not all, over the next years, be allowed their stupidities, their drunks, their randies, even their deaths, under the ever-changing sky?!

The bargaining was concluded. Bottles and money changed

hands. There was coarse laughter and most of the guards moved towards the guard room.

The guards remaining got the party to its feet again and moved it forward. Driven on by their curses, the prisoners pushed through inner gates, the mountainside moving in above them. Mathers looked up – saw a tribe of monkeys away above their heads, free to scamper over the slopes. He saw the shoulder of the mountain swing overhead, saw the sun, saw the sun eclipsed by mountain. He caught the expression on Joanna's face. Impulsively, they grasped each other's hands.

All the prisoners were clasping each other. No longer was there need for the guards to curse them. Shadow had fallen on them; they had no further will to resist. Now they heard the moan and grumble – rock itself complaining – of Khernabhar Prison!

That voice! It came from ahead, yet from all sides. They were moving in a tunnel now, and so had opportunity to note the sound well, to analyse – as the least intelligent among them must have done – how it seemed to comprise many of the noises of the animal kingdom, squeaks, squeals, moans, groans, bellows, chirps. They might have been entering some hideous underground farm in which everything from crickets and birds to sows and bullocks and still mightier animals were confined. Yet there was no noise but rock moving on rock. Nothing lay ahead but rock. There was no destiny but rock.

The corridor widened into an underground chamber. No daylight reached this far: the darkness was broken by torch-light and by a long gutter which ran with a tarry substance that burned. This tarry substance dripped into a tank sunk in the floor of the chamber. Guards were dipping wooden brands into the tank.

Now the noise was louder; its full melancholy din beat upon them like the wings of some vast and weary creature in flight – some reptilian prehistoric bird that screamed as it pulled its weight over lands unknown.

With the noise came the odour . . . and that too seemed
to move in from the reptilian distances of buried past-time. It
was an ancient and dirty odour, trailing across the back of the
throat a flavour of corrupt piscine flesh. Yet so great were the
other pressures on this doomed gathering, that it moved forward as if merely through a growing twilight.

*Now it's coming – it's coming! I have no fear. This is not
death for me, not death but a new chance. At last, I have this
chance to be better – inwardly to be better. Whatever happens,
an inner part of me can learn to be better. If I can stand it,
for my own good, as well as the good of the revolution. . .*

One of the guards thrust a torch into Mathers' hand and
pushed him forward. He noticed the girl took care to remain
close to him. She evidently drew some reassurance from him,
looking up now and then – but more with an air of appraisal
than appeal, he noted. Many things he noted; all were sub-
ordinate, mere insignificant details glimpsed under the skirts
of his black cloud of awareness.

What did overwhelm his attention was sight of the moving
prison itself. The guards were prodding Joanna towards it,
holding him back, holding the others back behind, separating
them. The visible part of the prison loomed before the girl –
they were thrusting her into a cell that had already half-
disappeared into squealing, grunting darkness.

It was an open cell with no front wall. A cell, then a thick
dividing wall, and then another cell. And then another dividing wall and another cell. Open cells: no doors, no front walls.
She was pushed into the first cell and Mathers into the next
one. The prisoner behind him was being readied for the following cell.

Clutching his torch, Mathers stood glaring out at his cap-

tors, at the dingy and muddled scene – but it was a scene from
life, it existed, however precariously, on the fringes of the
free world, it lay but a lung's breath away from open sky and
running animals and the elaborate affairs of men. As he stood
there, trying to memorise even the coarse faces of the guards,
the cell gave a lurch and, with grinding slowness, moved a few
inches to his right, reproducing all round him the noise of
tortured animals.

To step into the cells, it was necessary to walk across a narrow gap which separated cells from cavern. The cells containing Mathers, the girl, and the next prisoner ground and
bumped to one side. A pause, and then they moved again, an
inch, half a dozen inches, a few more, stop . . . After another
pause, this movement was repeated to the accompaniment of
more anguished squeals of sandstone on sandstone. Already
the cell containing Joanna had disappeared behind a wall of
rock and could be seen no more from the underground chamber.

The cells had only another fifteen or so feet to move before
Mathers too would find himself cut off from human view.
He stood – crouched, rather, staring out, wondering if he
should not spring forward and run for corridor and daylight.
But the guards stared back, for once looking orderly and
efficient, waiting for him to make a reckless move. He observed
that further guards were herding the rest of the prisoners into
a side-passage – perhaps to wait there until the slow progres-
sion of cells brought more empty ones into view. So he was cut
off from the poor specimens of humanity with whom he had
shared many painful days' imprisonment in the town on the
plains, with whom he had made the ascent to this more dreadful place; although he had no particular friends among them,
regret leapt in him as they were driven from sight.

The cells lurched again, roaring cruelly as they moved. Only
a few inches, painfully uncertain, but now on his right he

saw protruding the edge of the cavern wall that would eventually cover his cell and eclipse him entirely from the outside
world. He looked at it, reached out to touch it, saw how the
rock had been reinforced with heavy stone blocks, making a
pillar. As he touched it, the vibrations and squeals began again
and the cells again jolted forward. When the movement and
noise died, Mathers heard the man in the cell on his left weeping. He himself knew only paralysis, and could not weep or
pray. As for the girl, whose cell had now disappeared into the
rock, he heard not a sound from her.

*There is still time. Someone will come forward. My friends
will have managed to secure a reprieve. The guards will re-
lent. Or I shall wake . . Wake, wake, damn you, out of this
nightmare . . .*

Again the lateral movement, the pause, the movement again.
He roused partly out of his paralysis to take stock of his cell.
It was carved from solid sandstone, even elaborately carved at
its outer end, where pillars had been fashioned in the wall-ends
betwen cells, chunky pillars with an archaic motif binding
them. The cell held a wooden bed with a mattress on, and no
other furniture. At the rear of the cell was a double trough, its
two compartments, one below the other, filled with water that
trickled in from a groove in the rear wall; the overflow of the
water ran down into a hole in the floor evidently intended for
sanitary purposes. The side walls, roughly carved from the
rock, were covered with the graffiti of past incumbents of the
cell.

*Sandstone – weathered only by the hands of prisoners, hewn
eternities ago . . . And, if the rumours are true, a spell of
imprisonment here means ten years. Ten years . . . Oh, Lord,
ten years, where is Thy justice?*

On one wall was carved the figure of an old stooped man with a long beard, beautifully picked out in an antique mode. Mathers glanced at it in cursory fashion, reflecting that all prisoners would look similarly stooped by the time they emerged into daylight once more. He ran his fingertips despairingly over the surface of the rock, feeling the very texture of injustice.

God knows, I should not be here – I have done no wrong . . . Yet however false my conviction, all men are sinners. I'm guilty of many things. Perhaps we all deserve punishment . . .

As he was setting his torch in a socket in the wall, the slow movement came again; his small world grated forward inch by inch, as if the whole mountain of Khernabhar were in action. The movement spoke of a vast and weary suffering, the last tremors of a dying man; while the negation of movement that followed spoke of death itself.

And now the fourth wall had moved across the front of his cell more than half way. His view of the cavern, the guards, the trough of pitch, was through a gap of less than six feet. He felt his spirit drifting out of him like smoke.

How much time passed, Mathers could not tell. After a long lethargic pause – the short lethargic movement, and a further narrowing of his view of the outer world. He sank down to await the strong eclipse. The vigil was punctuated by a guard coming and throwing him a bundle of food and an unlit torch, and by a struggle between the guards and the captive next door, who tried to break out; he was badly beaten about the head and kicked in the stomach before being dragged back into his cell. Mathers heard him groan occasionally.

Again the shuddering movement, the screams from the rock. Over Mathers, an annihilating numbness.

Why do I feel as I do? Nothing so terrible has ever happened to me before, no, nothing ever approaching this . . . It affronts the name of humanity. So why am I possessed by the idea that this pain is something I have suffered before? When, where, could I have suffered anything remotely as terrifying? My dear mother took such tender care of me in childhood that I was never suffered to be shut in a cupboard or chest. Darkness did not scare me. I had no fears — why, then, along with everything else, am I forced to bear this burden of an unmindful familiarity?

Hardly aware that he did so, he wept for his parents, now dead, and for the life they had given him, now to be stolen away. When he looked up, the cells had jarred on again in their journey into the rock, and only the narrowest gap permitted him to look at the world of the cavern. In anguish and surprise, he jumped up, threw himself at the gap, thrust his arm through, gesturing at the mean company of guards. He called to them, begging for mercy. They looked at each other and grinned almost enough to reveal their teeth.

The grinding began again, and the lurch forward. As the gap narrowed still further, he had to pull back his arm quickly or it would have been wrenched from him at the shoulder between outer wall and cell wall. He stopped his cries and stood quiet as the vibrating movement closed the space inch by inch. When the movement stopped, there was a gap here and there, at no place wider than an inch, to which he could apply his eye and see the guards still there in the cavern, talking among themselves, more casual now he had been carried from their view.

Later, the grinding began again, and this time it carried him and his cell completely into the rock and away from the world of men. Mathers collapsed against one wall, burying his face in his hands.

The revolution must come! Some day soon, it must come! Our country cannot bear this oppression much longer . . . Help me to survive till then, oh Lord! The regime must be eradicated to the last man, and this hellish prison destroyed for ever.

Sinking into the well of his thoughts, he was a long time in realising that the tempo of movement and stillness had been broken. Now was only stillness. He jumped up in vague alarm, he stood there, he waited. Silence alone greeted him, pressed hard against his ears. The world of men was only a pace or so away – yet already it had sunk below the horizons of his awareness.

Movement had stopped. How long had it continued? Certainly not more than four hours, probably not less than two; for that sound as of animals being slaughtered had commenced only as Mathers and the others were ushered into the tunnel. From the legends he had heard of Khernabhar, he knew what this cessation meant, and his eyes turned instinctively to an object that had come into view on the outer wall, the rock face that cut him off from humanity.

The object consisted of an iron ring from which hung a length of chain. Mathers went over and lifted the heavy links. The boss that held the ring was firmly secured into the rock. He let the chain drop. The links clanked and hung still. He stood there motionless, his gaze locked to the dull length of chain. The horror of his situation was with him like a dark and invisible companion. His journey into the rock had begun.

At some featureless later moment in time, he came to himself again, his brain began to function along more normal channels, prompted by recognition of sound. When he turned his attention to it, a rush of small noise came to him, an underworld of sound that at first brought him only further terror.

Later, as the journey into the sandstone went deeper, after his torches had failed and died and he was alone in the dark of the mountain, he began to identify individual sounds, to force meaning from them, to hammer them into substitutes for those other senses of which he was bereft. Foremost among these were the sounds of water.

Mathers's water supply in the trough had its own collection of delicate noises. Its drips and splashes were close at hand, and generally as regular as clocks. They were busy and comforting noises, noises whose source he could verify by touch. Frivolous noises.

The next nearest water noises sprang from the first series. They were deeper in tone, on the whole continuous, and solemn noises. They flowed in particular under the mobile floor of the cells, as if some deep groove ran there to bear the water further yet into the stone heart of Khernabhar. These were lazy noises, which sometimes sounded reassuring, sometimes menacing.

Distant noises came into two categories. Ever-present but intermittent were various drips and plops that stirred Mathers's imagination when he lay helpless in the dark, listening; by concentrating on these distant sounds, he could imagine that he was not incarcerated in a mountain but stood in one of the rain-forests which covered the northern half of his country. These watery messages gave him illusions of freedom, as did other distant sounds, for they became voices of brooks, waterfalls, and torrents – interior brooks, waterfalls, and torrents, cascading through the entrails of Khernabhar, similar enough acoustically to remind him of waters washing slopes of mountain-jungles which he had explored with his father in his youth.

This last category of water-sound came and faded, and Mathers grew familiar with it only as day succeeded day, and week week, and the cells moved further into the mountain.

With other subterranean noises, he was less comfortable. Along with the prisoners in their cells travelled other living things, mice, spiders, insects, possibly even snakes and bats — but chiefly rats, whose activities roused him from many an uneasy sleep.

Sometimes, patches of strange light would float before his eyes. He imagined himself to be going blind until he discovered that the outer wall was sometimes smeared with phosphorescence and gave off a phantom light. He would stand with his eyes almost touching it, trying to imagine it to be the blessed glare of daylight that bathed them.

By this time, routine — the iron and remorseless routine of Khernabhar — had gripped him. The one focal point of the day came every morning with a scattered tapping, rapidly growing in volume. Although he was generally prepared for the summons, Mathers would start up and begin to hammer on the wall himself with a piece of rock. This was the signal to begin the day's haul!

He would then feel in the dark for the chain hanging from the outer wall. The chains punctuated the outer wall. Wherever the cell stopped, somewhere there was a chain to haul on.

The haul began. No movement at first, then a jerky start. Unison was soon achieved. The prisoners heaved on their chains together, unseen and unknown to each other. With squeals of protest rock began to grind over rock . . .

It was an enormously exhausting, an impossible task. Yet the cells moved. They moved only a few inches before rest was necessary. And then the effort had to be made again. And again. Over and over.

Being a methodical man, Mathers tried to keep track of time by counting. He came to believe that they generally worked for between two-and-a-half to three hours — nearer the latter mostly, but the strain varied according, he presumed, to the roughness of the ground underneath the cells.

The distance they moved was easier to compute, although it too varied. It was about twenty-two or twenty-three feet in one session. There was only one session a day: a morning's exhausting work.

When he had rested from the haul, Mathers habitually made an exploration of the newly exposed section of outer wall. He ran his fingers over the surface, arms outstretched. It was his way of mapping as best he could the dreadful journey inwards, and he worked his way along from end to end, from bottom to top, with methodical care.

The wall was by no means the smooth surface it had seemed at first casual glance. It had been scarred by numerous parallel lines, graphs of the moving walls, incised by small stone outcrops on the latter. There were other lines, too, and arabesques and patterns, carved by prisoners. Sometimes, a fault in the rock had caused part of the wall to crumble. In one place, the wall was extensively faulted, the fault extending over three days' travel. Mathers was as excited as if he had discovered a new landscape. He noted that the fault had been carefully patched with stone, with smooth blocks ingeniously inserted into the wall. At the end of the fault, his fingers discovered what he believed to be flints. He pulled them from their ledge and discovered they were regularly shaped; the knowledge, for some reason, made him uneasy.

With the flints, he made sparks, cascading like stars from his fingers. Using straw and shavings from his mattress, he was able to create fire. The straw supply was limited. He rationed himself to a few wisps at a time, and these he lit only when rations arrived, until he could create a better lamp.

Food supplies were irregular. Above the groove from which his water supply trickled was a larger hole, into which a man could insert his head. The hole formed the lower end of a tube boring upward through solid rock. Somewhere distantly up there was a gallery and a nebulous world of men — an ear applied to the hole could detect, on occasion, their comings and goings, their voices distorted out of recognition. Every so often, they threw food down the tube – and no doubt down the countless other tubes under their care.

Considering the poverty and discomfort of all other arrangements in Khernabhar, the food was tolerable, though always insufficient. It reflected the ample and various local resources; hard round loaves of coarse oaten bread; various fruits – coconuts, mango, satsumas, the thick-rinded mangosteen – some of which arrived well pulverised; and bundles of rice with shreds of meat in, knotted into fabric squares for their downward journey.

Mathers made it his habit to conserve his tiny fires for mealtimes, so that he could eat with a little light and feel he retained at least a shred of old civilised habit.

When I'm out of here, I will rejoin the guerrillas! I will lead a band on to Khernabhar itself. We will burst from its wooded defiles, destroy this vile machine, and release all the prisoners. This evil must be ended for all time. When I'm out of here . . .

He mused for hours at a time on the prison itself, hoping that he might be led to think of some way of escape. Escape was always in his mind, burning like a will-o'-the-wisp against the night of incarceration. He had to escape or go mad, and every day made the idea of getting free more urgent, because – yes, that was the supreme fiendishness of Khernabhar! – they were still – voluntarily, voluntarily! – hauling themselves deeper into the great mountain.

Shredding the hempen squares that wrapped his deliveries of rice, soaking them in the oil of the coconut, Mathers made himself candles and lit one with the flints. A tiny flame grew, flickered, fluttered, became oval, and maintained itself. Mathers was kneeling on the floor over it. He sat up and looked about. There was his cell, his home – its walls, its roof, the shadows, banished to corners. How sane, even welcoming, it looked!

He scrambled up with his candle. His determination was to examine minutely the inner walls of his cell but curiosity first deflected him to the water trough. There, holding his candle before him, he stared down and saw his reflection staring up – or not his reflection surely, but that of a savage, a hermit, with ragged beard and ragged eyebrows, with protruding cheekbones, with sunken gleaming eyes and corrugated forehead! With a gasp of surprise, he started back and could not look again.

And how long had he been here? He went over to the record of days he had kept in the dark, a row of scratches scored on the wall with a stone. The scratches were muddled together and numbered thirty-three or thirty-five. So little more than a month had passed since he was exiled from the world of men! Time, down here in this infernal darkness, moved as protestingly as rock itself!

At last, he took his candle up and began a minute inspection of the past as recorded about him. He had, of course, made such an inspection when his torches burned; but his agony of mind then had been such that only general impressions had registered. What he wished to do was to match the information of the rock against the rumours he had heard of Khernabhar and see if they shed some new light on the situation which would give him a key towards escaping.

To his surprise, his memory of the cell walls was largely false. His mood had been such, to begin with, that he had had eyes only for messages carved by recent tenants of the cell – cries of misery, revolutionary slogans, and a proclamation of vivid obscenity. His attention was now directed to marks of past time – in many cases, long past.

By the dim flame, no larger than a human eye, he read the

signs: the squinches or blind arches spanning the two inner corners and speaking, in their elaboration, of love rather than intentions of hatred; the sculpturing of the rock which showed no mark of the tools used to shape it; and the additions since, the mute voices of prisoners long dead! And how long dead? The earliest markings were in many cases obliterated by later additions, and the later additions by ones still later. It was noticeable that the most recent additions looked the roughest and least literate. Many of the earlier ones, faint though they were, were perfectly legible and perfectly formed.

Legible – but impossible to understand. For there was a script here that Mathers recognised but could not read. The Old Tongue! Men had written here using the Old Tongue as their natural language! Those prisoners must have died all of two thousand – perhaps as many as four thousand – years ago!

Many of the writings were records of individual lives. Where these were dated, Mathers saw that they went back many centuries. He read them marvelling, thinking how little life and consciousness had changed.

Frequently, the records were broken by the legend; CURSED BE THE NAME OF KHERN KAHZAA. This past tyrant, Emperor of the Eternal Wheel of Life and Death, had given his name to the mountain. His was the name most frequently invoked, until one got down to the present generation of scribbles, when the names of the hated dictator, Hener, and the beloved revolutionary leader, Reh – particularly the latter – predominated. The last occupant of the cell (so Mathers judged him to be) had scraped the revolutionary name everywhere. REH! REH! And on the rock of the trough was a large VICTORY TO REH!

That must have been carved at least ten years ago. Reh grows old. There are only white hairs in his beard. True, he survives, seems invincible. Yet victory is far from him. No

doubt of it, new leaders are needed. Perhaps better leaders,
perhaps better slogans. Perhaps better revolutionary material
and better thought behind them. Perhaps our people are less
than the men our ancestors were . . .

Only in one place had later scribblers been careful not to deface earlier writings. This was centrally, on the leading wall. Here an intricate figure had been engraved. Within a large circle, a double circle, slightly smaller, had been cut. Between these two inner circles were short radial lines, dividing the rim into a number of small partitions; the partitions were not completed all round the circle. The outer circle was broken in two places. At the centre of the figure were smaller circles, some intersecting, cut to different depths. The whole figure was intersected by a grand line.

Against this design were written various figures and notations in a corrupt version of the Old Tongue, of which Mathers could understand little. But he did understand that he was looking at a representation of the prison of Khernabhar. This was confirmation of the rumours he had heard: that the prison was a great wheel, rotating in the fastnesses of rock, the cells being mere niches on its perimeter.

He could not interpret the measurements on the incised figure, but he had heard that the diameter of the wheel was as much as five miles, and that the array of cells along its perimeter numbered as many as three thousand, although they were not always continuous. The great central axle upon which the wheel revolved rotated in the heart of the mountain. To this wheel of cells there was only one entrance, only one exit, as depicted in the design – the exit being sited somewhere on the mountainside before the entrance, so that those going in should not see the pitiful state of those emerging after their long ordeal.

That night – but in Khernabhar there was only night –
Mathers lay down to sleep with his head full of the image of
the great slow-grinding wheel, grinding men's lives away.
The wheel moved every day, had perhaps moved every day
since it was carved from the rock, for there were always wrong-
doers in the eyes of the state. It could move only in one direction, and therein lay its monstrous paradox: that the captives
holed like maggots in their cells were forced to propel themselves into the rock. Only by going deep into the mountain was
it possible to re-emerge, only by going deep into the mountain
was it possible to complete the revolution that meant freedom,
only by going deep into the mountain could hope of survival
be nourished.

So the prisoners hauled for almost three hours every day on
the chains in the well beyond the wheel, hauled till their sinews
almost tore, to get the wheel through its long and grudging
course!

*Sandstone grinding past sandstone . . . Ten years to a
revolution – I'm sure that's what I heard at university. Ten
years – about ten years, no matter who or what the prisoners
are. It might as well be eternity . . . How long is ten years?*

And what minor paradoxes were involved! This daily colla-
boration was an unspoken one between rebels and outcasts
of society. They were thrust down here precisely because they
did not co-operate: and only in their co-operation could they
drag their way through miles of rock.

Again: They co-operated even from the beginning, pulling
themselves *voluntarily* from the outer world, when they were
fresh and strong and healthy; yet at that period, inevitably,
they would pull with less than a whole heart – might, in some

cases, refuse to pull at all. Only later, when they could suppose that their call was half-way or more along the circumference of the prison – that, in other words, they were now *on their way out* – would they pull wholeheartedly; and by then, the evil regime would have rendered them aged, feeble, and sick, incapable of real effort.

And again: many of the prisoners, because they were the victims of a warlike state, were men of peace. Yet they, as much as the fieriest revolutionary, must have echoed the eternal unspoken wish that dominated Khernabhar: LET THERE ALWAYS BE WAR!

Only when there was war was the supply of prisoners fully equal to the supply of cells. Only then was there full man-power to haul on the chains and drag the wheel round through eternal blackness. Only then was there a chance that the tons of rock might be speeded and long years of imprisonment thereby lessened by a few days or hours.

The things that Mathers read in the rock, shocking as they were, brought him a truer realisation of his situation. They and the presence of a little light for a few hours of the day permitted him to consider others beside himself. He thought with some horror of all the other prisoners who sweated and festered in their cells; but a gentler concern filled him when he turned his mind to the two people who had been incarcerated with him. Of the man who had been thrust into the cell behind his, he had heard nothing beyond the groans of the first day. From the girl's cell – yes, Joanna was her name – he had heard some noises, scuffles as if she had been throwing herself against the walls in an hysterical effort to escape, and even perhaps a cry or two.

He set himself to make contact with her, and investigated the walls afresh. The distance between the leading edge of the cell wall and the outer wall – that is, between wheel and solid mountain – was generally no more than an inch: which said a great deal for the superhuman abilities of the architect who had designed Khernabhar! But this distance did vary to some degree, as if the wheel had a slight eccentricity and, when Mathers began his new investigation, it was enlarging to something over two inches. Since the walls between cells were about four feet thick, there was no chance of making contact while circumstances remained as they were.

Yet, even in this static place, circumstances were not unalterable. On the first day of this new investigation, Mathers found part of the outer wall had crumbled. Almost by the roof, there was a fault in the rock, into which he could thrust his hand!

Shaking with excitement, he lit a precious candle and pushed his bed over to the wall. By climbing on the bed, he could look into the hole. The hole was the width of two hands spread wide, irregular inside, going back not much more than arm's length. And two objects lay inside the hole.

He pulled the objects out. One was a length of roughly carved wood, a cudgel perhaps. The other was a skull.

He sat on the side of his bed, nursing the skull and staring at it with delight. It was the skull, he supposed, of a wild cat, paper-thin but beautifully formed, the lower jaw still intact, the buttresses of the eye-sockets exquisite. He cupped it in his hands as if it were a jewel. The hours passed as his mind travelled all the meanings of the life that, fading at last among the shadows of Khernabhar, had built and utilised this shell.

It was only later, when he had placed the skull carefully in a corner where he would not tread on it, that he turned his mind to the cudgel. It was more mysterious than the skull. He could accept that wild cats might be lured in from the mountainsides to hunt the rats living in the catacombs of the dark, scrambling in during the dry season down a waterhole. But where did the cudgel come from? Who had left it there?

In his solitude, he was making a mystery of nothing. The weapon had probably been tucked into the hole by another prisoner, tucked there and forgotten. What else?

Next morning, the signal came, the prisoners – each in the solitude of his cell – began their daily haul on the chains, six inches forward and pause, six inches forward and pause, repeated some forty-four times. And the hole in which the skull and cudgel had been cached slid away and was finally lost to view behind the following cell wall.

But a new and more extensive fault appeared. This one was less high than the last, and extended raggedly sideways. It had some depth and, examining it closely, Mathers deduced that it had been artificially deepened. Some of the rock glistened; moisture seeped from one of the cracks.

It occurred to Mathers that faults like this might one day appear on a much larger scale. He would then be able to hide himself in the fault. On the following day, when the wheel moved on, he would stay where he was and find himself in the cell of the prisoner following him. But the notion of being walled into a narrow hole, even for no more than a couple of hours, was enough to make him break out in a chilly sweat. Nor did he want to set himself further from Joanna. He would have to wait until a fault appeared large enough for him to squeeze forward between his cell and hers.

As chance would have it, the rock faults now stopped. Although the gap between cell and wall continued slowly to widen, it was still scarcely enough to thrust an emaciated arm through. Day followed day, each swallowed up by silent sandstone.

A plague of rats came upon him. They came swarming down the food chute and milling through his cell. They easily slipped between wall and wheel, and were gone, came back, whisked by, vanished. A day later, he saw his first cat. It was an intimidating beast, mangey, long in the leg, and boardlike in the body, with the expression of ferocity on its face heightened by a rat hanging from its jaws, which it wore like a military moustache. Mathers called a welcome to it. It disappeared with a look of unalterable hatred.

The animals came and went according to their seasons. He began to detect and was presently overpowered by an odour of corruption. A prisoner had died near at hand, to add his peculiar stench to the atmosphere. This prolonged corruption doubtless accounted for the influx of the rats and their enemies. It was dismaying to think of a sightless face a few yards away, staring into the night of Khernabhar and being dismantled as it stared.

He devoted himself the more sedulously to plans to reach the girl. Since chance counted for so much, his plans soon degenerated into dreams of what he and she would do when they were together; in truth, imprisonment might then be tolerable. But he added that he would be unable to forsake his cell permanently; it would be necessary to return frequently for food – two trying to live on one ration would starve; even love could not gainsay that. How could easy return be made possible? Clearly, only by breaking down a part of the wall between them.

The most vulnerable part of the wall was its outer edge. The chains dangling in the outer wall, by which the wheel was dragged round, were five feet in length. If Mathers could manage to prise a chain, boss and rivets and all, from the wall, then the chain could be used as a crude saw and, with him working at one end and the girl at the other, it might be possible to wear a groove in the separating wall deep enough for them to be able to climb through uninterruptedly from one cell to another!

Now every afternoon (to himself, Mathers still used the

diurnal terminology of the world outside) was spent with the cudgel, painfully attempting to prise a boss loose from the wall. Day after day, the bosses proved unmoving. The master-architect had had a skill that defied time.

Mathers's most terrifying day in Khernabhar began as wretchedly as any other. He woke from tantalising and instantly forgotten dreams of the world outside and paced round his cell as usual until the tapped summons brought him to his working position. With a rock, he tapped on the outer wall as heartily as anyone. Come on, you lazy swine! Get to those chains! Pull us to freedom! Since about two months had elapsed since his term of punishment began, there might be as many as ninety new captives behind him . . . little enough to set beside the three thousand-odd ahead, but at least a beginning.

The creaking, groaning, squealing progress was under way. How hateful the effort! How sickening, how weakening! How ill-matched was the human heart against the burden of night and sandstone! And yet . . . with cries of protest, the wheel turned slightly and the cells moved along.

When it was all over, Mathers threw himself on his bed. Exhaustion set in now, and he fell into one of those uneasy states between waking and sleeping which were a feature of his present life. A pair of rats chased themselves across his shoulder and stomach. He jumped up immediately, to sit shivering on the side of the bed.

Was there some faint light or suggestion of it about the cell?

Perhaps deliverance is here! Why not? The revolution has taken place. Reh has been successful! His men are in Khernabhar, slowly blowing the place up and rescuing all the prisoners . . . Or the evil Hener is dead, his henchmen killed,

*and liberty proclaimed from the palace! No, I'm just dream-
ing. But it could perhaps be a narrow shaft through the rock
– too narrow even to climb through, let's say, but wide enough
to let down a ray of light directly from the sun at a certain
time of day!*

He went to the outer wall. If there was light, it was uncertain, the feeblest glow. If there was light, it came from the
direction of Joanna's cell. He called her name, louder and
louder. The glimmer of light died. He pressed against the
rock, still calling, and felt it faulted beneath his hands, ragged
and recessed.

Although he had made a stern rule with himself to use his
limited candles only in afternoon and evening, he decided
this new factor warranted an exception to the rule. Kneeling,
he struck his flints together, sending the sparks cascading until
at last the hemp wick was touched and flickered into light.
He cupped it lovingly in his hands until it grew strong. Then
he carried it over to inspect the wall.

The fault in the rock was deep, tall, and lengthy; it extended behind the leading wall of his cell towards Joanna's,
beyond the penetrating power of his illumination. It had been
neatly patched with stones, beautifully squared cobbles, but
they had been prised away and the depth of the hole increased.
The hole was deep enough to hold a man!

*I could get to her! Now! No need to return here until
tomorrow morning, when the action signals start!*

To carry the candle on what would probably be a difficult
scramble seemed an unnecessary impediment. Mathers set it
down on the edge of the cell floor and climbed into the fault.

The rock had broken along its veinings, and the veinings
were irregular. There was plenty of room one moment, very

little the next. He chose to work his way along with his back
to the smooth inter-cell wall and his face to the ragged rock.
The fault twisted, and he was forced to push his way forward
lying virtually horizontal.

Progress became easier, the gap between wall and rock
widened, he regained his feet, shuffled forward, and soon the
edge of her cell wall met his knuckles.

He stepped out into her cell. Living darkness, strange smells.
'Joanna! Joanna!'

She flung herself on him out of the dark, kicking and
screaming. Or for an awful moment he thought it was her.
Then his hand, fighting to push her face away, met a bristling
crop of beard! Almost at once, his hand was bitten. He pulled
it back and struck out wildly. Two hands closed round his
throat and squeezed!

Electric colours punctured the blackness. Reaching forward,
he linked his hands behind his opponent's skull, at the same
time bringing his own skull violently forward. The bearded
man fell back cursing unintelligibly and then charged in again.
Mathers ducked, falling over with the enemy on top of him.
He kicked out wildly and was lucky enough to connect his
knee with something vital. As a howl of pain sounded, he
staggered and almost fell back into the rock fault.

Before he could pull himself to safety, his assailant was at
him again, this time poking a stick at him. It caught Mathers
painfully in the ribs before he managed to grasp one end of it.

'What's the matter with you? I'm no enemy if you're an
honest man. Where's the girl, where's Joanna?'

Savage growls and curses in a strange language were his
answer.

The stick was wrenched from his grasp. He scrambled back
to his own cell under a fusillade of blows. Never was refuge
more welcome, or light more blessed, than his. He lay for a
long while on his bed, trembling and gasping, clutching his

wounds, and peering in dread at the rock fault.

All that night, he could not sleep for fear of his unknown attacker, for the pain of his wounds, and for wondering what had become of Joanna.

Next morning, he worried about trying to make contact with the prisoner on the other side of him. Perhaps they might form an alliance – Mathers suddenly felt the need of company. But, when the cells next moved on, the rock fault would lie, not between his cell and the next prisoner's, but between the next prisoner's and the cell following that. There was no way of getting in touch. At least he had the consolation of knowing that the unknown attacker would no longer be able to break in upon him after this morning's work.

His candle was almost at an end – he had been unwilling to extinguish it – when the working signal came. Never more gladly had Mathers gone over to take his position by the dangling chain.

In the brief fight, he had sustained nothing worse than bruises. Even in his weakened condition, it took Mathers only a few days to recover from them. His mental state required longer to stabilise. He was now victim of fears and suppositions that almost took on their own life. Night after night, he woke screaming from dreams in which terrible things with faces all hair and snout and teeth flung themselves at his throat in paroxysms of fury. Sometimes these dream attackers were gigantic, filling the cell; at other times, they were no larger than a finger-nail.

All were equally terrifying.

His hours of candle-light were necessarily rationed but, light or dark, he would crouch with every muscle tense, staring towards those cracks round his walls from which attack might come.

Gradually, however, his fears subsided. The plague of rats

also died and, with it, the abominable stench that he imagined helped to distort his senses. The stench of Khernabhar was always permanent and corrosive; it ceased to be intolerable.

What has happened to me all these days? How is it I have been so preoccupied with myself? What about her? What has happened to Joanna? Is she still alive? She can't be dead, no . . .

One morning, he was his normal lucid self. The terror of the attack had vanished. He saw clearly, or imagined he saw, what had happened. That vile bearded creature was merely another prisoner, originally three cells ahead of Mathers, who had taken advantage of the rock fault to get back to Joanna's cell. He could be ousted if Mathers went prepared to fight. As for Joanna, Mathers had no proof that she was not still in her cell. He tried to avoid dwelling on the evils that might have befallen her.

What he needed was a weapon. Then he would be prepared for the next occasion on which it was possible to attack.

There were no metal objects available. But the cudgel was a fine solid affair, and one end could be sharpened into a point by the flints. By the time he had finished with it, it gave him added confidence.

But the grudging stone wheel of Khernabhar obeyed its own laws, turned at its own pace, unfolded its own possibilities when it would. Its rotation on its axis was like the slow turn of the centuries themselves, and its blind unchanging walls offered no chance of escape.

To divert himself, Mathers took to pacing the cell and to reciting such poetry and prose as he could recall at the top of his voice. By some insensible shift of his emotions, one poem in particular became his favourite:

Anna, thy beauty seems to bring
  Bewitchment of the world I know,
Spelling a change, till everything
  Is pale, impermanent, as though
  World were but raree-show.

O'er ravaged lands and prosperous,
  Countrysides of sun and shade,
Seascape or moonscape, without fuss
  Your dreaming eyes, your lips, have made
  Reality to fade.

So now before the bricks of town
  Palm trees advance or towers pace,
Wild mountains rise, breakers crash down!
  Unchanged alone where phantoms race –
  Thy love, thy face!

The Anna in the old poem became Joanna. The bricks of town became the walls of his cell. Then the poem was true, yes, yes, all else faded before the beauty of her face and all the intangible qualities her face stood for. No imprisonment could crush the budding of humanity's finer qualities. He forgot that the beauty of her face was something far more frail and transient than the beds of rock about him. Mathers was suddenly in love!

Over and over, he tried to trace all his memories of her.

Had I ever set eyes on her before we were assembled for the march up the mountain? Wait, yes, I saw her in the yard of the court on the day we were sentenced! Of course! She was standing in the cart as Hener's toughs thrust me down the steps! She in sunshine! Had she something round her head? A handkerchief ... Her hands up to her hair? Why didn't I pay better attention? The sun was in my eyes.

So many times did he return to the few fragments of memory
he had of her, that they became obnubilated. He was left
with nothing but a glimpse of her shoulder, the nape of her
neck, a curl of hair on it, the sight of an ear-lobe. And that
was all of Joanna that remained!

Through the days of progress and stillness through the rock,
in which he sought her essence and waited to seek her reality,
Mathers paced his cell and kept himself exercised. He was at
his exercises one day when a fresh aspect of the wheel design
on his wall caught his eye. Holding the candle up close, he
inspected it minutely.

It became apparent to him – and he wondered how he had
failed to observe the fact before – that the design was etched
over a much more ancient version of the same plan. What he
had previously regarded as construction lines or markings in
the rock were parts of a far older drawing, executed in a more
fanciful and decorative way. Allegory had been used, and he
realised that the old man with the beard, whose lineaments
he had admired, was part of this archaic design, and supported
the semi-obliterated wheel upon his shoulder.

Accompanying the design were hieroglyphs, faint, indeci-
pherable, and certainly of great antiquity. Mathers, gazing at
them, was taken back to a fine winter morning when he was
a young man, riding on horseback early through the woods
with his father. They cantered through a thicket of holly trees
which cut at their legs, up to an eminence on which stood a
dozen or so tall spruces, so old that they sprawled at angles,
often leaning their trunks against each other for support. The
hieroglyphs conjured up the intricate foliage of those spruces,
glimpsed in freedom long ago. Mathers and his father rode
up to the trees to enjoy the view and let the horses breathe.
They jumped down onto the soft ground, peering through the

mist across the valley.

'There's Khernabhar, the home of the ancient tyrant Khern Kahzaa!' Mathers Senior said. He pointed to a mountain that, from this distance, hardly looked bigger than others nearer at hand, up whose shaggy slopes the mists were drifting.

Leaning against one of the spruces, Mathers Senior spoke of the Saga of Onnias, which contained word of Khernabhar and its secrets. The Saga was of a great oral tradition, born long before the days even of Khern Kahzaa, before the days of written language; it contained legends that seemingly related to the coming of man on the planet. One legend spoke of a dynasty of terrible kings, father, son, and grandson, who imprisoned a whole nation in a mountainside because they were hairy and possessed six fingers on each hand.

'. . . ther peltts Like fiber were up ta eye-pits *On befor-heds thankly as arm-pits Sprooated while each furd' hand mounted extra furd' fingre*'

Upon imprisonment, this strange nation was forced to build a great wheel of incarceration inside Khernabhar, to symbolise the eternity for which they would be sealed off from the world. The last king of the dynasty sealed up the entrances to the mountain; but the nation still survived inside and would one day emerge to overthrow the world. So claimed the saga.

'The Saga of Onnias has been banned from our libraries since Hener came to power' said Mathers Senior to his son, looking across the valley. 'And perhaps before his day, too. Even very ancient and dead things can return to disrupt the present.'

The mist of that distant day faded into grainy sandstone; the sound of his father's voice changed back into the drip and boom of water; and the knot of trees became merely the hieroglyphs of Mathers's cell wall.

It's all older than anyone can guess at ... Reh, do you know of this iniquity? The revolution must come! Or perhaps it has come, and we prisoners are abandoned here. Perhaps the revolution has been betrayed! Then there must be another revolution ... I must get free!

Mathers stood for a long while, one shoulder against a wall, staring absently ahead, listening to the endless working of water all round. At university, he had joined one of the secret revolutionary societies, where he learned of another version of the story in the Saga of Onnias. This version also claimed a dynasty of three kings, father, son, and grandson; but it presented the father as an upright and religious man, founder of a Holy Order for which the great subterranean wheel was designed. This saintly ruler intended the cells for monastic cells; and the holy penitents intended to occupy the cells would propel themselves, generation after generation, revolution after revolution, reverently through the deep earth until, at the time of the final Resurrection, they propelled themselves direct into the presence of the Lord Almighty. The son of the pious dynast had been a weak and dissolute man, who allowed construction to go forward without his personal interest. He was murdered by his son, who indeed took personal interest in the vast wheel but subverted its sacred intentions and turned it into combined prison and torture chamber, which usage had been maintained into historical times and ever since. The legend had it that the enslaved wheel-builders turned against this wicked king, and that he was the first to be set to work in his own instrument of terror.

Whatever version of the legend was nearest the facts – and the truth would now almost certainly never be established – this much was evident: however far one might cast one's mind back into the history of civilisation, the wheel would always be there, turning, groaning, every day on its axis.

As for the possibility that an ancient nation, hairy and six-fingered, had been incarcerated here, that was probably an embroidery. Unless – and an idea so paralysing came to Mathers that he dropped the candle. It rolled on the floor and went out. As he scrabbled for it on the floor, he tried to recall details of the hairy man who had assailed him in Joanna's cell, trembling to remember how many fingers the creature had on each hand . . .

Shakily, he felt for his flints and re-lit his candle, looking round fearfully at the swooping shadows.

Careful measurements of the outer wall revealed that the slight eccentricity of orbit was still gradually increasing the gap between wall and cell-end. Mathers was sure that the maximum gap would be small and, once maximum was reached, would dwindle again; so that when the gap was barely wide enough for him to struggle through, he resolved that go he must. He had his cudgel – if he met his old assailant, he would be ready.

As to that old assailant, Mathers had a new theory. It was mere superstition to imagine that any of a prehistoric race mentioned in a long-forgotten saga could survive below ground – wasn't it? There was a more practical explanation.

The wheel of Khernabhar could not continue without maintenance. He had seen how faults in the rock had been repaired, and rock debris would have to be cleared away. Very well: then, just as there were passages to allow for water and food to enter the cells from above, so there must be ways for humans – guards – to do the same thing. His assailant had probably been such a guard; which might well mean that a passage-way to the world above was near at hand. If he could find Joanna, they could escape by that route and find their way to Reh's headquarters, there to help fight for the revolution.

In his pockets were flints, a new candle, and some food. He
went over to the water trough and took a last drink. He looked
round the cell and counted the scratches he had made in the
sandstone. His lifetime of imprisonment in the rock had in
fact lasted only one hundred and two days so far. Something
like one hundred and fifty-three prisoners would have been
thrown into the cells behind him – and the same number
released far ahead of him – several miles and many years
ahead of him!

He set his old candle down on the cell floor, since he would
be sure to drop it in his struggle to reach the next cell. Taking
up the cudgel, he pushed his way into the gap between cell
wall and rock face. Thin though he was, there was scarcely
room to edge forward but, inch by inch, he did it, cudgel in
his leading hand, face forward into the darkness.

In the vacant cell, the candle continued to burn for some
while. The marks of ancient occupancy stood on the walls,
water continued to drip. Shadows fluttered occasionally against
the roof of rock.

MELVYN BRAGG

HE felt trapped and boxed in by the place but repressed it and made a show of being as pleased as Margaret seemed to be.

'The point is,' she said, 'the flat is three times bigger than anything we could afford in any other central district. Besides, it's "coming up".' The flat was in a twilight area of Inner London where jerry-built victorian housing decayed in acres of treeless streets, like barracks long abandoned to the Natives who crept in and sought temporary shelter while vandals smashed windows and councils punched great gaps in crumbling terraces to make way for new blocks and towers. The few young middle class couples who moved in vowed that it 'would come up': it was near the centre of London, they pointed out, and what it lacked in amenities it made up for in convenience.

'You must apply a system of cross-benefits,' Margaret said. Coming as she did from an ordered and secured professional family she could also regard it all as a bit of an adventure. 'A London flat is a station not a terminus.' She was pleased with that.

The place reminded Alan of his childhood. Though born after the Second World War, his early life in the run down area of a large northern industrial town had been spent in a landscape nearer the depressed thirties than the more affluent fifties. So when, each morning, he found himself faced with some new occasion for distress, even if it was no more than a broken milk bottle, a swirl of litter or a sullen-faced child, a connection with his past was made; he had worked hard to break it.

'Another marvellous thing about it,' she would tell their friends, 'is that it's multi-racial. Pakistanis, Cypriots, West Indians, Indians – just a few, and Irish of course, if you can call them a race – they certainly behave like one! – it's extremely interesting.'

'Also of course,' Daniel had said, 'you have the advantage of actually experiencing this world-wide city problem. They're all in the shit. You can bring us the news. Guinea pigs.'

Daniel Ryan – the playwright and critic, several years older than Alan – lived in a neighbouring borough which had 'come up' years before and was now a forum for the successful, full of genteel animation. Daniel lived alone in a beautiful small Georgian house which he had bought cheaply. He and Alan had met on the television programme for which Alan worked: Alan had prepared the questions for Daniel's interview when his last play had opened.

Like Margaret's, Daniel's parents were of the professional middle classes: most of their circle were from that sort of background and their brisk competence constantly impressed Alan.

'I simply don't care where I live,' he had lied, 'as long as it's near the West End and I have a room to work in.'

In his mid-twenties, Alan Lawson was doing very well in television. He had done very well in the other institutions which had taken him from those dispiriting back streets to an enviable position in the communications media. It was in his nature to be grateful and he had been tempted neither to drop out, nor to hit out: the revolutionary politics of some of his contemporaries appeared to him as little more than a fashionable pose. Most of them, he would reflect, as he thought without bitterness, could well afford to be radical: the establishment would aways bail them out as daddy would pay the bills for the smashed up car. Alan was fully employed in getting a good education and absorbed in learning the ceremonies and rituals of the middle class he had joined. A flair for acting, briefly but brilliantly displayed at university had carried him away from the academic or industrial career he might have followed and into television where a lucky break had landed him on an excellent programme, full of opportunities.

His friends were far more pleased with his working-class origins than he himself could ever be; but although he was aware of this, they would only refer to it mockingly, and sometimes he felt attacked although he realised they would consider they were being affectionate.

They met in each others' flats and homes around the middle of London. Most of them had some association with television or worked there. They saw good films and good plays, read good books and the worthwhile weeklies and were rather self-deprecatingly beginning to distinguish good food and good wine. They took an interest in the opera and played competitive games based on pop culture in which all were delightedly erudite. In summer they went on good holidays and their careers were making good headway. Occasionally one of their number broke out and did remarkably well; more rarely someone would break down and drift away.

'Above all,' Margaret had said when getting the flat, 'we'll be able to have all our friends around without the whole thing turning into a children's party with everyone on the bloody floor.' She bought two sofas and six small armchairs in Junk City.

Alan was more of a listener than a speaker in these conversations, though his imitations were often called on, particularly the 'Boring Indian Sociologist', the 'Humourless Swedish Sex Expert' and the 'Blimp'. It disconcerted him how well he did the Blimp. That was their favourite, though: they enjoyed the idea of being English and Englishness, especially

in one of its more amusing manifestations, was endlessly fascinating. Margaret took an energetic part in any discussion. She
had a clear-browed seriousness, a clear-eyed devotion to the
point at issue 'out of George Eliot by A. J. Ayer', Daniel
would say, fondly. She was a liberated woman, one who had
gone manfully through a masculine education and come out
very like a male. She lectured in English at a College of Art
in the centre of town.

All their friends admired her and Alan was still a little
bewildered as to why she had picked on or rather plumped
for him. They felt no need to marry – or rather, Margaret
didn't. He let himself be ruled by her in this.

'You underestimate yourself so much that it's rather moving,' Daniel had once said to him. 'You take everything that
comes as a favour. It *is*, *really*, very sweet.'

He was a little uneasy when Daniel used such endearments.
The others scarcely allowed personal remarks to mark their
conversation. Daniel took licence for them all; and they were
rather thrilled by it, revealing to them, as it did, a peep of
that faster, richer, certainly not more intelligent but more
publicly acknowledged set that he also moved in.

'But it gets a little stuffy in the First-Class Saloon Bar,'
he once said. 'I like to have a whiff of the engine-room.' Of
course they did not let him get away with that but the term
stuck and they would ask each other what had happened in
'the engine room' should they have missed the latest evening.

To all appearances, they settled in quickly and well; had an
'open house' where the cars outside were so many and so vivid
that they could have been sent there on instruction during an
auto treasure hunt, having no real connection with the street.
The party spread into the downstairs flat too where a charming couple joined in. The harder-eyed acquaintances got out
the *A–Z* and worked out the proximity of this to other areas
which were 'coming up' or 'half-way up' or 'arrived': they

cross-examined him on rent and asked for the names of the local estate agents. Everybody agreed that it really was *London*.

Yet his stomach clenched each morning he went out, each time across the street he saw the dereliction caused by neglect and indifference. He was not trapped, he decided, but, paradoxically, cut off. That was it! His work in television – so far – was concerned exclusively with the studio side of things scarcely ever leaving the luxury and security of the liner-like building he worked in, concentrating largely on the arts or on joke items, witty, lightweight, tail-enders – this was not enough. He had to make contact with a world more 'real'.

Of course his friends would not allow this. The notion that the world of the unfortunate could be accounted more 'real' than their own world was soon chopped up and tossed away. They were interested of course and wondered why there was no contemporary Dickens to turn the pockets of undoubted squalor in contemporary life into a work of art. But that of course led on to the vexed question of the pressure, the density and quality necessary in an artist's relationship with society. Wallace Stevens and Borges provided useful guidelines; especially Borges, the Tower of Babel, the library, the labyrinth . . .

'I was wondering when you would get round to it.' Maxwell tilted back his chair and drew gently on his coarse Cuban cheroot. He was a lean man and he dressed with the restrained elegance which he admired in Alan. 'The Flying Scot', they'd nicknamed him as he'd rammed his way up this television organisation to create 'the best daily magazine programme on any network'. He was one of television's great figures and his sayings were the proverbs of production offices. 'Ideas,' he would say, 'intelligent men get them as easily as adolescents get erections.' Or 'this magazine holds up a mirror to society, laddie,' he would tell the eager young graduates littered on him annually, 'and society's no clutch of refined sensibilities playing with their pussies.' He enjoyed and exploited the contrast between a careful lowland enunciation and a bawdy vocabulary – it was a fastidious pleasure and he was gentle in it, considered just a little old-fashioned; endearing, it dated him.

'But what exactly do you *mean* by doing something more "to do with life". Whose life?'

Alan glaced at the walls. Neat as any General's Ops. Room they were papered with schedules, costings, maps, advance plans and everywhere red-headed, green-headed, yellow, black and white-headed pins secured all movements like friendly forts. The organisation was vast. There was one film unit permanently on world tours, another hitting trouble spots – Vietnam, Pakistan, Mexico, the Middle East – another circling Britain and a fourth based in London – the light cavalry for the delicate raid on No. 10 or the airport or Trafalgar Square. Besides this Maxwell had set up a number of stringers on the five continents and up and down the island. Apart from the film effort was the studio – a large studio available five days a week, and there they did the interviews with cabinet ministers and men in the news, discussion and analysis. Maxwell's weekly budget would have done credit, mutatis mutandis, to a Renaissance town, it was such a vast operation – not Urbino, perhaps, but every bit as devoted to capturing and transforming the world. The number of people he 'was responsible for' (only the organisation '*employed*' people) made up a fair force, easily a cohort – 'Maxwell's Clan' they were called, and there had been an abortive attempt by some of the younger directors to replace the 'Flying Scot' by the nickname 'Chief'. There was talk of chieftainship in his background; they were pleased at the possibility. They gave him tremendous loyalty and drew on great banks of youthful energy in pirating the world to bring back stories of the kind that fitted his rule. Maxwell called his directors 'the survivors': Alan wanted to be one of them.

'Whose life?'

'I just want a bit more action, I suppose.'

'Personally?'

'Yes.'

'You could join the territorial army in your spare time. They might even let you shoot a rubber bullet in an emergency.'

'I mean on this programme.'

'This programme,' Maxwell let his chair drop forward so that it thudded on to its forelegs, 'this programme does not exist to satisfy personal fantasies. I don't hire masturbators.'

'I've been inside that studio for over two years now.'

'Some never get in.' Maxwell smiled. 'And some never get out.'

Alan felt a break of sweat on his brow and was furious with himself for being so nervous. Maxwell had adopted his usual habit for important interviews and knocked off all phones, barred all interruptions. But the ten minutes was almost up.

'For two years I've written out questions for other people to ask, I've gutted books for other people to use, I've chatted up contributors for other people to produce, I've been a bloody page-boy and O.K., so the experience was marvellous but I want to get on to something and do it myself – prepare, produce, direct, edit and get it out – now!'

'What's your plan?'

'I sent you a memo.'

'I read it.' The pause was an old trick; an affectionate habit.

'Well. The report on the after-care of prisoners comes out at the end of next week. I'd like to find some prisoners' wives and ask them how they cope while he's in and when he comes out.'

'We've done it.'

'I know. February 1968, and This Week touched on it in their programme on Prison Visiting in May 1968. But there's been nothing since and this campaign by prison wives has gathered momentum. Besides we can ask different questions now. We needn't speak in a whisper and shoot it in silhouette. We can ask them what they do for sex – that's what we all want to know, for a start?'

'Why?'

'Well. If you believe Freud, that sex affects other actions directly and fundamentally then perhaps we are damaging these people and making them worse by denying them sex.'

'Nuns don't become criminals.'

'No, but that doesn't mean criminals should be forced to be monks.'

'Why not? So far I don't like the idea.'

'Look. This report will say that many, the majority of marriages of hardened criminals break up after a man comes out. Why *after*? Sexually, if they *could* get together wouldn't it be a better method of helping him to come back smoothly into society?'

'You mean have Screwing Rooms in Her Majesty's Prisons?'

'Yes. And most important, what's to be gained if a family breaks up – more kids more liable to be criminal and more criminals more likely to fall back into their old ways.'

'I'm not convinced.'

'Look. Prisoners are institutionalised – they're more like patients in a hospital than *criminals*. But the wife, in open society, she suffers – is seen to suffer the loss of privileges and capacities; in some primitive societies they made the criminal the pariah – remember? – well, here it's the *wife* who becomes the pariah. Although society likes to keep its streets clean and institutionalise its pain, it can't do it – it still must have its wounds in the open. We need to see criminals in order to react to them in order to keep the idea of Law intact: things are strengthened by their opposites. And with *him* locked away it's *she* who acts out the criminal for us – it's her we shun or neglect or befriend as the case might be. I mean, perhaps we need to bring prisoners into the open not to cure *them* but to help keep *us* healthy.'

'The stocks on the village green.'

'Exactly.' He shook his head instantly. 'Of course not!'

'Dangerous ground, laddie, and you don't need any of that speculative baggage to do a seven-minute story for a magazine programme.'

'The point is, why should the wife and children share the sentence?'

'Because their man committed a crime against society. Our audience want to sleep safe in their beds at night. So do I.'

Alan was silent. He had muddled the arguments set out so neatly on the memo; forgotten the statistics, only half-remembered all the tips he had received about how to 'deal' with Maxwell, and was now left with the sense of a cliché powerful in his mind – battering against a brick wall. Maxwell enjoyed silence, and drew on his cheroot. Alan waded on –

'Look. Everywhere there's the most fantastic violence and we know we *have* to cope with it otherwise we're finished. We have to find ways of controlling population growth without wars and yet we always *have* had wars: we have to find ways of fighting without hydrogen bombs. On every continent there's black against white and in every city there's a plague called loneliness and a holocaust called nervous breakdown. Right? Now this is part of that bigger situation: but we can limit it, we can see it clearly, it can be a test case. One man's violence – how does a civilised (no sarcasm intended) society cope? We lock *him* away and we make *her* an outcast. That's what we *do*. Jesus Christ, if we can't do better than that in small things what can we expect in big?'

'Prove your point,' said Maxwell very much with the air

of merely giving someone a chance, 'and we'll show it.'
Rapidly he outlined Alan's shooting schedule, his resources, his
budget, named his cameraman, his editor and his production
secretary; checked up on his knowledge of cut-aways, film
stocks and laboratory processing speeds and then nodded. Alan
stood up. 'A concrete case,' Maxwell said, 'we can't solve the
problems of the world. A specific instance. Show me first
rushes next Wednesday and we'll see how it stands up. And
how it stands up depends on how much you want it, laddie:
the same rules for work and play. Now – out!'

His left hand tugged at the bottom of his neatly fitted
waistcoat: then trailed up to pat his well brushed greying hair:
his right hand reached out for a pen and on the way knocked
the telephone into action. His eyes were firmly concentrated
on the papers before him. Two phones rang simultaneously.

Alan was shaking but exhilarated and he went first to the
lavatory, both for relief and to savour in solitude the fact: 'I'm
going to direct a film,' he said to himself in the mirror and
squeezed his eyes tight shut to let the words percolate slowly
through his mind.

He did not always go into the bar. Drink at lunch-time
made him fuzzy headed and besides he could not afford the
large rounds, but on this day he did and went right into the
'clan' who were gathered in their usual corner. What a great
lot they were, he thought! They were better looking, faster
witted, more hard-working, bigger drinkers, they had prettier
secretaries, told funnier stories than any comparable group
in board-room, common room, club, canteen or cell anywhere! And all around the bar were others in television, men
who made films, directed plays, covered events: worlds of
theatre, politics, big business, sport, archaeology, comedy, pop,
technology all spun around this central illuminating screen,
and in command of the planets were these men here, in this
bar, remarkably independent in all but a few areas which

Alan had not yet tested. He bought himself a half of bitter and went to listen to tales of Prime Ministers and missed opportunities in Katmandu, of the asides of great men and the hassles of hounded directors. Just as the organisation itself elicited vivid comparisons (now they said it was like the medieval papacy, now like the communist party, now like the East India Company), so this surge of fashionably dressed and vivacious, widely travelled and hard-working men drew out similes just as easily – commandoes, cavalry, and there was the unkind cut about their being the storm troopers of the communications system. They knew their place and images of themselves lapped them around. Occasionally, Alan felt sickened or intimidated by them, just as the whole world to which his education had led him could appear a strain: that was when he was feeling weak, he thought, and it was accompanied by long verses written in the early hours of the morning and unhappy introspection. He was afraid that in succumbing to institutions he had lost his intuition and often in this busy, wordy, exciting place he missed the slack and flux of those intense relationships experienced in the tight community of a working class family and area. But he would soon throw it off he thought and hoped, inject himself with the attainable fantasies of these other lives and join in. He sipped the beer.

Soon he was 'doing' his Indian Sociologist for the clan. 'As – a friendly alien,' he said, each word at once accurate and mocking the accent it imitated, his tongue clicking softly on his palate: lips faintly popping: as for the content, he let it come from where it would, 'I would like to express my cumbleet aggremont with thee las spekker. On this matter of race relations we hab to be very careful, very careful that in gainin' ower liberties we are not at one and the sem time lockin' up our freedom. Tank you. O yes my goodness, gracious me. Thee black man, id mus be recognised, here un now in present civilised company, is not thee same as thee brown man or thee white man or thee yellow man. China has a great cultural heritage and Japan almost half as long. And so we are faced by a difficult-y at thee outset . . .'

When, later, he came to remember what he had actually said, he was ashamed of himself. He had given a racist entertainment to amuse those he wished to impress, he thought, and described the situation to Margaret who enjoyed being his confessor.

'Nonsense,' she said. 'If we aren't allowed to make fun, then it's too bad. Besides which, what you're really worried about is not what you said but what people thought of what you said.' He gritted his teeth as she drove into the solar plexus of his anxiety. 'Not to worry,' she added. 'They probably didn't give you a second thought.'

And he felt in some way absolved. Margaret, who knew so well the working of the world in which he had found himself – its moral checks and balances, its personal demands and prejudices – was to be trusted over this. He handed her his social worries as she gave him her personal uncertainties; for Margaret was unshakeably convinced that she had no talent whatsoever and equally committed to the idea that Alan had talents which would rise to any demands made on them. She was very pleased that he was making new demands.

They were cosy in their flat this chill early summer evening. Purcell's Golden Sonata spilled out of the stereo; a real fire burned in a new grate; side lamps lit the large room giving it a richness it lacked in daylight; the four prints and the paintings by friends looked elegant: Margaret sat across from him snuggled in one of the two massive armchairs, himself in the other; she reading 'Two Nations' resolutely and pointedly; he drawing up his plans, equally self-conscious.

Sometimes he thought it was an imitation self who was alive, a stand-in, playing the part while the *real* actor – did what? His friends from primary school worked as labourers or mechanics – fitters, plasterers, electricians: the grammar school set seemed equally remote, still back there as accountants, civil servants, teachers: even the majority of his university acquaintances appeared distant, doctors, dons, young executives, foreign office, abroad with oil companies; only the handful who had drifted into the metropolis, usually for journalism or the theatre shared a life he now led. But where was its centre? In this flat furnished in a style he liked and admired but was no more his own than the trappings of Blenheim Palace? In the television building where work was so joke-laden and exciting that nothing in his experience could connect it with his life's meaning and dread of the word? There seemed more a centre in those bleak streets beyond the flower patterned curtains and that was why they jarred him.

Margaret refused to wear her spectacles and so the book was all but pressed against her nose. She was slim, wandily slim and her hair waved gently, auburn. Her expression was easily severe but when she smiled she yielded everything as her body did in all its unguarded movements. He had met her at a party, feeling foolish after drink had encouraged him to do his imitation of Mick Jagger: but she had praised him and drawn out the sting of embarrassment and when he had heard himself say 'shall we go back to your place?' she had nodded as unfussily as she had undressed soon after their arrival. Until then, Alan had fought every inch of the way with girls back home whose life depended on their virginity and then thrown himself sodden with drunken misery on to the waters: but here he was sober and the girl was attractive. Moreover she was unembarrassed about sex and enjoyed it; as she enjoyed a good dinner, he had sometimes thought since but repressed the thought. She imagined he had taken her hand and that she had guided him since, over-grateful for the tit-bits of form and manners which she threw into their common dish, over-grateful for her concern for him, the intelligence of her interest in his affairs: or perhaps not grateful enough, he could not be sure.

It was not often he thought about it. Their time together was so rarely spent together. Most often their intimacy was never allowed to develop intensity but generalised in parties, or groups, dissipated in cinemas or concerts and other events. He did not feel that he could reach out for her instinctively as he could even now for girls he just passed in the street. But Margaret was good.

'Maxwell said he was wondering when I would get round to it.'

She knew all about Maxwell.

'He always likes to pretend he anticipates what happens.'

'Do *you* think it's a good idea – this film?'

'I've told you. I think you should have stuck to your own sort of subject for your first film. You're good at the arts, writers and painters, that sort of thing. Daniel says you have more of an idea than any of them.'

'It's too cut off, Margaret. Besides – they don't *need* another director for that. And this *is* more *real*.'

He could say that to her when they were alone. She disagreed of course and talked about 'art' as a *central* 'reality experience' but he knew she would accept what he had just said: she gave him a lot of rope.

'I think it's very brave of you,' she said, later, when they were in bed. Still reading the book she was also puffing nervously at a cigarette and knocking off the ash over-frequently into an enormous ash-tray which featured a caricature of the Prime Minister on its inside base.

'It depends on who I can get.' Alan was still tense from his success. The entire day, since receiving Maxwell's go-ahead, had been such an effort to contain his euphoria that he was tired. 'I need someone who can really *talk*, you know, *speak* it.'

'Yes but darling, it's documentary isn't it? You're not look-ing for performers.'

He screwed his eyes up in the way Maxwell had. 'That's a varra moot point, the noo,' he answered, mocking his chief's accent. 'Varra moot t'indid,' he paused, 'Indeed,' he explained.

'You let him take you over like all the others,' she fretted. 'It's quite obvious he's just an entrepreneur. Maxwell uses your talent and works the system. He's a fixer, that's all. You shouldn't let yourself be influenced by him.'

Alan loved it when she ran Maxwell down although at the same time he considered her opinion on the man and his job to be childish and utterly worthless.

'Come on,' he said, having to make more of an effort to be jocular than he could have wished. 'Come on.'

She stubbed out her cigarette, put the bookmark carefully in place and turned, bumping into him rather heavily. 'Oh, I've forgotten my glasses.' Swinging round to place them on the table, her thin breasts swung across her chest and Alan's desire was threatened. She beamed to him and whispered 'Try to make it longer this time, will you darling?'

Her remark shuddered into him and yet he was so well trained that he found himself trying to do as she had asked, grateful, yes, pass exams, wear a suit for university, work hard, be careful about the way you talk, don't let them know you've never heard of Winnie the Pooh and *The Wind in the Willows*, if in doubt play the fool: a good life, a damned good life. She moaned in disappointment and he rolled away.

When she was asleep he got up and made himself some coffee. The failure had not moved him. Success there did not move him much now either: not much at all. 'Aged 24,' he said to himself in his Deep South accent, 'Al's sex life was over.' He opened the curtains of the sitting room and looked out on to the stricken street. The obscurely rooted sense of desolation clenched inside him: that was real.

The springy turf of his life since seventeen, the mossy banks
of ease, copses of curiosity, all life an extended simile of verdant opportunity weighed now too heavily now too lightly.
He hated this place. He hated the poverty, the dirt, the
desperation: he hated the knowledge that his kind of past
people lived there and he hated the fact that his kind of present people would drive them away, even from this. Yet he
had to stay: just as he had to do this programme for which he
was not really fitted. Only a mild disturbance, he told himself;
it was only that, no more than the common intimation of an
approaching depression – which until now was usually avoided
by the leap into a new interest, new company, a new shuffle
of the cards on the programme, a new edict from Maxwell.

But it was different this night. Or he wanted it to be different. And making a film, his own statement, could make it
different. Yes. If he had the courage – he wanted it to be
different. He had served well for long enough. And somehow
the accidental move to this place had shown him the extent
and the nature of the change such service had caused in him.
These streets had brought up the idea of prison.

He went to the bathroom and looked at himself. Hair flop-
ped attractively fair; clear grey eyes and a slim face; well built,
broad shoulders flat stomach. He tensed his muscles and bared
his teeth. In his old dialect, a thick Cumbrian accent, he nodded at his image and said: 'Aa've bin wundrin' when thou'd
get reound ter it, lad. Now then. Set to.'

His father's voice spoke that: he must go and see his parents
again: he'd neglected them lately.

The phone rang at seven the next morning and Alan was
asked by the sound recordist where and when the first location was to be. He had not worked it out.

'But I'm going gliding,' the man said with just a little pride:
both of them knew he could just have said 'I'm going away';

'what I mean by that,' he went on, picking up the dropped stitch, 'is I'll be uncontactable until, you know, I mean I won't come back unless I have to.'

'Monday then,' said Alan, briskly, wide-awake. 'Ring here at this time and I'll tell you. It'll be in London. It'll be in the morning. I'll want us to rendezvous about nine.'

'Thanks.'

'Happy Landings.'

'I landed in the bloody English Channel last time.'

The cosiness of the previous evening with Margaret, the fire and the Purcell seemed now to have been a gulled prologue, a trick which an outmoded scene or style had played on circumstances which simply did not fit. In some imperial fantasy you sat in tranquil contemplation of the great events which would soon unroll according to an inevitable and triumphant pattern. Becoming a 'film director' had sprung open such hopes. But any notion that he was an imperial majesty controlling events from a great height was soon dislodged.

He had thought that having been intensely involved in studio work for so long he would be subject neither to strain nor surprise in the making of a short film. But the words 'film director' were so powerfully glamorous that his poise was shaken, with pleasure, but still shaken. And as for the comparison with the studio – that soon went –

'In a studio,' he said to Margaret after the first day, eagerly bringing her the news, 'everything comes to you. People, ideas, contributors. And the cameras are there, the lights and sound and make-up are there, you have this great cavern of facilities, you're an airline pilot and they have to climb aboard if they want to get anywhere. Film makers are fighters – they have to sweep across the ground, looking for their target, searching for their material.'

Guady images coloured his hours.

Above all the difference centred in the fact that he was in

charge. If I don't do it, he thought, with an enormous sense
of exhilaration, nobody will.

That first morning telephone call triggered off a 'total in-
volvement' as Maxwell, in his even more sober moments,
would denominate the immense work he exacted from his
staff: they prided themselves on their capacity for work.

'How's your show comin' along, laddie?' Maxwell asked in
the bar that lunch-time and Alan blushed that the secret was
out. The others derided him, benevolently. He bought the
drinks. Before he sipped from his glass, Maxwell raised it an
inch and nodded at Alan and smiled: the man had a very
rare smile, it seemed to burst on to his face as if a flower had
thrust itself open in fast motion, even his skin seemed to
become younger and fresher: Alan knew he had been smiled
on.

His production secretary was a middle-aged woman who
had been with the programme since its beginning. She knew
so much about how to handle the organisation that Alan soon
abandoned any pretence and asked her what he should do: she
led him through the Byzantine bureaucracy as neatly as
Ariadne laying out her thread. She knew which police stations
were friendly about filming in which areas at which times: she
always arranged for there to be parking spaces: she would
check up on the availability of local cafés and pubs: she could
complete the various forms which the servicing departments
sent along, forms so long and complicated that the only valid
comparison was supposed to be that diabolical examination
necessary for entrance to the Chinese Civil Service: she
mothered him when contacts broke down and suggested he talk
to this other man she remembered from years ago: she made
coffee and knew when answering the phone whether he was
'in' or 'out': she had worked with all the crew before, several
score times, and they relaxed when Alan passed them over to
her: Doreen she was called, grey haired, very attractive, cheer-

ful, slim, astonishingly a spinster and once Maxwell's secretary but she preferred to work with directors who went out filming and he used her shrewdly to carry the young. It was a widely remarked fact that Doreen was the only person in the entire organisation who could bring that rare smile to Maxwell's face whenever he saw her. Alan wished that she had been younger and he would have married her. Just like that!

The whole world was – 'just like that!' – on those first couple of days. He was Orson Welles, he was Duncan Webb, he was a troubleshooter, he was a searcher for truth, he was William Wilberforce, he was a future Maxwell, he was the lean young still-eyed director unafraid of danger and obloquy raking the metropolis for examples of injustice which he would reveal to the public at whatever cost.

The excitement interfered with the expedition of his plan and again and again he forced himself to sit down and write out his schedule, his objectives and his 'line' on slips of paper.

'What it comes to in the end,' he said to Doreen, 'is that I must find somebody the viewer can sympathise with. Maxwell's right. We must never forget that for most people criminals appear as society's enemies. But what *I* want to show is that we need to see those we condemn, we *need* to have it in the open and so we *also* punish a criminal's dependants.'

Doreen nodded; her typing never stopped.

'*I* don't *know* anybody who's in prison or anybody who's *got* anybody in prison,' she said. 'So I suppose your argument doesn't apply to me.'

He checked a rush of irritation and the tapping typewriter was all the sound between them. It was a major objection to his line of philosophical enquiry.

'What I really think,' he said, flatly, 'is that if we're going to pretend that we want to help criminals then we should help them.'

'They should help the people they've harmed, that's what I think. They should be *made* to pay back the money they steal and support the people they do an injury to.'

'A lot of them *want* to.' He let his hand drop on a sheaf of newspaper cuttings. 'But why not do both? – help them and encourage them to pay compensation.'

It sounded terribly woolly.

'It should be interesting,' Doreen said; rather too loyally, Alan thought.

They were the only two in the vast production office: everyone else had already gone up to the studio to work on the build-up to the evening's transmission. Doreen and Alan went at the last minute – they saw the programme through, they had drinks with all involved afterwards, and throughout the confident, exuberant occasion Alan was gloomy. None of his leads had been successful and he dreaded being asked about his 'show' by Maxwell and despaired at the easy and accomplished chat of so many around him with such solid achievements to their name. The talk, which switched from public politics to organisational manoeuvres, and included one generously bawdy story from the successful novelist who had dominated the programme (even Maxwell had to admit the man's quality) was like Babel as he paid attention to the nagging inside his mind which was trying to strain a seven minute film out of the waves of information and impulse which broke over him.

He was glad to be out and decided to walk part of the way to his appointment. He got off the tube at Tottenham Court Road and began going north. As he strode up the Tottenham Court Road, he was inflamed with eagerness to be about his work. The noise of cars, the polluted air, the flak of images which streaked across his mind, shops blazing with underwear and jokes and magic toys, sex devices, erotica and the bazaar of affluent goodies, to his left the cinemas supported

by huge billboards of naked and titillating flesh, pillars of
enticement promising a Roman carnival inside the cavern's
mouth, coloured light bulbs raw as teeth and on his right, in
the east, the once sedate squares of Bloomsbury, the British
Museum, the University Library. New Values for Old – this
and the density of people on the street, each, it seemed this
night, alive with excited curiosity and so open to approach that
his skin prickled to make the welcome violation of their mystery – (and his eyes trailed so greedily after the women who
passed by – yet there was no thought of *not* returning to
Margaret) the whole feeling of the seedy, splendid, littered,
teasing, rackety, grand street, flanked by pools of learning and
acres of quiet habitations contentedly embedded in the city,
fed his mood and he hoped his film which sucked all his life
into it now, he thought, was become a vortex, himself willingly
trapped in the centre: he wanted to spin and be spun and
not to know the number which would fall.

Graham lived in a side street near Mornington Crescent
Tube Station. As much a twilight area as his own Alan
thought and he felt sturdy in their similarity. All those who
lived in such streets by choice were affirming something, Alan
thought, his head still singing from the cacophony of excitement stirred up by the walk along the city street; like the bar-
barians come upon the ruins they camped in the old places
and dreamed to begin again. He walked up the narrow steps
to the top flat.

'You looken for Gray-ham, mister?' A young West Indian
girl came on to the pink, peeling landing.

'Yes. I am.'

'He say you gotta see him in de pub. De Public Bah of de
Falcon; turn lef and all along you can' miss it.' She beamed
and then giggled. 'He says tell you he have a big black beard.
You know like a pirate.' She stroked an imaginary beard

and he returned her courteous laugh.

'The Falcon. Turn left. Thank you very much.'

'An' you tell him Maisie say "Sorry". You tell him that?'

'Maisie says she's sorry.'

'Yep. Just that. Nothin' further.' He nodded and felt really compelled to stay as long as she was standing in front of him. When he did remember himself and turn to leave, it was awkwardly done. He felt her eyes on top of his head, like midges in the thatch, as he trotted down the uncarpeted wooden steps.

'Hey mistah! Mistah!'

'Yes?' His head was thrust right back on to his shoulders.

'I ain't Maisie.'

'No?'

'*Hell* – no.' And she laughed again and again he had to laugh with her.

The Falcon was as broken down as any neo-realist could have wished and the inside was as neglected as the outside. If you knew anything about beer you stuck to bottled in a place like this and if you knew anything about self-preservation you kept the bottle handy before leaving after a briefly decent interval. In the public bar a juke box squatted on the red linoleum, lightless and silent but gleaming with chrome, a computer of song waiting for its supper. The bar was even now at this mid evening time disfigured by slops and the wispy lampshades gave no protection to bare bulbs which brutally displayed the poverty of the place and with their little light chased out all warmth. How, in such a spot, could he feel happy? But he did. It was edged with nervousness and relied on a great bank of securities built up over years and still available a short taxi ride away where in well dressed public houses well dressed men in public raised the hops and tapped the barley and culled the vine. Perhaps, he decided, it was only that he was so different here and what pleased

him really was the sense of himself clearly defined. The barman wore a brilliantly white sweat shirt which displayed the
weight of plump muscles once well groomed.

No one with a beard.

He stood at the bar and felt the lack of a foot-rest, staring
at himself in the mirror behind shelves holding a few half full
bottles of spirits and some old champagne glasses set out in
pairs: he counted fourteen. His bottle of beer was quickly
finished and still the sullen juke box had not stirred. He went
and fed it. The harsh music made more sense of the place.
He ordered a scotch and took it to a corner where he could
see all exits and all entrances.

Eventually, on his way to top up the juke box once more
he considered himself to have been nodded at by the barman.
He went across.

'You er, lookin' for a fella name of Graham?'

'Yes.'

'Biggish fella? Beard?'

'So I'm told. Yes.'

'He, er, said he'd be there,' a slip of paper was handed over,
'about now, about nine. That's an address.'

'Thanks.' Alan looked at the address.

'Is this near here?'

'No.'

'Have you an *A to Z*?'

'No.'

'I see.' Irresolutely Alan looked at the paper.

'Ask Jackie,' the voice behind him belonged to an old man
whose face was clenched white. 'Jackie knows whereabouts.
Arsk Jackie.' He was hoarse.

The barman nodded and briskly removed the paper from
Alan's grasp. He turned to nod gratefully to the old man.

'Jackie used t' be on the cabs, see. He 'as The Knowledge.'

'I see. That's handy.'

'Like an encycleepeed. Nothin' gets away.' The voice was badly strained.

'It must be hard to learn it all.'

'Some never do. They give up good jobs but they can't get The Knowledge and so where are they?'

Alan had nothing to answer.

When the street's location was found, he discovered that it was only half a dozen rows away from his own. He took a taxi.

There was laughter coming up from the basement and he stood for a moment to let it find a place in his mind. It was the most desolate street he could imagine. The taxi belted away rapidly, as from a bomb target. Eerily noisy in the empty street. Most of the houses were boarded up, waiting demolition. A long broad street, it held two cars, black, and one motor-bike; the few lights were dim and rare as camp fires across an embattled valley.

He knocked with unfelt heartiness and the laughter was guillotined. The man who opened the door was tall and brown skinned, his beard clipped and neat as a sailor's, his simple outfit of dark sweater, dark jeans and dark boots emphasising the neatness and the blue eyes keeping to the idea of the sea.

'You the T.V. man?'

Alan nodded: he felt that to say anything would be to say too much.

'We don't need no T.V. man.' The female voice was breathless, not recovered from the laughter.

'Who sent us a T.V. man?'

'Well?' Graham smiled and Alan returned it: not because the action was irresistible but because even so early and even in such a small matter he already felt in some way under the influence of this calm contained man who stood in the half-light at the half opened door; he smiled obediently.

'Alan Lawson,' he held out his hand. 'Graham Dixon?'

His hand was taken, lightly clasped, released.

'I have something to finish here. It'll take about an hour.'

'I could go to a pub.'

'Who *is* it?'

A blonde bush of hair bobbed over Graham's shoulder and curiosity was instantly transferred to welcome when she saw the good looking young man:

'Which pub?' said Graham.

Alan hesitated: on the choice of a pub so much could depend. He did not want to appear to be slumming it and yet he knew that all the pubs in the immediate neighbourhood were poor. The only 'decent' pub, however, was a rather notorious male pick-up place.

'Ask him in,' she said. 'Come on Graham,' she split up the name into two syllables, mouthing the last as 'yum', 'he looks harmless. Come in,' she said and pulled Graham's guarding arm from the door. 'I'm Betty.'

'Alan. Alan Lawson.'

'Betty Whitby.' She smiled and this was a warm smile, all easy to return. 'Pleased to meet you.'

'We could go out now and I could come back later,' Graham said.

'Oh no you don't!' She tugged at him, half-playfully. 'You said you'd do them shelves, Graham Dixon, and do them shelves you will.' She looked at Alan conspiratorially. 'Men'll try to dodge any work, won't they? Come on,' she pushed Graham and he allowed himself to be pushed. 'In and finish them, come on, come on!'

He went into the basement and was forced to stop by the sight of the walls.

'It's only water,' Betty said. She also stopped. Graham went ahead and a small boy dodged past him to fling himself at

Betty. 'But let's be fair – there aren't any rats in this place, are there, eh?' She cuddled her son, 'there aren't any silly old rats there then?' She looked at Alan. 'They used to run all over us in Leamington Street, that's where we moved from. Graham found us this. Come in. Have a cup of tea.'

He went into the room in which she lived with her three children. Graham was putting up shelves in the corner. The two beds were separated by packing cases and tatty chairs. Alan felt his heart lurch with a pity which overwhelmed him.

Betty chattered while she made tea: Graham worked efficiently and rapidly on the shelves, refusing Alan's offer of help (no offence taken, Alan thought, offended, though there *was* nothing he could do): the children bounced on the bed, white strained faces split to excitement over these two men in the house, and in the fireplace sat the television, shiny, new, out of place.

She made it easy for him. Her vivacity was in itself a great welcome. She was attractive: her breasts were rather too big for the modern fashion but with her thin waist and good legs she made her own fashion: the slovenly and careless dress appeared, to Alan, to suit her although he came to this conclusion greatly tentative: all judgement and assessments were threatened with the curse of being called patronising by a self-conscious censor which thrust itself to the front of his mind.

'Can you mend T.V.'s?'

'No. I'm afraid not.' Speak! Speak! His voice hammered his brain. Give! Give! Give!

'I had a boyfriend – I mean I knew a boy, once, he *could*. He could mend anything you cared to name. He mended my mum's radio once that hadn't gone since before the war but he just mended it. He used to nick spare parts – I mean, everybody did – from this electrical shop he worked in and all sorts of fiddly things he always could get hold of that made it work.' She paused and Alan plunged in.

'I – I work *for* television, I mean I make, *help* to make television programmes. I – you – do you watch?' he named Maxwell's programme.

'Who is it on that who, you know, talks on it?'

Alan gave her the name of the presenter and though she nodded pleasantly and politely it was without conviction. He suggested that at that stage in the evening her children would be more likely to be watching the other channel: she accepted his explanation gratefully, looking for presents.

'Do you meet everybody that's, you know, famous and stuff?' She giggled at the possibility and her eyes sucked at him, he thought, what force she had, the longing stretched out and clutched and drew.

'Who, in particular?'

She named some popular names. He said he knew them all, out of a desire to be friendly – or was he placating his conscience or her imagined fury? Or was he, in trying so hard, being merely banal and boasting? These questions swept across his mind like a hail of morse and the words he spoke could not wipe them clear. He invented inside information, saying that this one was good at cricket and that one wore a wig, this one had been married twice and another never drank – slanderless, harmless stuff, based on bar-gossip and good guessing. Soon she was watching him as raptly as her children were watching the gangster film on television. He was uncomfortable under such surveillance but that had to be borne: it was the least of things. He told her whatever he thought she most wanted to hear and later he thought that his half-truths were like the sickly, sweet food she stuffed the children with for treats. Their badly nourished and gaunt little bodies were pouched here and there by a sort of poisonous puppy fat: so too her strained and hungry mind by his gossip.

Graham's silence and his unobtrusive but intensive work made a contrast with Alan's picture of himself which was hard to bear.

'What 'you want to see old Graham for?' Betty patted her hair and glanced over at her helper with sly coyness, 'is he gonna be a T.V. star?'

Alan knew that Graham would resent his revealing the reason for seeking him out. But he himself resented being bullied by the other's indifference. In the silence between them he made his first stand against a force he considered in all ways superior.

'Maybe.'

'Really!' Betty was as alert as a startled hare. 'What for?'

Alan felt Graham's privacy clench around him.

'Well. He – we haven't discussed it yet – but he might help me on a programme I'm doing.'

'What about? Eh?'

Graham had not quite finished the job but he laid aside his tools most deliberately. Alan was aware of an inexplicable tension between himself and the other man.

'I can finish this tomorrow,' Graham said.

'What about this programme? Graham!' she appealed, almost wailed. 'Gray-yum. What about you being a T.V. star? Please.'

'I'll be no star,' he said, grimly. 'We'd best go.'

'Without telling me! Without telling me about the programme. That's mean.' She tugged, gently enough, at Alan's lapel and mocked a beggar's plea. 'Come on, mister, I'll not be able to sleep for not knowing. I'm terrible for worrying about things that I don't know. You've *got* to tell me. I won't get a wink, really.'

'It's a programme about prisons,' Alan said.

Her expression fled to Graham and in him found reassurance for her fright. Alan was bewildered.

'I'm doing a short film really about wives of men in prison. How they suffer, you know. What their life's like.'

Betty glanced at him suspiciously. Then, her expression switching with violent rapidity yet again, she released large tears.

'Their life?' she said. '*My* life you mean.'

Alan was filled with painful embarrassment and unable to get on top of it until they had walked a while through empty streets.

'Do you like West Indian food?' Graham asked.

'I've never had it.'

'It's cheap and it's open.' He went down some steps into a basement similar to Betty's. The restaurant was half-full. People knew Graham. Reggae music played on a tape: there were only two other whites there, young girls.

'It's my fault,' Graham said. 'I shouldn't have asked you to come there. I thought I'd be finished those shelves before now.' He looked at his hands: large, working hands but long fingered, graceful. 'I'm getting soft again.' It was difficult to look at him for any time without feeling pinned by those eyes, blue white, arctic. 'Her husband or whatever he is, he's the father of her youngest, Danny, he comes out in about ten days. Robbery with violence. She's been through it.'

Alan nodded. He wanted to ask Graham so much at once. He knew that he was a welfare officer: that before that he had travelled a good deal and that he painted and had exhibited quite successfully. Alan felt he had never met anyone who was so firmly right; whose passage was so independent: Graham seemed to him to be doing and acting while he observed and mirrored. Within an hour or so of meeting him, Alan regarded this man as a hero; an 'instant hero', he said to himself, hoping to break his fall by the usual self-conscious mockery but it was no use. Others too, he could see, felt Graham's unperturbed singleness: his was no special insight though it felt like one.

'It's, I mean, Betty would, I think, be exactly right for

what I'm trying to do.'

'Why?'

'Well – she talks very vividly. She could say what it was like.'

'Why should she?'

'I think imprisonment is bad for the man and worse for his wife and children. It's worth bringing it to people's attention.'

'It wouldn't do her much good.'

'Wouldn't it? She'd be paid. She'd enjoy the filming part, I think. And most of all she might welcome the chance to help.'

'Help who?'

Alan grinned: in his terse interrogator he had found a point of relief.

'I though you were going to help me.' He waited. 'Well that's why I came along to you.' Again he waited. 'Why did you agree to see me then?'

'I wanted to find out what you were up to.'

Alan relaxed. It could be a straightforward fight for a while.

'Why?'

'Too many of you lot buzzing around with your little meddling stings. Who needs you?'

Alan nodded and waited again. And waited.

'There was a film done in Manchester,' Graham began eventually, conceding with the faintest nod, 'Your people went along, taped hours, used minutes, cut out all the really important bits, made everybody over excited, confused all the local efforts and ended up with the usual mournful liberal slop about how sad it is to be sad, how poor poverty is – that sort of circular exercise. The point is there was a local group going there, getting organised, getting militant. These people have had enough pity. They need to be helped to organise themselves into action. They need to strike and to march and to demonstrate like the oppressed forgotten minority they are. They don't need pity. And they don't need tearful publicity.'

'I know about that film.' Alan pushed the plate away, undemonstratively but firmly. He had been trying to like the food from the beginning and could not. No point in pretending any longer: continued politeness would have made him sick. 'But I'm not dealing with the Poor or the Homeless or the Dispossessed . . .'

'If you're talking to Betty you are . . .'

'No I'm not. I'm setting out to do a specific job in a short film timed to come out on the day an important report is published and aimed at raising interest in a subject which needs attention. That's all.'

'If you say how sad she is, would you get someone to say how angry they are?'

'What about you?'

'No.'

Alan had found some sort of equilibrium. He felt clearer about his idea than at any time since it had occurred to him.

'I don't *need* your permission to talk to Betty you know,' he said. 'And I certainly won't put anything into the film that I don't want to put in.'

Graham pushed aside his naked plate and poured some more beer from the can.

'Yes,' he said. 'I hadn't much of a bluff. If you point a camera and wave a tenner down these streets, they'll smile, why shouldn't they?'

He said no more but sat back indifferently and glanced around the small restaurant quite carefully. Alan felt that he was again in the position of being somehow unworthy and parasitic and yet, simultaneously, he was determined to go through with his project and angry that he should be so easily and strangely baulked.

'I *will* be interviewing her,' he said. His voice was rather hoarse. 'If she agrees, of course.'

Graham nodded and bounced to his feet.

'You'll be on expenses?'

'Yes.'

He smiled, ruefully it seemed to Alan, and left.

He would have appreciated a word with Maxwell but the next day was Saturday and although he knew that other directors rang him up at any old time he did not think himself important enough to do that. But he was looking for a hand to steady the wheel, a pilot to check the course... Most of that day was spent searching. He raced around London fixing up his locations, his interviews, his alternatives. He had hoped to let Doreen alone for the week-end but by mid-day he needed help: she was only too pleased, she said.

He took her to Betty's with him. She organised the filming there for Wednesday evening: she managed to give Betty some of her fee in advance without fuss: she was efficient and businesslike and made the occasion work. Alan's confusions were unwrinkled by the practical difficulties she raised for his consideration: Betty was calmed and convinced by Doreen's brisk certainty. Towards the end of their stay, Alan found himself, most unfairly, sneaking a conspiratorial smile at Betty: she was inflated with pleasure and it came back to him like a charge. He resolved to buy some present for the kids: he corrected himself, the 'children'.

It was after seven by the time he and Doreen had hammered out the final schedule: she would type it on the Sunday: Alan was most embarrassed about this but there was nothing he could do to help, she assured him. They were in a Wimpy Bar: she preferred to have 'on the spot planning sessions' *out* of pubs she said: it was one of the few matters on which she was emphatic; Alan suspected a history of evenings which had sprawled long through drink. Though she was willing to work all hours she was not pleased to work unnecessary hours. She refused a Wimpeyburger and had only one cup of coffee. When she left him he went across to the nearest pub as a gesture of independence, perhaps: a forlorn gesture. He downed the drink rapidly and went to meet the gang.

They had a meal in a cheap Greek restaurant in Charlotte Street and enjoyed the overcrowded decor, the Greeker than Greek waiters, music and food: it was an example of 'good bad taste', the place, and at that hour they almost had it to themselves. The late film they went to was Japanese and brilliant. For drinks they pushed up to Daniel's, who had invited them to drop in 'very late'. They discovered that he had given a dinner party and his guests, he whispered in the hall, were 'very rich but just a *tiny* bit boring': they arrived just in time to blow on its past midnight embers and give it some last flames of interest. Daniel was very proud of his small, elegant house and they spent half an hour before they left looking at two new works by Colin Spencer and commenting on some samples of wallpaper which *had* to be chosen for his study. In bed Margaret was tired but not irritable: the knowledge of a free day following relaxed her: she was considerate.

Yet again and again, throughout the amusing and replete evening, Alan's thoughts were tugged back to his film. He would shut one eye, screw up the other until what he saw was a 'frame' and then slowly scan the room, seeing what the camera could take in: he did this most surreptitiously but even so they caught him at it and laughed. And then the meal – he could not erase the image of an opened can of beans on the packing case with a teaspoon jutting out of it: Betty's youngest had been feeding himself with them as if they were sweets. Their dinner in the restaurant, that 'simple meal', would have fed her family well for over a week: there was no equation that he could see, none. If only his film could make a difference. He went to sleep with the thought that he had forgotten to pass on the West Indian girl's message to Graham.

By Sunday afternoon he was far too fretful and impatient to stay among the sargasso sea of Sunday papers. They rang up people and went for a walk in Regent's Park.

In the sunlight the newly cleaned Nash Terraces gleamed with elegance and through the new leafed trees the white paint almost glittered. An army band played beside the boating lake and at the end of each piece when the audience in deckchairs applauded the conductor saluted them. The sound of their applause was like the clapping for a good shot at cricket. Children were well-behaved. The sun was not too hot but there was no wind. Small yachts drifted on the lake and crowded rowing boats bumped into each other heartily: they could cheer. It was calm and complicated and heavy with Englishness; they used the ugly word to break the awkwardness that such a contentment was to be found in such a scene.

There was a strangely unattractive tea-hut in the middle of the Park. Alan did his Blimp: Margaret liked this best; it reminded her of an uncle.

'Thing is,' he said, 'Chips shoved up this damned hutch in the war as a NAAFI for Elsie Froog and her gals – you know Elsie? Calls herself Lady Whatnot now, married a chappie in tinned food – so Elsie got on to these Housing Chappies and said, you know, dammit, if you expect the gals to patrol Regent's Park at dead of day against the dreadful Hun well they simply *must* have a tea-place for a chat and brush-up. Absolutely *no question*! Of course Elsie pulled a few ropes – matter of fact after the war she became quite a notable bell-ringer – and bless me if they didn't rattle up this old hutch, what? Of course it was unusable until 1948 because they couldn't lay water on. No tea without water, what? Another department what? Elsie had no ropes in that lot: jumped up bureaucrats, she called 'em, not a family I knew among the whole damn lot of them. Still, it was a nice thought wasn't it? And Royalty opened it, o yes, no less; soon after El Alamein.'

Alan arrived in the viewing theatre too early. Novices were supposed to take care to enter unobserved. It was bad form but he ignored the danger and stayed. This was the engine room. Here came films, uncut, just printed in the laboratories, 'rushes' these lengths of celluloid were called, which had been sent back to Maxwell's show from the world over and here too Maxwell himself, smack on nine, having read six newspapers from three countries and been through all his mail.

Between nine and ten Maxwell saw and commented. One of his secretaries took down the resulting messages which were later sent to the film editor, the cutter, to the producer concerned, to the cameraman, occasionally to the laboratories, to the interviewers and directors. Here Maxwell was in as near total control as he could get without himself going out on all the stories: he would have been in at the initiation, he would have given a briefing, he would have asked for reconnaissances where necessary and fussed over questions, he would, later, be in at the first assembly and the writing of the commentary, the presentation and the final cut but this was the hub of the film operation: here it came in as material and Maxwell shaped it for his programme. The demands of his show and his own style of journalism came before the desires of the director on the location and any aspiration he might have towards a personal character in his films: 'Metteurs-en-scene,' Maxwell would say, the voice grinding the French phrase to dust, 'Or Filum directors as the commonalty prefer to describe them – are all spare pricks at my wedding: *baby*!'

'Young Lawson itching to look at his mess, eh?' Maxwell grinned. The secretaries flanked him at the control panel. The others, if they noticed, gave no sign. It was too early: Maxwell's morning manner was borne dearly by his men.

Alan had shot film for two days, the Monday and Tuesday and seen nothing yet. He had not filmed Betty and not succeeded in getting in contact with Graham although he had spent a lunch break trying to trace him: there was nothing specific he wanted from him but somehow he *had* to see him . . .

'Right. Let's go.'

Alan's cameraman crept in beside him as the lights dimmed; Doreen sat at the back with the other secretaries, taking advantage of the light from the control panel to check her timings and her shot lists.

Maxwell accompanied the rushes with a low commentary, almost ceaseless, clearly indicating when he wanted a note taken. Alan's came up after film of refugees from Pakistan and a report smuggled back from a black penal settlement in South Africa. Yet he could scarcely pay attention to them.

When his own film came on! Oh – that shot of the row of houses, the camera sweeping relentlessly along the broken façades, dirty lace curtains twitching nervously, giving an effect, he thought, that the very buildings were poised between pain and embarrassment! And the interview with the two prisoners who talked about 'going mad' for lack of sex and how it made you either bottled up or homosexual – strong stuff! Shots of statistics, of more dilapidated houses and a short interview with a sad woman whose husband had emerged from Wormwood Scrubs impotent.

'A lot of material in two days,' Maxwell spoke louder for Alan's benefit. His tone was warm. 'You've had a rocket up you all right. There's no centre Alan, no interview with a woman we can believe in. The Wormwood Scrubs thing is too near farce: it shouldn't be: but in a 7 minute film it *will* be. I'm sure you have somebody else up your sleeve. The prisoners are good but your questions were too soft. When a criminal says he feels like killing somebody you must challenge it. That shot along the front of broken down old houses has been done a thousand times. O.K., next.'

On it went and Alan there trying to digest what he had been told, to suppress his appreciation and control his indignation, to concentrate on the film *now* being shown because that director too was there. He had somebody else up his sleeve all right!

He chose to walk part of the way to Betty's flat. The crew would have arrived already and begun to 'set up' but there was no need for him to be there. He had asked for a simple interior situation and it could be done just as efficiently without him.

As he dragged his feet through the streets where no trees grew, where no flowers were, where the only green came from weeds growing out of cracks in walls or bushing on roofs as if the earth had sinuously thrust itself through all the flaws and would soon once more cover the ground, streets which could be numbered in hundreds along a broad arc of London, streets which lay as some exhausted carcass of rubble curled about the sweetly rich city centre, like the dead hulk of a fated mammal used even in its death throes by the new conquering species of warmth, streets which broke with windows and with the scattered fright on children's faces – the heavy thought of his indifference sucked at him like guilt.

He was unprepared, he felt, for such a confrontation. He wished he had come on it gradually or could trace an emerging pattern in his behaviour: instead, it was as if his eyes had blinked open, closed again but were now unable to blot out the sight. And Graham, or what he believed of Graham, whispered to him of a world he had so far only brushed against or laughed at: an area in which the strong men were, he now thought, those who were prepared to search for alternatives, in ways to aid the distressed, ways to lead a private life, ways to interpret a man's concern. Only the independent had the courage to alter, he thought; and the feeling of independence he got from making this film, a feeling which could draw on years of self-help and apparent self-propulsion through university and immediately afterwards, this very feeling led him to question the limits set on it. The limits were defined above all by Graham who was outside them.

The thought of Graham had become a fixation: he saw him as a free spirit, a man of ringing justice, a sane secular missionary, a man able to be at ease in worlds of toughness and terror, able to enter violent bars and from there go tenderly to ruined lives in cramped spaces, in some earned and deserved way a man without any need to apologise or be afraid. His first encouraging schoolmaster had been something of a hero to Alan and so was Maxwell – but nothing, it seemed now, nothing like Graham: for Graham was the man he should have been, he thought, if he had been less concerned with career and comfort; and braver. And when he looked clearly into himself, at this film where all came out of him as from a pool and every moment he gazed Narcissus-like at his own image, then he remembered, clearly and painfully, the hotness of his younger passion for equality and fairness and saw how thickly coated with sugary success he had since become. Graham's concern, and by extension the concern of all those who worked in the shadows knowing that to change the image was the first way to change the object, all those who had deliberately climbed outside the security fence of privilege and secure organisations now appeared to Alan to be the achievement to be admired: he could broadcast that.

Betty's home was crowded.

The camera and the lights, the sound equipment, the expensive objects and their busy manipulators warmed and filled the basement which had been so desolate. Outside the door a crowd of children had gathered around the television vans and the drivers were answering questions cheerfully: inside,

Betty's children so cowed the nights he had come previously, so crouched so mousy before the snow-flaked television were beaming and proud, the pets of the Unit. Doreen had brought them all sweets. The electrician had repaired both the television and a faulty kettle. The assistant sound recordist was fixing a stiff window. This place in Alan's mind the very symbol of poverty and deprivation, of public squalor amid private affluence, this plague on England and nightmare of his last few days was lively, jolly, as full of Bank Holiday spirit as a crowded beach on a hot summer's day. And Betty looked stunning.

'I went to my friend Ellen's,' she said, seeing his eyes on her lavishly dressed hair, 'she used to be in the business, you know. She was up the West End doing all the big names at one time and when I told Graham he said yes, go, treat yourself, use some of this money on yourself because the rest's going on the kids every penny on clothes and shoes, especially that, don't they look nice? I thought I'd get them in advance ready for today to surprise you.' She swivelled on her toes, her hands on hips, and, having sensed his confusion and smelt that it was tinted with resentment of some sort, she looked suddenly guilty. 'Didn't I ought to have spent the money before I earnt it? . . . O Christ! Don't I get it unless I'm any good? Maybe I won't be, O Christ! I should've thought of that.'

'No. You'll get the fee. Of course you will.'

She was not convinced or rather she would not be convinced, wanting to root out the anger in him.

'You didn't want me to look nice, did you?' she said.

Alan looked around, unable to take a grip on the situation. They had a measure of privacy in the hall: how could he tell her that she was right? And further confusion, that her attraction reminded him so piercingly of the manner in which the girls he had 'fancied' in his own town in the past had been attractive: for to tell her that she was attractive would be a declaration: one which she longed for as she looked at him, so openly and

'You look fan-tas-tic – Oh! Fan-tas-tic!'

Graham pushed past him, picked her up and swirled her around the small space: yet though she kicked her heels with pleasure, Alan knew that the longing for *his* resolution of their knot was not erased. His pity the previous time had been interpreted as affection, perhaps even as love: he thought little of himself for being so sure but he had to see clearly and that was the fact. Perhaps, in some way, unconscious but definite, he had encouraged it: for she *had* the sort of loose loveliness, slovenly-sweet, that he had always lusted after and all Margaret's sensible permissiveness had not washed it away. Something in the smell. He smiled at her as Graham put her down, being unable to do anything else, smiled as he felt, warmly and lovingly: and she blushed with pleasure.

'Well,' said Graham, 'I heard you went into a prison.'

'Yes.'

'And you no doubt think they should be abolished.'

'Don't you?'

'No. We'll need them for the politicians, come the revolution, and all you lot.'

Alan shook his head. He could not cope with such chat. Casual talk of revolution was, to him, like giggling in church during holy communion.

'We're ready,' said Doreen, 'when you are.'

'Would you sit in please?' Alan asked Betty. 'Doreen will show you where. Then they can line up the shot. Medium Close Up!' he shouted the instruction needlessly down the stump of a corridor. Betty meekly followed his request.

'Doesn't she look great?'

'Yes. She does.' Alan's hopelessness was being rapidly healed by the realisation of how comical his confusion would appear to Graham. 'I suppose you encouraged her to dress up.'

'Well I knew you'd want her to look her best.'

'And I suppose you've told her what to say.'

'Just a word in her ear.'

'That's,' Alan felt himself taking a great stand — yet why should he cede all righteousness to this man? Why was it so difficult to find a moral centre in his own work? 'that's very thoughtful of you,' he said, 'although I think that you might have granted her the intelligence to make up answers for herself.'

'No need to be pissed off. You must have guessed I'd want to help her.'

'D'you think I want to harm her?'

'You might do it without intending to. This is a great event for her, you know. You're a great man. Television is as big as God Almighty. You can't resent her being helped. Can you?'

Alan shook his head and went into the room where Betty was seated like a nineteenth-century royal personage posing for an official photograph. Everyone smiled at Alan. He sat down, at the side of the camera.

'Won't they see you?' Betty asked.

'No. I'll ask you questions and then cut myself out.'

'But he'd look great, wouldn't he?' She appealed to them all, earnestly. 'I mean better than that one they have now; who wants to see *his* miserable face in the wallpaper every night? You should ask them to let you try, Alan. *I* would watch.' Her voice was firm and urgent and Alan was touched both by its innocence and by the general understanding of the crew who desisted from adding taunts to this vulnerable declaration.

'We take more than we'll use,' he said, 'much more. About five times more if necessary so that you needn't worry about stopping or saying something again: and don't worry about the time it takes, I can always cut it.' Why had he not said 'we' can always cut it or 'it can always be cut'? Inside his skull questions churned incessantly, drawing at him. Pathetic, he thought to himself, to be so unsettled by what was after all a bread and butter film on a straightforward issue for a no nonsense programme on a well-established network.

'Right. How long has Danny been in?'

'Nearly a year,' she whispered.

'Could you say that as a statement, please, Betty, you know: "He's been in for nearly a year".'

'He's been in for nearly a year,' meek, obedient she repeated his words. He went on, relaxing himself to relax her, mentally noting that she was saying nothing usable and able to record that fact without self-conscious nervousness because the nature of the job made his function a serving one.

They changed reels. The room was quiet – businesslike. A new magazine of film was loaded. The cameraman re-checked the light: Alan let the connection between Betty and himself go dead. He was exhausted already and knew that he had to re-charge their relationship entirely if he were to get anything from her.

'I suppose,' he said, when the soft whirr of the camera alerted him; he had not asked for the clapper-board which was such a slam of nervousness; they could put that on at the end – 'I suppose – well, most people would imagine it difficult for a young woman, an attractive young woman like you . . . there must be plenty of men want to, as it were, take your husband's place and you could scarcely be blamed for wishing that place to be filled from time to time.' The attempt to be tactful complicated his question and he feared he might have to ask it again. But he waited: the oldest rule of interviewing, Maxwell had told him, 'wait' – they'll always talk, just wait, 'silence works in favour of the one with the authority,' he used to say, 'expect an answer and you'll get one.'

Betty was absorbed in her effort to be helpful. For the first time in the interview she was sufficiently detached from the

burden of her superficial appearance to look natural: she
brushed at her hair with her hand and flicked it, lightly: and
then she smiled.

'Well you do miss it,' she said, so gently that Alan held his
breath: it was like carrying a rim-level cup full of water over
bumpy ground and not being allowed to spill a drop. He
could feel the crew, also, leaning with interest, and by that
attention easing and encouraging the words, the confession, the
performance. 'I mean I'm a fully normal woman and who
wouldn't miss it, sometimes? At nights you just cry and count
the days. I have a calendar to mark them off and sometimes I
bring one of the children in just for to have somebody there
and you think about it, you know.'

'Do you wonder if he's thinking about you?'

'Well, from his letters he is if you can believe them and
there's no reason you should tell lies or rather write them
down on paper when you're in a prison, is there? He doesn't
say as much, you know, but then I don't either, not as such.
But he's just as normal as anybody else. You would *think*
in prison they have no normal feelings but why shouldn't
they? Mind you I think it's the best part of the punishment,
that is the hardest. He says they all say that.'

'Of course *he* won't have any problem about being faithful to you.'

'Oh no.'

'Whereas you might, well of course you *would* from time to
time be approached by people in the natural course of events,
in pubs, dances . . .'

'I haven't been dancing since Danny went inside.'

'Wherever it might be.'

'I wouldn't go to a pub except with my mum and her man.
And my sister. You lead a very cut off life from entertainments
when you have three kids you know.'

'Harder,' Maxwell would have said, he thought, 'don't

draw back now; harder'. Alan spoke caressingly gently.

'But it must be very lonely for you, sexually lonely.'

'Yes.' She looked at him so openly that it was like a bright light and he blinked. And waited.

'And you make up your mind that you've *got* to put up with it,' her expression was as earnest as her tone, 'you've *got* to.' She paused. 'But you can't,' she added simply. 'Or I can't. Other fellas come along and ask and I try but they say why not, you know, we would enjoy it and I know we would.' She was concentrating so hard that her eyes had drifted away from his face and stared abstractedly. 'What I say to myself is that I'm no good to anybody if I'm not happy, nobody is, I'm no use to the children, it's no good, I've tried but I want it more since he went away than ever, for the comfort of it. You see,' now she turned to Alan and there was that heave inside him which experienced interviewers had told him about, like the time when the analysand transfers his emotions, like the time the penitent makes the real confession, like the time the suspect talks – he *knew* she was telling him everything and at that moment too, a sensation mixed with bewilderment and shame, his clearest thought was a prayer that the camera would have enough film in it. Yet how could he when she gave him trust like this? 'You see he's father to the youngest, you know that, well, I didn't want any more but he said he had to have one of *his* if he was to have a family life and I could understand that. But it's put me right off him. I didn't know how to tell him and then he was put away so I couldn't – but when Jenny came I went right off him because it was the usual thing, *I* was left with it all to do, know what I mean? He *meant* well but there was no regular money and no decent treatment. I don't mind him knocking me about but not the kids, I was glad they put him away really or I would have called those Cruelty to Children people to stop him. So it's been a blessing in a way because one thing about *most* men –

in the beginning, they're great. They are. They're really great
to a girl, they're smashing and they bring presents for the
kids and *I* don't mind giving them what they want. I mean
I've got it, haven't I? being honest, why shouldn't they have
a bit? It's when they get steady things go wrong and that's
the time to get out. Anyway *I* think so. But how can you say
all that when he's in prison and thinks you're faithful and
true – of course I tell him I am, it would break his heart –
what can you do? I dread him coming out. When I come from
the visiting with the other women there's a lot says the same.
He comes out in six days and he can't be counting the days
as hard as I am. But he'll want it, won't he? He'll be mad for
it. How can you tell him at a time like that?'

The camera whirred in silence. No one moved. Then there
was the 'flip' as the end-pieces of film went through the magazine.

'I had her in big close-up for most of that,' the cameraman
said quietly.

Alan nodded. Betty looked at him tentatively, seeking a
smile.

'Thank you,' he said.

'We have nineteen minutes thirty of material altogether,'
Doreen was briskness, sensing that her briskness was needed.
'That should be enough, shouldn't it?'

'O yes,' Alan replied. 'Yes that's fine.'

'Wrap?' The sound man.

'Yes.'

'Want to listen to your mummy?' he asked the boy and to
the child's unspeakable delight, fitted him into the earphones.

'I'll make some tea,' said Doreen.

'Was I all right?' Betty asked, anxious now, out of it. 'Did
I say what you wanted me to say?'

'Every blessed word!' Graham came across to her; his bitter
joviality alerted everyone in the room but Betty herself who

was too concerned about her performance to be open to anything else.

'Really?'

'O yes,' Graham stood beside her and patted her shoulder – patronisingly, Alan thought, wanting ammunition for an attack or rather for his defence – 'you said everything. They'll love it when they see it, all the voyeurs in the television world. They'll think you're the authentic voice of individualism and a great little piece of television.'

Betty took in a sharp breath and glanced wildly at Alan whose face was expressionless. The crew still went about their jobs of wrapping up the equipment but they were as alert as they had been during that last speech of Betty's in the interview.'

'Have you signed a contract?' Graham asked her.

'Have I?' . . . she asked Alan. He nodded.

'How much for?'

'It was – what was it?'

'Twenty-five and fifteen more on transmission. Plus a facility fee. Forty-five altogether.' Alan tried to be angry at Graham for what he was doing: but the emotion would not come.

'I can get forty-five pounds together,' Graham said. 'It'll take a few days but I can do it.' He glanced at Alan. 'Would you destroy that piece of film for that?'

'No.'

Betty now looked scared.

'You realise you're the worst sort of gutter puked journalist if you show that, don't you?'

'Whether I show it or not isn't your business.' His voice was shaky.

'Will you show it?'

'That'll depend.'

'On – on its "production value". Is that what you call it?

You're a tenth-rate rat. You know that? You're worse than the rest, pretending to care. Gutless, scavenging, liberal shit. I'll give you fifty. Make a profit!'

'Grah-yam. Please.' Betty tugged at his pullover, distressed and wanting peace.

'Tea,' said Doreen, carrying the tray before her and obliging Graham to move.

He stepped over to where Betty's son was standing in earphones, his face flushed with private and privileged enjoyment. Graham smacked his fist down on the spool of tape, ripped it off the recorder and snapped it in two, throwing out the thin yards of brown tape all across the room. The silence was stern. Then the frightened boy began to sob. Betty went to him to comfort him and the look of compounded affection and misery which Graham gave to the mother and son pierced Alan. But he had nothing to say.

'Excuse me,' Graham edged his way around Doreen and left.

'It's all right,' said the sound recordist. 'I always make a copy on another machine.'

By mid-evening he was so restless that he was unable to sit in a chair for more than a few moments. Inside him was an open cry of uncertainty which sucked in everything. He had begun suddenly making a savage attack on the flat, the street and the district the moment Margaret had arrived.

'I'm sorry,' he said, 'it's weak and foolish and so on but the place depresses the hell out of me. It's all very well for a slummer like you: to you this is a foreign country. To me, it's home and I got out of that long ago. We're leaving.'

'O.K.' Margaret replied, sing-song as she did whenever he was angry. 'O.Kay do-Kay. But this time – you find the flat. Not so easy, peasy weasy. Have a plum – catch.' She threw him the brown bag and he caught them too firmly. His hands were sticky.

'Right!' he said. Her casual responses always halted him.

'Are we going out tonight?' she asked.

'We *always* go out. We live like bloody aristocrats – out every night, seeing everything. We can't afford to go out.'

She opened her purse.

'I could buy you fish and chips and front row of the stalls.'

'That's not the point.'

'I see. You're in a Oh-how-dreadful-that-we-have-money-while-millions-starve-mood are you? Well – give all you've got to Oxfam and calm down.'

'Don't be so bloody flip. You think it's showing a sense of proportion. It's just educated frivolity. Flip with an honours degree.'

'*Work* for Oxfam then.'

'Oh – stop being so bloody practical! Everything can't be solved by the brisk application of commonsense, you know. You're like a thickheaded old man I once knew who trained our rugby team and slapped embrocation on everybody whatever happened without fail. Some things didn't respond.'

'There's bread in the bin,' she said. 'Stuff *that* down your throat. Bye!'

She came back in an hour or so, having walked to a pizzeria and had her supper.

Alan would have liked to make it up to her; he knew that she was right to be sensible, that her sense of proportion was a very desirable and proper limitation on self-interest – and yet he could not at present like her for all he might admire her. She was very skilful at keeping things together and he was overwhelmed by her sexual willingness and, to a great extent, shamelessness: besides which she had guided his way safely through the labyrinth of make-do, transient, youthful middle-class London and he had relied on her for that although he would have denied it. But this first film, himself the director, *his* statement able to be made and his responsibility brought into play: he had been waiting for this to mark his independence.

He would have liked to make it up but he sat on ignoring her even as she stood awaiting no more than a kind word at the half open door.

'I went for a pizza,' she said. 'They do one with bacon now.'

He did not reply, sick already at his boorishness but unwilling to give when giving would have appeared hypocritical.

'If making a two-penny half-penny film turns you into this, thank God you didn't direct *El Cid*, that's all I can say.'

She had found the line which released the knot. 'El Cid' was one of his favourite films. He had taken her to see it four times: it was a perfect example, he claimed, of great Pop Art, on the very highest level. She was helping him.

'I'm sorry,' he smiled rather glumly. 'I *did* have a bad day.'

'Surprise, surprise. Now *who* would have guessed? Can I get your slippers, sir?' She clumsily played the Geisha Girl as she came across to him, and then landed very heavily on his lap. He winced but masked it with a kiss.

In less than an hour he was as bad as ever.

'I'm going to see Daniel,' he said.

'Can I come?'

'O for Christ's sake! Can't I go *any*where on my own?'

'I'm beginning to think you find me just a tiny bit of a drag. Yes – no?'

'Look. I want to walk through some empty streets to see if Daniel's there. I don't want to phone him. I couldn't give a damn if he isn't in his house when I get there. It's that kind of a visit. Right?'

'Take a walk, Fido. Mind you don't foul the pavement and obey all the bye-laws.'

Again her jokiness and her acuteness could have released this hugged intensity he so desperately wanted to nurture.

But it was not release that he sought.

It was between two and three miles to Daniel's house and much of it went through the twilit area which was now in his mind as powerful a landscape as any in his childhood. It seemed he walked the streets alone for few were out on this sultry night and the greatest contact came from the accumulative pressure of thousands of dimly lit curtains, thousands of broken wall faces, litter, slight, sweet-rotten stench, half-glance and the burst of noise from a juke box or a public bar or a siren. Somewhere in this dense variety, somewhere in this poverty and unhappiness and confusion was the confusion he felt for Betty and the complex longings she had aroused in him and the flagellating conscience roused from years of safe deep freeze. He went to see Daniel so that he would not go to see Betty. He did not trust himself with her. Cats yowled as they were caught in backyards: he had once thought their cry like a baby's cry but tried to disassociate the two sounds ever since he had once seen the painful assaults made on the yowling shes.

Near Daniel's home the pattern changed, quite suddenly, and soon Regency cottages and Queen Anne terraces, pretty little early Victorian squares and high Edwardian grandeur occupied the tree-filled streets. Gardens sprang up as if a magic wand had been waved and the air was perfumed with the lush wet smells of the closely cultivated gardens of this highly metropolitan central suburb, expensive stocks and well bred plants. The ease and the elegance of it ought to have soothed him but even the mildest stimulus by now excited the singing tension in his head.

Daniel was rearranging his glass paintings. He had what he described as a 'fairly interesting collection of these pictorial perversions' and they went very well with the small chic rooms, the greens and the reflections giving peace and warmth to the rather predictable excellent taste of the furnishings. His ambition was to collect historical ones, 'Kiss me Hardy', that sort of thing, but they were outside his pocket at the moment and he bided his time with sporting scenes, concentrating particularly on boxing.

'It's very like you to have a bloody collection,' Alan said as he hooked yet another painting into yet another position for Daniel to judge its effect. 'Most people would just buy the odd thing because they liked it.'

'Cultural kleptomaniacs, my dear boy, those are your collectors. Civilisation needs misers. A little to the left.' His tone was much softer and plump with innuendo as the two of them were alone: he loved to tease out sexual ambiguities and Alan was such an easy screen on which to flash and flicker his patterns.

'Miserliness? *Greed*. You don't want a picture, you want an investment.'

'Quite right too. A sense of property is essential to civilised man. A little, symbolically, to the right – that's it.'

Alan climbed down the dainty library steps.

'I like their long johns, don't you?' Daniel smiled at the painting of the two moustachioed pugilists face to face in ancient pose. 'It somehow gives a sense of proportion to the whole business.'

'It was a *sport* then.'

'Exactly. That's the word I was searching for my dear. *Sport*. One last one – up there, over the door, a sort of surprise for the exeunts.' It was a painting of six angels blowing trumpets and the clouds parting. 'The last call,' said Daniel. 'I always wonder who posed for those camp little cherubs, don't you? I mean, Western Art, as our great Sports commentators would say, Western Art is full of the most corrupt and fleshy looking boys you could meet outside a Turkish market and they're all, *always*, shamelessly pretending to be rooting for Jesus. A more deceitful crop of hypocritical little tarts cannot be seen nay not in all Israel. Up a bit. There. All done. How nice it is to have a big strong man about the house.'

It was not often the two of them were alone together and on the other occasions Alan had found the banter greatly to his liking. He enjoyed his search for a role and his discovery of an exactly appropriate response. The game allowed the expression of mock witticisms, 'bastard neo-Wildisms', Daniel called them, 'a bastard destined to be passed over for the legitimate Oscars of the day but still . . .', and Alan liked the sense of control, of being above and outside the combat which such remarks induced. It was as much a tone of voice as a turn of phrase but he liked to try to catch both, wanted to ensnare that mandarin disdain as another of his 'turns'. Even now, despite the urgency he felt inside himself, he was caught in the play, and as it went on he felt obliged to explain and excuse himself and did so by deciding that this represented sparring, looking for an opening; not knowing his prime need of Daniel he could use the preliminaries to discover it.

'This whisky,' said Daniel, as they sat in the pleasant Edwardian armchairs – the snug room he called his study 'this whisky which I pour like liquid – which metals are light-brown? I don't want to use such a vulgar analogy as a metal, both copper and gold would lead you to think I was implying how expensive the stuff is, so, it must be a mineral, but brown jewellery is so rare, now why? Do our ladies fear the earth? Very well. The whisky must be the whisky must be the whisky. I call to your attention, anxious and unsecure host that I am, that this whisky is rare. This is no Auld Lang Syne and up your kilt for a last wee fling only, but something distilled in Fingal's cave when the spirit of Rob Roy stalked the outer Hebrides and the Lion of the North turned twice in its ancient tartan sleep. Music?'

'No thanks.'

'I approve. If it's good we cannot talk and who wants bad

music?'

'I don't mind Bach in the background.'

'Background music, my dear boy, is for people who live background lives.' He was warming up; enjoying himself.

'You sound sixty-six and satiated.'

Daniel smiled.

' "SATISFATA SED NON SATIATA" – Do you know that mot of Messalina? Never mind. Alliteration, ah me, that takes me back to the *Angst* of Anglo-Saxon and the thrash of adolescent verse. Mid-thirties, Alan, and well-preserved. Cricket and worry. No cornflakes.'

'That's new.' He pointed across the room, suddenly irritated by this self-concern.

'Yes.' Daniel got up and went over to the painting which practically filled a wall. It was an oil, a landscape, the dark tops of mountains, a brilliant white dominated sky and a sun red and slashing the sky with its last hail of power. 'Yes. This is my non-jokey work. It's an oil by a man called Terry Lee. He used to exhibit a lot in London late fifties early sixties but over the last few years he's been in the north working out a new way for himself. Teaching and so on, he has a good job. He's preparing for another assault on London. I bought this directly from him. It's quite simply staggering. And how he has the guts to compare with Turner by putting that sun in that shade just there! – o yes, he's serious. And expensive. I like that. He keeps his prices at a good market level. No loss of nerve. I approve.'

And Alan could relax because he too liked the huge and dramatic canvas in the same way as Daniel did: he could relax in the similarity because by revealing such a strong genuine response Daniel had put the earlier patter in its place.

'I wish to Christ I knew *my* market level,' Alan said as Daniel returned to his seat.

'Hm?' The sound was meant to encourage but Daniel

could not yet give Alan his full attention because his own still lingered on the painting and went from there to the adored objects, a washed silk rug, first editions of books on gardening, mexican statuettes, a set of early nineteenth-century brass rubbings ... the room, lit now, a light which brought out the richness in the deeply patterned dark green wallpaper, was truly like a cocoon, quiet, rich, cossetted, one of the cradles of stylish comfort, one of the many boxes of contained and concrete fantasy which were slung throughout London like loops of lit bulbs on a great ocean liner ...

Alan began to outline his thoughts.

'What's this Graham person like?'

He described him and was more wary: as if by personalising it Daniel had at once diminished it and somehow 'brought it out into the open'.

'You see,' he concluded, carefully, 'I think that what he's doing is right and really I ought to be doing the same sort of thing.'

'You'd be miserable,' Daniel replied, briskly.

'Do you think so?' Alan was greatly relieved and then, wearily he noted it, ashamed of being relieved.

'Unless, that is, you have Hidden Resources. I expect you believe you have. You must do. So you *could* be capable of it if that part of you I don't know is unexpectedly different from the part I do.'

'In what way different?'

'Tougher. Less reflective. Oddly enough, less compassionate. Your pin-up Graham must have a thick skin.'

'Oh – that's all ballocks, Daniel. It's the usual feeble self-indulgent romantic face-saving ...'

'Steady on.'

' ... notion that those who do good are necessarily less "sensitive" than those who cultivate their sensibility. Sensitivity is not the most important thing.'

'And there we disagree totally. It is far and away the most important thing. Without it all other qualities are a knot of muscle-bound behaviour patterns. Sensitivity, as I see it, is like the sensitivity on the plate which catches the picture. It's the magic that makes the world appear.'

Alan did not reply. How easily they fell into the same old rut! He predicted Daniel's next point and he was correct.

'And the world of course is inhabitable only in so far as it can be imagined. Just as Medawar says that scientists can consider only soluble problems, so human beings can exist only in possible conditions. And possibility is a gift from the imagination. "We are such stuff", you know the old line – "as fictions make us" it could be. What people call "harsh reality" is in fact a world without shape or form: they find it harsh because there is no frame and so confusion or rather mere nature is in control. And none of us know what nature is or what it will do. We have to imagine what it will do and the better our imaginations the more accurately we can predict. That's what Henry James was talking about when he said something to that effect about the immense comprehensiveness of great art: just as great life. In crude terms we admire a man who does a lot. In the highest terms we worship the creations of those, like the Renaissance men, who bring together so many elements into their one life that they, truly, create new lives for us all. The idea of grace for example is an invention: jaguars have grace but it is hardly probable that they admire each other for it. Someone, it is always an individual, once said "Look! how graceful he is" – and a world was born. Heavenly choir. End credits.'

'Look – Daniel – the point is that while I've been – I'm not following up your point and I'm sorry to appear boorish – but while I've been doing this film I've come up against a world which has been around for some time. We've laughed at the tatty productions of the underground press, we've argued away the extremist politics of the gilded New Left and the reductive radicals, we've pissed on these experiments at communal living and rejected acid and pot and street demonstrations; and so on and so on. But it seems to me from what I've seen that added together it makes more sense being like them, being part of the Alternative Society, they call themselves, than being like us, me anyway.'

'Yes I see,' Daniel replied. 'I know some of them. It's an interesting area. There's a landscape there I'd like to write about because it includes disaffected fugitives from the aristocracy – you've surely heard the one about the girl who put the Che in Cheyne Walk – and self-educated apprentices as well as old thirties shop-stewards and many of the most vivid of the younger lot, joining hands in a daisy chain that takes in rock as well as soft drugs, women's lib and black is beautiful, housing associations and popular poets, it's the alter ego of the wealthy jet set and just as international and exciting, it could be the jet's shadow on the land, and full of sexual experiments and a life style which ignores institutions and corporations except to feed off them as shareholders or as parasites: or to use them as enemies. And in so far as your organisation and your work is at all relevant to these people it is as an enemy. All that you want, a career, a chance to "do things"– within an institution, nice possessions, a viable long-term relationship with one person, a continuation of a long accepted outward form of manners and so on and so on is just so much bullshit to these people who'll laugh at you all the way to the couch.

'Now the main point is that *this* society anyway could in one limited but useful way be seen as a large body most of which is concerned to keep itself going and devoted to that end, caring much more about means than ends. The alternative society, your Graham, is an anti-body. It wants to infect this society. It wants to bring it a plague of "happiness, liberation,

justice, pleasure" – whatever – in the terms in which it appreciates those things. What has happened to *you* is that you
have taken their basic assumptions for granted.

'But who supports Graham? Who, to be terribly simple,
who pays his wages? Who sees his electricity comes out of the
plug? Who brings the wool for his sweater from the Canter-
bury plain to Marks and Sparks at a very reasonable price?
Joe Soap – yoked and driven of course by another Alternative
Society – the Boss-Men. But Joe Soap is part of it.'

'I wish you wouldn't say Joe Soap.'

'Fred Bloggs. So already your Graham is relying on a lot
of help. Now he acts as he thinks – that's true. Should we
all? Would it have been *"better"* if Dickens had dropped his
novels and devoted his life to the causes he after all only
touched on in his fiction? Civilisation is not a one track mind.
A truth is not the whole truth. Who knows that some final
Jehovah figure might find Dickens more *socially* useful even
than Wilberforce?'

'You're just playing around.'

'It wasn't Damascus you came from, was it?' Daniel paused:
Alan took note of the edge in his voice. 'I mean if I'm going
to be asked to give your concern a context, I don't see why in
exchange I should have all the righteousness of the ages poured
all over me.'

'I'm sorry.'

'I was finished anyway. Let us pray or, a quotation.

>   Nor love thy life nor hate; but what thou liv'st
>   Live well: how long or short permit to heaven.

That's all.'

'That's enough.'

'Milton.'

'Thanks.'

'The whole point is,' said Daniel, in gentle peroration,
coddling his glass and rocking the whisky from side to side,

'that if you decide to, you can ask yourself fundamental questions in any situation. Yes, that is we, the Between-Men have
that privilege: stronger men describe it as a vocation.'

Alan nodded. Daniel's play was called 'The Between Men'.
It was concerned with the choices available to those – like himself and his well heeled contemporaries – able to exercise a
wide range of possibilities and sympathies. He had hoped the
title would have a life of its own and it would become a catch
phrase like 'The Angry Young Men': it hadn't. Nevertheless
he himself would use it as such at times of relaxed intimacy
and it was a kindness to accept it for what he intended. In a
way, it was payment for the whisky, Alan thought, suddenly
light-hearted as he left Daniel's, clear and confident about what
he would do and impatient to do it instantly.

He took a taxi to the end of the street and walked: her light
was still on. He hesitated but the decision carried him on: it
was late for other considerations. He *had* to see her before the
end of this day to put *this* day right.

'I *knew* it would be you,' she said. She opened the door
fully and stood dressed exactly as he had left her so long ago
in the afternoon: no trace on her of the evening which must
have been the usual battle to settle the children and manage
the cooking which she did so ineptly.

Her certainty disturbed him.

'I needn't come in,' he said. 'I can say what I have to say
here.' The thrust of excitement which had sprayed throughout
him as he had come down the steps condensed before the
actual situation and it was as if a cold trickle went down his
mind.

'O, come in.' She thought he was being no more than polite
and walked ahead of him.

He followed her and saw in the room that all the children
were asleep; their new toys were beside their heads.

'The excitement tired them out,' she said, 'lucky them. It

always wakes me up. Was I all right *really*?' She sat down forcing him to do the same; her appeal jarred him.

'You were fine.'

She smiled at him and stretched just a little. There was no question that he had walked into a situation which could slither into complication so easily that it would appear unnoticeable. The whisky seemed to dry and burn in his head as he set himself against Betty's increasing attractiveness; so soft skinned, so open, so welcoming.

'It's silly of me to come here so late with the children asleep and so on,' Alan heard himself talking as if the voice had belonged to someone else; a clam, dry-sensed man detached from the entanglements of smell and sight and need in which the two bodies were intercoiling, 'but there was something on my conscience. You see – Danny will undoubtedly *see* this programme – he's bound to. They have television there and an item of this nature is bound to be seen and of course what you said this afternoon will upset him.'

It worked. Betty came out of her succumbing dream and paid attention to what he had actually said.

'I never thought of that.'

'And so if it is not what you want, I won't use it.'

'Is that why Graham offered you the fifty pounds then?' She was timid with the question.

'I suppose so.' Alan overrode a desire to justify his action in his own terms. 'Yes.'

'When will it be put on?'

'The day the report is officially published. Tuesday.'

'Danny comes out Wednesday.'

'I know.'

'I was going to meet him. You know. Just to show there are no hard feelings. But it's just as well you *told* me because I was going to see him this Saturday again – you know, like usual, I take the kids, they have a place for kids there now, it's very nice, they're very kind . . . I was going to tell him to look out for it.' She paused. 'I never thought of what I'd said hurting him. It will, won't it?'

'If he doesn't know about that it will, yes.'

'But it was good. You said it was good. It *was* the best bit, wasn't it?'

'It was good, yes. Maybe there were other bits just as good.'

'No, that was the best.'

She got up and in that action was self-consciousness. A natural reaction was heightened by the knowledge of a public and drama became part of her experience of the scene. She went and found a bottle of sherry which was about a quarter full. Alan checked and castigated the sentimentality which was pressing him to weep at her mock Hollywood mimicry, the sad charade of anxiety which covered real pain.

'We need a drink,' she said and emptied the bottle, with scrupulous justice regarding portions, into two willow-patterned cups. 'Cheers,' she said. 'My sister brought this round last time she came. Cheers.' Another gulp: she grimaced. Alan sipped.

'It'd be better if he got to know without me telling him,' she said. 'When I look him in the face I can't say it. I mean my mother and sister would have taken me back long ago if I had given him up but I couldn't, could I, with him being put away?' Her loyalty beat into Alan's head like the sound from a drum: how could he 'fancy' her? How could he not?

'They *hate* him, you know. He bashed up my brother-in-law once. He had fourteen stitches down his face. Here.' She drew a line from eye to mouth: the action was like that made by children shivering in the exciting mime of cutting their throats with their fingers. Alan felt closer to the violence, to the criminality of this 'subject' he had taken on as a task-to-be-accomplished, closer than at any time since he had begun. In the prison, the stench of doused disinfectant and the solidity of the bars and the warders had erased all notion of crime: it was punishment which dominated that scene. But here as Betty remembered the occasion when her man had slashed a long wound across the face of her sister's husband, here was the hushed reverence, the awe, the smack of heroism and the thrill of evil. He began to understand that she was as open to that as to everything else.

'He used to bash me as well, you know.' She leaned forward in her seat and pored over her cup of sherry. 'I didn't need to have to say anything, he would just "turn".'

'Why did you stay with him?' No – no – questions could only lead to knowledge and the bond of common confession. She hesitated. 'Why?'

"Well. For one thing he was good, you know, at *that*. And sometimes he was nice. He would bring presents and I knew they were nicked but sometimes they were nice.' She reached out and touched his face. 'His skin wasn't like yours though, Alan, not soft like yours.' His stomach, his whole body regis-tered a silent tremor of fear and lust – he could not deny it. He wanted her. She put down the cup and her arms reached out for his neck. He let her cling for a moment and then stood up. She was dragged up with him and felt him harden as she pressed herself against him.

'Alan, oh, Alan, Alan . . .'

His jawline ached. His legs were unsteady. Had she resisted his feeble fingered attempt to loosen her grip he would have been finished. But she was still afraid that he would reject her out of hand, that he would find her 'not good enough' and that terrible humility allowed him to escape.

'Not. Not now,' he said: and he even had the treachery to glance at the children. She blushed and nodded and he left.

On the street he walked like a man past drunkenness and did not know why he had not made love to her, taken her out on the town, danced, laughed, treated and enjoyed the night, the time.

Margaret was asleep, the light on, her book tumbled on the bedroom floor.

For the next few days and over the weekend, Alan had the legitimate excuse that he was cutting his film. He had taken far too much and was hard pressed by the editor who flung the black celluloid around the minute cutting room like a mad Father Christmas hurling out streamers. In fact, despite his huge Bakunin-black beard and his anarchistic jokes, the film editor was rather *like* a benevolent Liverpudlian Santa Claus, taking Alan gently through the festival of cutting, presenting him with viable alternatives as helpfully as Doreen had presented him with viable possibilities. At one stage the entire business of film making seemed to Alan to present itself as an incessant clamour for decisions: what to shoot, who to interview, where to set the camera, what lens, what movement, which angle, which shot to print, which to keep, which to shave, which to extend, which to juxtapose with which, which soundtrack to overlay, where to put the commentary, whether to have music and where, whether to have charts, whether to have photographs, where to intercut, whether to superimpose, where to cross-cut, where to cut away; and at each stage, though nursed and led by willing auxiliaries, the system was such that Alan was both primarily and finally responsible: a fate which he greatly desired. But as, in addition to this, Maxwell demanded he set up studio interviews with a new mixed media syndicate who were to stage their first exhibition in one of London's most famous stores, Alan had no time between bed and bed for anything but frantic work. For which he was glad.

He needed an excuse not to see Betty. He sent her a note. He was glad that he had a reason to postpone a self-promised confrontation with Graham. He could legitimately avoid

Daniel and the gang (even the Sunday congress was side-stepped because of a necessary visit to a warehouse in Putney where one of the mixed media syndicate had developed his latest 'Liquid-Lighting' Technique: three hours in a technicolour cavern of squirming pond life projected through art nouveau patterns on asbestos walls). While the pressure was so obvious that Margaret's irritation was transformed to concern and by the Sunday night she was clucking with contented alarm. He was in bed by ten sipping cocoa and right out until the morning's alarm.

Maxwell saw the first cuts after his session with the rushes. There was always a hiatus, like the intermission between the cartoons and shorts and trailers and the main feature film. Coffee was brought in; chastened directors fled to put yet more of the world on to film, and the first cuts and final cuts were loaded on to the projector. On that Monday morning, Alan was deeply relieved to discover that his was the only first-cut. Maxwell saw final cuts in the afternoon.

In the theatre were Dave, the editor, Doreen, as bedecked with ribboned stopwatches as any sports day vampire, Alan and Maxwell and Maxwell's production secretary. The film was shown. The lights came on.

'That's a very guid first assembly, Alan.' The name was pinned on to the sentence like a decoration: the level lowland tone seemed to hum in the small space, replacing the projector's clatter. 'The people are interesting and the argument is sound. I like your voice on the guide-track but Alex will read it. The music is unnecessary but it was worth the go. You'll be taking three minutes out of it and I expect they'll come chiefly from that woman – what's her name?'

'Betty,' said Doreen.

'The blonde?'

'Yes.'

'She was disappointing. I'll come back to her. The two

prisoners are better shorter and that comment from the warder is excellently used. Have you any more of him?'

'Just a bit where he says a bit more of the same about it being worse for the man. Nothing that adds.'

'The passage where he implies that he only makes love to his wife once a month – that's very well done. No one can take offence and it emphasises your point with humour. I still think the long panning shot across the terraced frontage is as old as documentary films and I can't see why, laddie, you need that sort of dallying with the tits when you're already down on the nest. Cut it out.'

'Yes sir! Right away sir! Off with her boobs!'

Maxwell nodded, as at a solemn rejoinder.

'Now, that blonde. I felt you were about to get something really extraordinary from her – and that's what the film lacks. You give us a very competent run around a representative section of the course and it will set up a discussion well enough when you've done the alterations and Alex and myself have worked on the commentary, but there's no real magic in the film as a film and that's a great deal to hope for but I thought you were capable of getting it. Some directors can, some can't. I'm disappointed. You can tell from the start those who can. I had a hunch – and I *still* have that hunch. You've time to get more from that blonde – you should try. She was working up to give you something really exceptionally good. What happened?'

As Maxwell had been talking, Doreen had been dipping her head more and more earnestly over her notepad, Dave had been glancing around wildly, bursting to talk but restrained by Alan who felt quite chill with determination. In the silence Maxwell sensed something was on.

'Well?'

'There was some more but it's unusable.'

'Why?'

'It would get her into trouble with her man. She says she's been unfaithful to him and so on, that she can't help it, you know, what you'd expect in a way from a sexy, honest woman; and I know that if he sees it he'll beat her up.'

'What does she say? About using it, I mean?'

'She's in no real position to help. She wants to be on television. She kids herself this is the best way to tell him "good-bye" which she intends to do anyway.'

'I've tagged it on to the end of the reel.' Dave could keep silence no longer. 'You can see it if you like.' His scouse accent made the attempt to suppress his excitement comical.

'You think it's good do you, Dave?' Maxwell asked. Dave looked hopelessly at Alan. Maxwell nodded and pressed the intercom. 'Run on,' he said.

They saw Betty's 'confession'. There, in the viewing theatre, plush on seats of old red velvet, watching a battered print with an inadequate soundtrack, she 'came over' like a punch in the face. She had opened up completely, and the camera had gone right in.

Once more the lights came on.

'I see your problem,' said Maxwell calmly. 'It's a bloody marvellous piece of film. I knew it was there. Why *should* this guy see it?'

'If *he* doesn't, his mates will: or somebody'll tell him when he comes out.'

'She's going to leave him anyway?'

'She says so.'

'We could hold it up for a day,' said Maxwell.

'We'd miss the publication date of the report.'

'Her piece is worth it.'

Alan shook his head. Maxwell stood up.

'Your problem, laddie.' He buttoned up his waistcoat, straightened his tie and then put on his jacket – always worn outside the office. 'But those few minutes of hers are the best material I've seen for quite a wee while. Work at it.'

The decision was made and put into effect by Wednesday lunch-time. The film was to go out that evening. He gave himself his lunch hour to get across London to Betty's place, explain it to her, and be back for the rehearsal of the studio discussion.

The basement door was opened by a small Indian man, middle-aged, neatly dressed, a relaxed, quizzical expression on his face which made Alan conscious of his rush, of the rather over-colourful combination of silk scarves and denim and of the taxi above them, black through the railings, ticking away like a time bomb.

'I was looking for Betty . . .' O Jesus Christ! He had forgotten her second name! Damn him. Damn! Damn! Damn!

'I believe there was a young lady used to have the flat before I moved in,' the Indian replied, strictly polite. 'But I'm afraid I never met her.'

'And you've no idea where she went.'

'None at all I'm afraid. I'm awfully sorry.'

'Please. It's I who . . . did a man called Graham help you to . . sorry, thank you.'

He leapt up the steps and directed the taxi to Graham's flat. He forced himself to walk up the last flight of stairs. The door to Graham's flat was half-open. His knock was answered by a pleasant 'come in.'

The West Indian girl he had seen on his previous visit was nursing Betty's youngest child.

'Do you know where Graham is?'

'He be back here soon.'

'Is he at the pub?'

'Sorry,' she shook her head.

By now Alan felt cooler and he paid off the taxi and walked quickly to the pub. The juke-box thundered and the pub

rocked with the exuberant mid-day drinking of an Irish building force which had come over from the new block of flats
being erected in the middle of the derelict area like a Peel
Tower in a wasteland. Graham was at the corner of the bar,
on a stool, reading a small book which was undoubtedly just
the volume that every man of spirit ought to be reading, Alan
thought with poorly attempted mockery – Third World Politics, Debray most probably, the scholarly revolutionary. Alan
could understand why the establishment so hated those who
were so few but so against it: it was the glare of righteousness
which caused the fear. And Alan, too, felt outside the sympathy of this righteousness as he stood for a moment and looked
across the jostling bar to Graham. Within that righteousness
was right, Alan thought, but it was not necessary for everyone
to be a fundamentalist. There was no one true way but many:
not even justice could be worth the denial of different means.

Graham looked up, saw him and without hesitation grinned
and beckoned him over. Alan was immensely relieved and inflated with pleasure as he pushed his way through to the
corner.

'What d'you drink?'

'Just a half please. Draught Guinness.'

'If they've any left after the wild geese have been at the
taps. Half a Guinness Eric, thanks.'

'Do you . . . do you know where Betty is?'

'Yes.'

'Where?'

'Safe and sound.'

'You won't say.'

'No. Now then – one half of Guinness. Famous television
man here, Eric, give him a smile – you'll be on the box.
Cheers.'

'Cheers.' Alan sipped through the froth and felt stupid for
having been so easily gulled.

'It's all right,' said Graham, 'they won't turn on you. Just the Labouring Classes in their Leisure-Hour, you know. Something to tell your chums about. They're your Audience, aren't they? Get some research in at the grass roots.' He slid off his chair and moved to edge past Alan who put his glass on the counter and laid his other hand on Graham's tense arm. He had to find a line to keep on his feet, to keep this man from walking all over him. Graham paused for a moment.

'This Guinness is a bit sour,' he said. 'Sorry.'

He walked out, depressed that he was so despised by someone whose life he admired so much, someone who had not only finer feelings but tougher reactions to them. It was a shameful luxury to catch yet another taxi back and throughout the afternoon as the studio clanked into operation like a fanciful ship's engine room suddenly seconded by a showbiz tycoon, as the questions were rehearsed and the carefully balanced contributors sat on each side of the impartial chairman like stereo loudspeakers flanking the turntable, as the time for the transmission of his first film drew near and he caught a glimpse of his name on the credits during the final run-through, as he hoped his mother had got his letter and felt anxious that someone might uncover his filial vanity, as he went over the film frame by frame and saw it fall apart in his mind, as the time came and then passed when his footage was on the air, he could not stop thinking with shame about Betty and with uncertainty about Graham.

'Do you think,' he asked of Maxwell afterwards as they had a drink, 'that it's more important to make a film like that or to actually do something about it?'

'Making a film is an art, laddie. We're not artists.'

'But doing something I mean directly; there; so that something has changed. Say, organising a sort of trade union for prisoners' wives for example – that sort of thing.'

'You're asking the question they all ask at the beginning.

Should we do or should we report? It's should we stay or should we leave?'

'And what's the answer?'

'That's your affair, laddie.'

'Who leaves?'

'Some do. Some go.'

'And those who stay?'

'Other questions come up.' Maxwell grinned and Alan was embraced by that famous beam of genial good nature.

'How about a drink? – that kind of thing.'

Margaret was desolate. She had been obliged to work late and then trapped in an underground train for half-an-hour between stations. She had missed it.

No one rang.

They went to the New Cinema to see the latest batch of underground movies. On the way back in the tube, Alan fell asleep, his head bouncing on Margaret's shoulder as the empty tube rattled along the tracks.

Just as they were going to bed, Daniel rang. After giving Alan the most welcome congratulations and expertly picking on just the right points and appreciating precisely the right nuances and cross-references and above all the ironies both in the film and in the discussion, he said:

'I was rather surprised there was no Betty after all you'd said about her.'

'It didn't work out.'

'I missed her. You know? Silly, isn't it? – probably because you'd led me to expect so much, the film lacked a sort of *positive centre* in the full meaning of both those words. It was excellent – and do believe that – I wouldn't lie – it would be too easy to say I'd not seen it at all – but in those studio things you arranged on Arts subjects there was always that little *touch*, *some*thing, you know. It could be quite irrelevant: as Betty sounded. It wasn't there in quite the same way.'

'Maybe I should stick to art.'

'Maybe.'

'Well. Thanks for ringing anyway.'

'Frank's on Saturday?'

'Yes. See you.'

'Take care. Bye.' Daniel's farewell was rather breathless and the phone clicked down most gently.

I'll make love to *you* tonight,' said Margaret, heartily. 'You look whacked.'

'Just let's lie. Just, lie. Shall we?'

She sighed and nudged her head under his chin. Uncertainly, her fingers trailed up and down his spine.

He woke at half past five and got up, instantly alert. Margaret was in a deep huddle of bedclothes and undisturbed by his departure. He left a note downstairs on the kitchen table.

His street looked better in this early dawn light than at any other time. It was as if full daylight depressed and dispirited the place: for these bricks, though battered and neglected, were well enough at dawn. It would be cowardice to run from them. For reasons he could not entirely deduce this particular band of London, this twilight stretch was some sort of battleground and he was in it. Beyond it lay the grace and favour villages of London which were as desirable and interesting as ever, but this was the analogy he needed if he was to do anything at all.

Milk carts and police cars, paper boys and sudden articulated lorries; the metropolis slept through sunrise. He walked.

Outside the prison he took great care to take up a safe position. He had recce'd it before going back to a transport café for some more tea and another bacon sandwich and now it was ten to eight and he was watching.

Graham pulled up the van directly outside the prison gates and then drove off a little way, parking down the main street which led to the place. She had brought her two oldest children. All three looked very small and comfortless beneath the high walls of the prison. She tugged at the children's clothes, making them tidy to divert her nervousness. As the clock struck eight the doors opened and he came out.

For a moment he stood there and Alan could see that he was steadying himself. Then he set his face hard and walked to her, no opening of arms, the mackintosh still carried neatly and in the other hand the case. It was Betty who opened to him and he stood rigidly while she embraced him. When she turned to lead him to the van he saw that she was crying, her face shining with the tears. In his own throat there was a lump and he breathed deeply while in his mind, so clearly that it might have been spoken aloud, he heard: 'Good. Good. Good . . .'

When the noise of the van had died away he began to walk and after only a few steps felt very tired. He made for the main road where there might be a taxi and found that he was beginning to think over a film which would attempt to show the *real* effect of locking a man up for a long time. To show the full man, as people tried to do in a novel. The point would be to begin it on the day a man was charged with a serious crime which would be likely to result in a long sentence – he would have to be someone with a record – but how would the sub judice ruling affect starting so early? Anyway the point would be to visit the prison regularly with a camera crew. To build up a portrait over about a two-year period. Of course the only way in which this could be done logically would be to have regular access to a unit through a regular programme such as Maxwell's. The crew would have to do other things in between. The point would be, though, to get say a psychiatrist, a social worker and perhaps a writer, to examine the film shot as you went along and to intersperse their developing comments with the film. Who knows, perhaps you could *stay* in the prison for a while and shoot what had never been seen before. Not just an interior – document the whole texture of a prisoner's life – were the cliches true? was it so vile? alternatively, was it more like other institutions than a separate institution?

On the main road the traffic roared into London. The rush hour was on. The city had to be fed. Alan found a bench on a stretch of roadside grass which this local council preserved along its busiest highway to remind the metal boxed worker of nature and the alternative. As the traffic increased he began to make his notes, occasionally glancing up to see if there was a taxi.

FREDA BROMHEAD

MRS BARBIZON was walking up and down her warm room when John Askew arrived at the house, about twenty minutes before dinner-time. Outside, London was gripped by windless, cleansing cold; pavements had been velveted with frost all day. In the distance she could hear the stoical intermittent growl of buses, and sometimes there were nearer sounds of taxis scuttling through the bitter streets.

Nowadays one did not trail, but she walked as though she did, past three long windows, shuttered and curtained, to a sculptured fireplace in one direction, and then to a wall of bookshelves in the other. Above the books her own portrait – a triumphant-looking girl painted years ago by Orpen – watched her rhythmic pacing, the prelude to what was to be an evening alone, a silent meal, and a time afterwards when perhaps her thoughts might relax into the laziness of weeds in a stream.

John was shown into the room – for there was still someone to show people in – evidently tidied and nerved to play his social part, nose and ears stung by the sharp air on his walk from the underground. Mrs Barbizon was quite able to dissemble the fact that she had no idea who he was, but even she could not soften the truth, when it emerged, that her husband had asked this young man to dinner, and then completely forgotten to mention the invitation and gone out.

'Unforgivable! But, Mr Askew, we shall just have to forgive him and be as cheerful as we can together. But of course you mustn't go away again! No, no, I wasn't expecting anyone else, simply an evening by myself, with a hard choice between correcting proofs or playing patience.' (She saw him look at the galley sheets that streamed over her desk and remind himself: 'Oh yes, *she* writes too.') 'Do sit down. It's dreadful to face proofs, but then I have puritanical regrets about playing patience – won't you come nearer the fire? – though Tolstoy used to, they say, and I was encouraged to read somewhere only today that Gordon Craig was sometimes riveted by it. I do wish I knew what kinds they played.'

She knew she was prattling, but he looked now as if he had been slapped across the face, and she was trying to get him away from the rueful moment to a stage where they might sit drinking sherry and feel pleased with each other for being blameless and behaving well.

He was standing uncertainly, ignoring the chair and her talk. 'Is there a . . . Would you mind if I washed my hands?' he asked abruptly.

'Yes, of course. Across the hall – I'll show you.'

She took the opportunity to go and persuade her kitchen to improvise something, for the honour of the house, and to choose a bottle of her husband's more cherished wine to see them through whatever kind of ordeal the evening might prove to be.

The sitting-room was empty when she returned to it, and she went over to the desk and folded up the galleys – her memoirs – with the irrational feeling that they were still private and if anyone else glanced at them it would seem like eavesdropping. He was away so long that she began to feel concern, and then to wonder if he could have let himself out of the house. After all, he might have been hoping for some reinforcement of the personality from being accepted on dining terms by James Barbizon, and from whatever summing-up of the confusion of existence the older man would offer him to take away. Instead, he found himself cruelly diminished, unmemorable and disregarded.

She felt the poignancy of this, but feared that she could do very little to help it, and began pacing up and down again as she waited, wishing that her part in the evening were more predictable. If it were written in French, she thought, it would lead to her consoling him with the revelation of mature physical love (timed to fit between the departure of the domestic staff and the return of her husband). She recalled a phrase from such a passage describing an 'accessible bosom' – but her own did not feel at all accessible to John Askew, though she was sorry for his slapped look and prepared to shelter him from the cold night and from what she guessed was a rather exposed life.

She paused by her desk and was verifying in a diary the time of next day's unwelcome appointment at her bank when he came back. Although it was obviously an ordeal for him to have to make an entrance for the second time, he was now resolutely at ease.

'I find your house most excellently warmed. It feels as if it's never been allowed to get cold.'

'Ah, yes. Our fires have been maturing here for twenty years. It makes a difference.' (No need for him to know how soon those fires might have to go out.)

'Even this enormous room – you can use every corner of it, like a stage set.' He began to prowl, carrying the glass of sherry she had passed him. 'It's rather a splendid room. I suppose you hardly notice it any more.'

'When you came in before I thought I saw it for the first time, as you did, and I liked it. It was caught unawares and found satisfactory. That's one of the pleasures of people coming to see you.'

'I expect it is. At present I live in a guest-house in Earls Court.'

'Tell me about that.'

'Oh – Yale locks and meters in every room, you know. Very clean. Unfortunately there's a leaping mauve plastic greyhound fixed quite immovably on my wall. I've covered it with a Christopher Logue poster but a bit of tail still protrudes. The other people are either very ordinary or most peculiar, but they come and go rather frequently, so we don't get to know each other much, though we all eat in a dining-room in the basement. The landlady says: "There you are, little one," when she puts the plate down in front of you. She's very kind. She was in the A.T.S.'

'Will you stay there long?'

'Who can say? That portrait was you, wasn't it?'

'Yes, it's me,' she answered, noticing afterwards that they had used different tenses.

'I'm afraid,' he said, doggedly getting it over, 'that I've never read any of your books.'

She asked smiling: 'What do you read?'

'Oh, American writers. No one else appears to have any life in them. Fitzgerald, Henry Miller, Bellow.... I except the two I've read by your husband. He may be traditional, but he does seem to notice what goes on.'

'He would be glad to know you think so. He sets great store by being aware.'

'A friend of mine maintains that there are two kinds of novelists: one says: "The butcher was bad-tempered", but the other writes about a bad-tempered man and may incidentally tell you he's a butcher. We prefer the second approach.'

'It's the view you have of people when you go into a hospital ward – very striking, especially when they're women, to see them stripped of circumstances, one to a bed. All the same I can never write about anyone unless I know what they do, or what they live on. What do you do, Mr Askew?'

'Well, I'm with this printing firm. Also I'm Treasurer of the MS. Club, which your husband came to speak to last week.

He asked me a great deal about printing. He's going to set up a press of his own, isn't he?'

'It was an idea . . . He's been having a bad row with his publishers. Damn you, he said to them at one point, I'll print my own books in future and distribute them myself. But it's patched up for the present.'

'Oh. Then if he's given up the idea of the press, I dare say that's why he didn't remember – '

'Certainly not. He has constitutional amnesia. He'll be sorry to have missed you because apart from anything else we both think it's absurd not to know more about the printing of books.'

'I did make some notes . . . And I brought some examples of type-faces.'

'Do show me.'

At once he became mature and fluent. His exposition, which lasted until their meal was ready, made her consider skill and judgement which she was ashamed of having almost disregarded until then. At one point he went to the shelves and chose an example at random. It happened to be one of her own books, and while he discussed its page-area, head and folio lines, allowance for 'take-up' at the back margins in binding, and criticised in passing its insufficient leading between lines, she thought again of the unusual aspect of people seen in hospital, isolated from personal connections.

'Printing will be your honourable profession, as well as your business, won't it?' she said, when they were at table.

'It's the thing I have an aptitude for. My father runs a newspaper in East Anglia, so the interest started a long time ago. But of course it is an obsessional occupation, and – as this friend of mine says – it's only a secondary activity, not really creative.'

'Is your friend creative?'

'He's an artist.'

'A painter?'

'He doesn't *paint* any more!' (This enthusiastic repudiation made her instantly up in arms on behalf of works by the Camden Town group which hung round the dining-room walls.) 'He's having an exhibition next month of his new strip-offs. It's a method he invented himself. He pastes a lot of sheets of paper one on top of the other on a board – any colour, patterned or plain, it doesn't matter, so long as they're all the size of the board. When they're dry he strips them away unevenly, and he gets marvellous free effects. The idea came from the hoardings on the underground. He used to travel a lot on the District Line when he was teaching at the St Giles Art School – he says he collected enough material on those journeys to last him for years. I expect you've seen his sprinkle designs for textiles? Those came from the random spirals on the platforms when the station staff had gone over them with watering-cans. He uses just the same technique himself.'

Mrs Barbizon helped him to cheese soufflé, murmuring: 'There you are, little one,' as she passed the plate, less to amuse him than to keep up her own spirits.

When she had helped herself she decided to tell him: 'It's a curious thing. I can be quite hardy about your not reading me, and not being American, and not even the right kind of novelist – but when you tell me about an artist who does non-paintings I feel as miserable as if all the masterpieces of the world had been thrown into the sea.' She saw that he was looking both appalled and wary, as if he found himself alone with someone gravely ill, and added: 'I expect it's an elderly form of sulking. Because honestly I respect your friend for finding his visual material on the District Line instead of going to Capri for it. Let's finish this wine.'

The wine floated them away from potential rocks and on to the end of dinner, and when they crossed the black-and-white squared hall back to the sitting-room, where coffee was waiting, she was calling him by his first name, and he was talking again with his constrained unconstraint.

'I know now what made me say this room was like a stage set – it could be the scene for one of those very good Shaw revivals. I've been to one or two. Such a surprise to me to find that the famous red revolutionary was absolutely embedded in upper-middle-class form: libraries and parlourmaids and so on. Probably never even realised it himself. And so pathetically timid about sex.'

'He knew quite a lot about love, I think. But you wouldn't expect me to be objective about Shaw! He was a father figure to my generation.'

'Well, of course you had to take your father figures as you found them,' he said sympathetically.

Mrs Barbizon poured the coffee. She had known Shaw, not very well, but he had given her wise help during the upheaval in her life before her second marriage. Those days of agonising and daring, and the achievements that followed, were all in the folded galley proofs on the desk. By now she was feeling that John Askew had come to the house on purpose to make her see that they were too faded and faraway to have been worth writing down. In spite of the wine, she felt cold and pinched. It would have been embarrassing at that moment to look up at the portrait of the girl confidently wearing her old-fashioned hat.

Still, she had to move within their social trap. 'John, when we have had coffee would you care to play chess?'

'I'm afraid it's a game I've never taken to.'

'Perhaps you would like to look through my husband's record collection and see if there's anything you want to hear.'

'Thank you – but if you don't mind I can never listen to music with just one other person. It has to be either by myself or in an audience. Do you know what I mean? If I'm to be watched listening then I don't know what to do.'

She nodded in answer to his question, and then the conversation died down as suddenly as a fire of paper. They were drawing near a moment of agonising blankness, but her sense of having to act in the nick of time showed only in the brisk way in which she said: 'Well, I'll tell you what *I* would like to do – but I don't know if you'll approve. Ever since you explained the technique, it's been growing on me that I want to make a strip-off picture.'

'Why? Just as a joke? I thought you said –'

'With no ulterior motive, really. Not to prove anything. But of course you may feel that it would be a sort of betrayal of your friend's idea.'

As if this irritated him, he instantly changed his ground. 'I don't see why I should mind. I would quite like to see how it does work – on a purely experimental basis.'

It was not the way in which either of them had expected to spend the evening – kneeling on the floor with left-over wallpaper and Christmas wrappings and copies of *The Times* between them, and a pastry-board which she had fetched from the kitchen – and almost at once it altered their relationship. Latent antagonisms, which might have been played off in a game of chess, simply lapsed while for the following hour they cut and measured and pasted. Gradually a kind of sympathy grew up between them; they consulted in a companionable way about the next layer to be chosen. In their semi-silence they heard the general grinding of the city round them, a sound of time being used up and the future being got ready.

When the last sheet had been smoothed on to the board there had to be an interval to let the paste dry, and at the end of a train of thought which had been absorbing him he asked, on a sigh: 'I wonder if you would tell me something?'

Whatever he wanted to know was serious. She was prepared to be questioned about her fear of death, but he went

on, with some difficulty in getting it out: 'Is it your impres-
sion that I have a loud voice – that in fact I'm inclined to
shout? I've been told that I do and it's a thing one simply
can't trust one's own judgement about. Likewise that when
one gets voluble one reveals an East Anglian accent.'

She could not take advantage of a lowered guard. She
answered truthfully: 'I flinch from shouters. You would have
noticed it. I think you speak in a perfectly well-modulated
way, with nothing at all rustic about it.'

This satisfied him, but it seemed to lead to a rearrangement
of ideas that still was not comfortable. For a moment his
cheek was dented by that assertion of the jaw which is so
revealing that an observer may feel that he should not have
seen it.

'Has some young woman been teasing you, John?'

'Not precisely in that way . . . It's a person I've known for
years. He grew up in the same town.'

'Is he at your guest-house, too?'

'He's got a house of his own at Islington, with a studio
built on. It was the only London household I knew when I
first came. I was, in fact, at his wedding; hardly anyone was.'

Mrs Barbizon leaned against the warm marble of the fireplace; perhaps a splendid passivity was what the evening had
really demanded of her.

'Of course, he outgrew our town very soon . . . He has an
immensely positive personality. He had ideas about absolutely
everything. I knew because I never lost touch with him . . .
When he was having his long analysis he wanted to walk in the
dark, night after night. Sometimes we didn't say a word for
miles . . . It always ended in talking like maniacs. I remember
once we found ourselves practically in the country, discussing
symbols and the unconscious mind . . .'

At last John leaned over and tried one corner of the pasted
papers with a fingernail. 'We shall be able to begin tearing

off in a minute. I've never seen him do it, and I believe he usually leaves them all night, but I don't think that's really necessary.'

When the time came to finish the experiment they each ripped carelessly at random layers of paper, and then set the board on top of the bookshelves and stood back to consider the result and to decide which way up it should read. Their reactions were sharply different.

John said: 'It's absolutely authentic! It might be from the studio of the great man himself,' and gave an excited laugh, as if he were unused to the pleasure of a small disloyalty.

Mrs Barbizon was bewildered: 'We used no skill and no thought, and yet it works! You can look at it. You could look at it for quite a long time. But it can't possibly have any meaning.'

The thing seemed alive. A corner of newsprint showed under a layer of transparent green; that green was vivid over a black and white pattern, but reappeared cloudily under a sheet of thin white. Textures were multiplied. All the colours and jagged shapes flowed together, as if they were floating and organising themselves of their own accord. She was disconcerted by the pleasure it gave her.

'John, tell me, how can you explain – ?'

But he was of no use to her, for he had taken the length of the room in great free strides and was now laughing in earnest. There was a kind of mottled radiance about him as he stood grabbing at the mantelpiece, swinging to and fro and guffawing in the same rhythm. She heard him pause for a moment and snort to himself: 'Creativity! It takes more to print the page of a book!' and he shot a confident look into the mirror over the hearth, as if congratulating himself that he had broken old habits of dependence and survived disillusion and was never going to be taken in any more. (Of course, he also had to laugh away the humiliation of his arrival that evening.)

She was left to her resentful enjoyment of the strip-off picture, and it was a problem that could not simply be dismissed. She wished that it had not been added to her other worries at this time. Was it art? If so, lifelong convictions were in tatters. It took a resolute moral stiffening to realise that the longer she persisted in living the more perplexities life was bound to provide. Theories would always be turned inside out, accepted answers inevitably be seen not to be final. The process was not going to stop because of her diminishing time and strength.

The small mantelpiece clock sweetly but firmly pinged eleven close to John's hand.

'Oh, but I ought to go!'

At least he was grown up enough to know not only when but how to take leave. Soon, in the hall, he was hunching into his coat and wrapping round himself the elation which would keep him warm when he went out. It was unlikely that he would ever come to the house again, and his brief appearance there reminded Mrs Barbizon of those young men in cotton running-clothes who sometimes dash across the streets at night, their unfinished faces lit up in headlights before they disappear. One is left behind troubled, almost sad.

But he was coming towards her, hand outstretched, beaming with assurance: 'Now I must say good-night and thank you for what was – after all – by no means an entirely wasted evening!'

The opening and closing of the front door a few minutes later let into the house a column of cold air which took a little time to disperse.

The Mystery of the Missing Cap

MANOJ DAS

IT is certainly not my motive, in recounting this episode of
two decades ago, to raise a laugh at the expense of Sri Moharana or Babu Virkishore, then the Hon'ble Minister of Fisheries
and Fine Arts of my state. On the contrary, I wish my friends
and readers to share the sympathy I have secretly nurtured in
my heart for these two men over the past two decades.

Sri Moharana was a well-to-do man. His was the only
pukka house in an area of twenty villages. Whitewashed on
the eve of India achieving independence, the house shone as a
sort of tourist attraction for the villagers nearby. They stopped
and looked at it whenever they passed by, for none could
overlook the symbolism in this operation that had been carried
out after nearly half a century.

Sri Moharana had a considerable reputation as a conscien-
tious and generous man. He was an exemplary host with two
ponds full of choice fish and a number of well-cared-for cows.
He was a happy villager.

Came independence. As is well-known, the ancient land of
India has had four major castes from time immemorial. But
during the days immediately preceding independence a new
caste was emerging all over the country – the caste of patriots.
The Fifteenth of August 1947 gave a big boost to their growth.
In almost every village, beside the Brahmins, Kshatriyas, Vais-
yas and Sudras, a couple of patriots came into being.

It was observed that the little fisheries of Sri Moharana were
often exercised in honour of these new people. And observers
began to notice that Sri Moharana had become a patriot. As I

discovered later, he had even nursed the ambition of becoming a Member of the State Legislature. The incident I now relate occurred at the outset of the endeavour in that direction. I witnessed the incident as a small boy (my maternal uncle's house which I frequently visited being just near Sri Moharana's house). When I narrate it, I am obliged to do so with the understanding which has matured in me with time.

In those early days of national ministries there were no deputy or sub-deputy ministers. All were full-fledged Hon'ble Ministers, and Babu Virkishore, who held the portfolios of Fisheries and Fine Arts, hailed from our district. The sponsors of Sri Moharana thought it proper that his debut into politics should have the blessings of Babu Virkishore.

In those days a minister's daily life was largely made up of speech-making at public receptions. A reception was arranged for Babu Virkishore with Sri Moharana as the Chairman of the Reception Committee. Sri Moharana's huge ancestral cane chair was laid with a linen cover, upon which the best village seamstress had laced a pair of herons with two big fishes in their beaks. For a fortnight every day the village lower primary school children devoted the afternoon to the practice of the welcome song. Among the many strange phenomena wrought by the spirit of the times was the composition of this song; for the composer, the head-pundit of the school, had lived sixty-seven years without any poetic activity. The refrain of the song still raises echoes in me. Its literal translation would be:

> 'O mighty minister, tell us, O tell us,
> How do you administer this long and broad universe!'

The rest of the song catalogues the great changes nature and humanity experienced on the occasion of the minister's coming: how the sun almost blushed in romantic happiness that morning, how each and every bird recited a particular *raga*, and with what anxiety the womenfolk waited to blow their conch-shells when the minister stepped into the village.

I know that nowadays ministers do not enjoy such glory. But it was very different then. We the rustic children wrangled over several questions: What does a minister eat? What does he think? Does he sleep or not? Does he ever suffer from colic or colds?

Sri Moharana himself was hectically excited. He used to sleep for a full hour in the afternoon. But he gave up this habit at least ten days prior to the reception. All his time passed in examining and re-examining details of the arrangements. Yet he seemed nervously uncertain.

At last the big day came. The minister got down from his jeep when it entered the very first welcome arch on the outskirts of the village. There he was profusely garlanded by Sri Moharana and then was requested to re-enter the jeep as the destination was still a furlong away. But the minister smiled and made some statement which meant that great though destiny had made him, he loved to keep his feet on the ground! Moharana and his friends looked ecstatic.

While hundreds applauded and shouted *Babu Virkishore ki jai* and *Bharatmata ki jai*, etc., the elephantine minister plodded through the street, to the embarrassment of the poor, naked earth.

And I still remember the look of Sri Moharana when the minister's long round arm rested on his shrunken neck – a look which I have seen only once or twice later in life in the faces of dying people who have lived a contented and complete life. Sri Moharana's look suggested: 'What more, what more, O my mortal life, could you expect from the world? My, my!'

All the people – even invalids – for many of whom it was the experience of a lifetime – were alternately shouting slogans and gaping. We, the half-naked, pot-bellied, uncivilised chil-

dren, walked parallel to the minister at a safe distance and
felt extremely small and guilty.

At Sri Moharana's house the minister and his entourage
were treated with tender-coconut juice, followed by the most
luxurious lunch I had ever seen, with about twenty dishes
around the sweetened, ghee-baked rice.

Soon the minister retired to the cabin set apart for him.
Though it was summer, the cabin's window being open to a
big pond and a grove, there was enough air to lull this giant
of a man to sound sleep. Volunteers had been posted to see that
no noise whatever would originate from anywhere in the
village to disturb the minister's midsummer dream.

I had by then separated myself from my companions. Being
ambitious, I was eager to be as physically close to the great
man as possible. And the minister sleeping seemed a most
ideal condition for achieving my goal.

Mustering all my self-confidence, I slowly approached the
window facing the pond. This was the rear side of the house.
The minister's P.A. and entourage were on the opposite side.

While I stood near the window, suffering the first shock of
disillusionment of my life regarding great men – for the
minister was snoring like an ordinary man – something most
extraordinary happened. Speechless I was already; the incident
rendered me witless.

Through the window I had observed that the minister's egg-
bald head rested on a gigantic pillow while his white cap lay
on a table near his cot. Now I saw the notoriously irresponsible
Jhandoo bounce towards the window like a bolt from the blue
and pick up the cap. Throwing a meaningful glance at me,
he disappeared into the grove.

Even when my stupefaction passed I was unable to shout,
partly because of my deep affection for Jhandoo (knowing that
the consequences of his crime could be fatal to him), and
partly for fear that the minister's snoring might cease. At that

time I was in a dilemma as to which I should value more –
the great man's cap or his snoring.

I returned home pensive. But before long I heard a suppressed yet excited noise. Crossing into Sri Moharana's com-
pound I saw the minister's P.A. flitting about like a butter-
fly and heard his repeated mumbling, 'Mysterious, mysterious!'
The minister was obviously inside the cabin. But nobody dared
go in. Sri Moharana stood thunderstruck, as did the other
patriots. The Public Relations Officer was heard saying, 'The
Hon'ble Minister does not mind the loss of the cap so much as
the way it disappeared. Evidently there is a deep-rooted con-
spiracy. The seriousness of the matter can never be exaggerated.
In fact, I fear, it may have devastating consequences on the
political situation of the land.'

I could see Sri Moharana literally shaking. He was sweating
like an ice-cream stick, so profusely that I was afraid at that
rate he might completely melt away in a few hours.

When I saw Sri Moharana's condition, the conflict within
me as to whether I should keep the knowledge of the mystery
a secret or disclose it, was resolved. I signalled him to follow
me, which he eagerly did. A drowning man will indeed clutch
at a straw.

After I told him what had happened he stood dumb for a
moment with eyes closed. Then wiping sweat from his forehead, he smiled like a patient whose disease has been accurately
diagnosed but is known to be incurable. He then patted me
and said, 'My son, nice you told me. But keep it to strictly
yourself. I will reward you later.'

The incident had thrown a wet blanket on the occasion.
From the sepulchral silence of the minister's room only his
intermittent coughing could be heard. And every time he
coughed, anxiety damped the spirit of the people in the courtyard and on the veranda.

I went over to join my friends. They were full of anxiety.

One said that if the thief were caught, the police would hang him on the big banian tree beside the river. 'Some twigs have already been cut off,' someone said. 'Perhaps all the villagers will be thrown into jail,' said another. Among us there were even such naives who believed that the minister's cap was a sort of Aladdin's lamp, that anyone who put it on would possess ministerial power.

But the situation changed rapidly. I saw the minister and Sri Moharana coming out to the veranda. I did not know how Sri Moharana had explained the matter to the minister. But the minister was all smiles. It was the most remarkable smile he had hitherto displayed. By then at least half a dozen caps had been procured for him. But he appeared with his head bare. Even to a boy like me it was obvious that his bald pate wore an aura of martyrdom.

Not less than five thousand people had gathered before the specially constructed pandal when the minister ascended it, that remarkable smile still clinging to his lips. Sri Moharana's niece, the lone High-School-educated girl of the area, garlanded the minister. A prolonged thunderous applause greeted the event; for, that was the first time our people saw what they had only heard in the tales of the ancient *Swayamvaras*, a grown-up girl garlanding a man in public. Then the chorus 'O mighty minister' was sung to the accompaniment of two harmoniums, a violin and a *khol*, because it had been tuned in the *kirtan* style.

Then it was Sri Moharana's turn to say a few words of welcome as the Chairman of the Reception Committee. I saw him (I was standing just below the pandal) moving his legs and hands in a very awkward fashion. Certainly that was nervousness. But with a successful exercise of will-power he grabbed the glittering mike and managed to speak for nearly an hour giving a chronological account of Babu Virkishore's achievements and conveying gratitude, on behalf of the nation, to the departed souls of the minister's parents but for whom the world would have been without the minister.

I was happy that Sri Moharana did well in his first public speech. But the greatest shock was yet to come – in the concluding observation of Sri Moharana.

Well, many would take Sri Moharana as a pukka politician. But I can swear that it was out of his goodness – a goodness unbalanced by excitement – that Sri Moharana uttered the lie. He said, his voice raised in a crescendo, 'My brothers and sisters, you all must have heard about the mysterious disappearance of the Hon'ble Minister's cap. You think that the property is stolen, don't you? Naturally. But not so, ladies and gentlemen, not so!'

Sri Moharana smiled mysteriously. The minister nodded his big, bald head which glowed like a satellite. Sri Moharana resumed, 'You all are dying to know what happened to the cap. Isn't that so? Yes, yes, naturally. You are dying. Well, it is like this: a certain nobleman of our area has taken it away. Why? Well, to preserve it as a sacred memento. He was obliged to take it away secretly because otherwise the Hon'ble Minister of Fisheries and Fine Arts, who is a burning example of humility, would never have permitted our friend the nobleman to view the cap as anything sacred!'

Sri Moharana stopped and brought out of his pocket a handkerchief full of coins and holding it before the audience, said, 'Well, ladies and gentlemen, our friend the nobleman has requested me to place this humble amount of one hundred and one rupees at the disposal of the Hon'ble Minister for some little use in his blessed life's mission, the service of the people.'

Sri Moharana bowed and handed over the money to the minister who, with a most graceful gesture, accepted it. Applause and various words of wonder and appreciation broke out like a hurricane. Even the minister and Sri Moharana clapped their hands.

Then, of course, the minister spoke for two and a half hours, drinking a glass of milk in between, at the end of which he declared that as a mark of respect to the unknown admirer of his, he had decided to remain bareheaded for that whole night although the good earth did not lack for caps and, in fact, a surge of caps had already tried to crown his undaunted head.

Soon my shock gave way to a double-edged feeling for Sri Moharana; an appreciation of his presence of mind and a sadness for his having to spend one hundred and one rupees to cover Jhandoo the monkey's mischief.

That night all the respectable people of the area partook of the dinner that the Reception Committee gave in honour of the minister. Glances of awe and esteem were frequently thrown at the minister's bald pate and homage paid to the honourable thief.

But when I saw Sri Moharana in the morning, I could immediately read in his eyes the guilt that haunted him – at least whenever he saw me. Sri Moharana perhaps had never uttered a lie; but when at last he did, he was forced to utter it before thousands of people. God apart, at least there was one creature, that is myself, who knew that he was no longer a man of truth.

The minister, however, looked extremely delighted. He did not seem to notice with what constraint Sri Moharana was conducting himself before him.

At last came the moment of the minister's departure. He was served with a glass of sweetened curd in his cabin. While sipping it slowly, he said, in a voice choked with curd and emotion, 'Well, Moharana, ha ha! the way things are moving, ha ha! I am afraid, ha ha! people would start snatching away my clothes, ha ha! and ha ha! I may have to go about, ha ha! naked! ha ha ha! But I don't mind! ha ha! That is the price of love! ha ha ha!'

The minister finished his curd and came out to the rear

veranda facing the pond and the grove to wash his mouth. Sri
Moharana followed him with water in a mug. There was nobody in the veranda except me. My presence there was not
accidental. A few minutes before I had observed that the rascal
Jhandoo, playing with the minister's cap was slowly approaching the veranda. Seldom had I wished for anything so ardently
as I wished then for Jhandoo to go unnoticed by the minister.
He was a monkey not in a figurative sense, but a real little monkey. When he was an infant his mother had taken shelter inside Sri Moharana's house in order to save her male child from
the usual wrath of its father. Sri Moharana had not been at
home and his servants killed the mother monkey. Sri Moharana became extremely sad, did not eat for one and a half days
and, to compensate for the wrong done, nursed the baby
monkey, christened Jhandoo, with great affection.

After Jhandoo had grown up a little he often escaped into
the grove. He was half domesticated and half wild. He played
with everybody, and everybody tolerated him. We children
were extremely fond of him.

Then to my horror, I saw Jhandoo rushing towards us from
the other side of the pond. I made an effort to warn Sri
Moharana but in vain. Jhandoo got there in the twinkling of
an eye. He sat down between the minister and Sri Moharana.
He put the cap once on his own head and, then taking it off,
offered it to the minister with a very genial gesture.

My heartbeat had trebled. Looking at Sri Moharana's face
I saw an extremely pitiable image – pale as death. The surprised minister mumbled out, 'Er ... er ... isn't this one the
very cap taken away by the nobleman?'

And something most fantastic came out of the dry lips of
Sri Moharana who seemed to be on the verge of collapsing.
He said, 'Yes, yes, this is the nobleman ...'

His eyes bulging out, the minister managed to say, 'What?
... What did you say? ... Well?'

But Sri Moharana was no longer in a position to say anything. He broke into tears. Next moment I saw the Hon'ble Minister of Fisheries and Fine Arts weeping too.

The P.A.'s voice was heard from the opposite veranda, 'Sir, the jeep is ready.'

The minister gulped the mugful of water and walked towards the jeep. Sri Moharana followed him. Their reddened eyes and drawn faces were interpreted as marks of sorrow of separation.

Sri Moharana's political endeavour is not known to have gone any farther. And it is strange that the Hon'ble Minister Babu Virkishore who was willing to be robbed of his clothes was soon completely forgotten in politics. I strongly feel that it was this episode of the cap that changed the course of their lives.

ANDREW GRAHAM

IF I could have foreseen the – how shall I put it – the eerie experience which awaited me I should have tried to get out of going. Francis Destrel, a widower cousin of two generations back, had died. I was his godson and the obvious person to represent the family at his funeral. I was seventeen.

When the day came I got up early and took the breakfast train to London. It was a dank January day with a nippy east wind. St Pancras smelling sulphurous: a taxi to Paddington with that stale sweet stench which taxis used to have: early lunch with no appetite at the station hotel, and then through fog and engine smoke to the Oxford train.

Glancing through the papers I saw, in Peterborough's column: 'Francis Destrel, the explorer and naturalist whose death was recently announced, was greatly respected as an authority on the birds and mammals of New Guinea and Kamchatka. His book *The Cruise of the Contessina*, published over forty years ago, remains one of the best informed works on the subject.

'At Arlingford, his lovely Georgian house in Oxfordshire ...'

How odd, I thought, to see it all in print. Cousin Francis saying: 'When I was in Kamchatka ...' Cousin Francis sitting over his after-dinner claret, and Oliver, his superlative parlour-maid, rustling in at a quarter to ten with hot peeled chestnuts in a napkin on a silver plate.

I closed my eyes and was back in the candlelit dining-room with furniture shining as mahogany used to shine in the brave old days of housemaids. Cousin Francis with his neat beard, and a hand with a cameo ring fingering the stem of his wine-glass, and the rosy glow from the red lining of his waistcoat reflected on his starched shirtfront. I don't know if this was thought to be a vulgarism – I'm inclined to think it was – but the effect was charming.

When I had stayed at Arlingford as a child I had had plenty of time to explore. I liked best the museum room which was a sort of mummified chapter of my cousin's life, of the years in the eighteen-seventies and eighties when, in his friend Sir Henry Loveday's yacht, the *Contessina*, he had gone on voyages of exploration. There were framed maps with a thin red line showing the route the yacht had taken, glass cases containing curious objects, or huge butterflies or exotic birds. I remember with affection the racquet-tailed kingfisher and the whiskered puffin.

In a corner of the room was a second door with a velvet curtain in front of it. I cannot remember why I had been reluctant to open it. Nannies and governesses were fond of telling children what not to do. Had one of them once put a prohibition on it? Or had I myself decided to keep the room behind the door behind the curtain as a private mystery?

When I was about ten the word 'funk' must have become part of my vocabulary because I remember deciding that next time I stayed at Arlingford I must conquer childish fears and see what lay behind the door.

I had opened it gingerly, the curtain moving with it on a brass rod held by brackets, and found a small uncarpeted room lit by a bullseye window partly obscured by ivy. In it were two things: a black japanned deed-box and, on a shelf, a glass-fronted case with curtains drawn in front of it, presumably to protect the contents from direct light. There was a labelled key in the lock of the deed-box and on the label was written: 'for Messrs Dennehy, Robinson and Kildahl. To be opened immediately after my death. F. G. R. D.'

The word 'death' gave me a shiver. Ten minutes before, I had been having tea with cousin Francis and his guests under the cedar on the lawn. I turned to my other discovery, the glass-fronted case, and drew back the curtains.

Inside was a bird which seemed to me at the time to be the most beautiful thing I had ever seen. It was labelled: '*Paradisea regia* (Genus Paradiseidae) The King Bird of Paradise.' It must have been two feet long with a spectacular plume of pale yellow feathers spouting up from under its wings and cascading over its back. I was gazing at it so raptly that I didn't hear cousin Francis come in.

He said nothing. There are times when telepathy takes over, specially between blood relations, specially perhaps when one of them is a child. I remember that he looked infinitely unhappy, and I remember that I knew that I had done one of those things I ought not to have done. I drew the curtains.

He took my hand. Together we went out into the garden.

People were playing croquet. Gardeners were watering the geraniums and heliotrope. The sun shone as it did in everyone's childhood and the little cold room with the black box and the marvellously beautiful bird began to evaporate as dreams and mists evaporate with the dawn – but not entirely.

The train drew in to Oxford station. At the exit I met great-aunt Effie (known as 'The Trumpeter') and great-aunt Adela, both in black fox furs and huge timeless funeral hats. They pecked at me through their veils. We got into one of the black Daimler taxis which had been sent to meet the train. I sat on a tip-up seat with my back to the driver. We jolted our way through the town and into the leafless country. I felt sick.

'I hear poor Francis has left some very odd directions for his funeral,' said aunt Adela, 'really very odd indeed. A lead-lined coffin with special silver mountings and . . . and . . .'

'Oh dear, oh dear,' said The Trumpeter, 'I shouldn't have thought that was quite "the thing".'

I knew that note of disapproval. It was often sounded by the less glamorous (and poorer) members of the family when speaking of cousin Francis's grand manner, the panache with which he had lived.

The Destrel family (originally d'Estrelle) were Huguenots who had taken refuge in England in the 1690s. Francis Destrel's grandfather had bought Arlingford when he ceased to be a silk-merchant in Spitalfields and, with the help of the prevailing nineteenth-century wind, this family of hard-working northern French tradesmen had, in two generations, become leisured English gentry.

Perhaps cousin Francis had slightly overplayed the part. I'm sure he saw himself as a seigneur and that explained the lead-lined coffin and the silver mountings. It is by such durable accessories that, when civilisations are exhumed, the grave of a seigneur is distinguished from others.

We drew up by the lych-gate and got out. I still felt queasy. Aunt Adela took smelling-salts from her muff. I sniffed and felt better. Aunt Adela was a dear. Her face was as wrinkled as one of last year's pippins. Her black-gloved hand squeezed mine and we exchanged such smiles as are permissible before funerals in January churchyards. We walked up a flagged path between dark Irish yews to that most melancholy sound, the tolling of the tenor bell.

Inside the church there was a strong smell of coke fumes and mothballs. I spotted various relations and the tall figure of Harry Loveday, son of cousin Francis's old friend.

The cortege arrived. I was next to the aisle. As the coffin was wheeled past, I caught sight of an emblazoned silver plaque on the lid and those fitments which were not quite 'the thing'.

The rector read the service in a slow quavering voice. It was before the days when Anglican services were taken at a hand-gallop, cutting corners wherever possible, so where the directions say: 'one or both of these psalms following', we sang both.

Uncle Hugo Destrel, a well-nourished dean, read the lesson and I remember what a comfort it was to hear that porty Oxford voice and catch glimpses of his scarlet D. D. hood, the only splash of bright colour in the church.

The first part of the service came to an end. To the music of a funeral march, the cortege moved the other way. Aunt Adela and I paired off in the procession of family and friends.

We were standing round the grave, two or three deep, and I was in the rear rank. We waited for the last mourner to arrive and then the quavering voice started to read the final prayers.

'Suffer us not at our last hour for any pains of death to fall from Thee.'

Then we saw, slowly rising into the air (it was, I learnt afterwards, being lifted by Harry Loveday) the magnificent Bird of Paradise, its great plume of golden feathers tossed about by the wind like the waters of a sunlit eastern fountain. All this in a muddy Oxfordshire churchyard under a moleskin January sky.

I shuddered. I suppose we all shuddered. I heard a little restrained throat-clearing but I'll bet aunt Effie wasn't the only person present to be murmuring: 'Not at *all* "the thing".'

My cousin, as an heir to Huguenot tradition, had always kept strictly to low Anglican custom. Much more than that, he had again and again given proof that he was a convinced, if conventional, believer. Yet, at a moment when he must have known that his mourners' minds would be fixed on the central Christian idea, he had left special directions for the introduction of something at whose significance, whose symbolism we could only guess.

It may be that most of the people present dismissed the matter afterwards with a brief: 'Very bad form, I thought,' but surely I was not alone in wondering why he had done it.

Why?

For years the incident lay unconsidered at the bottom of my mental file of 'Inexplicable Oddities.' Then in 1952, on a steamy evening in Haiphong, a port at which the *Contessina* had put in, I took it out and dusted it.

I had been talking superficially about religion to a Tonkinese gentleman, a Roman Catholic of the third or fourth generation.

'But the rickshaw coolies, *les gens de la rue*, what do they believe?'

He laughed a little oriental laugh of politeness rather than amusement.

'*Pauvres petits*,' he said, 'they are mostly animists. They believe that when they die their soul enters into a bird.'

In so far as the idea might have affected my cousin, I couldn't make it hold water. A King Bird of Paradise might have been a suitable receptacle for the soul of a seigneur but even so, even so . . . the bird would have to be alive. Transferring one's soul to a stuffed bird out of a glass case wouldn't get anybody anywhere. Or indeed any soul.

For twelve years more, the memory lay dormant and then, in 1964 I stumbled on a clue.

The year before, I had been instrumental in getting a book published which illustrated family life in the 1860s. On the strength of this a relation of the family in question wrote and told me that his wife had just inherited an illustrated diary kept by her grandfather in the seventies and eighties. Would I like to see it?

I went to stay with them in Wiltshire. They met me at Salisbury and, as we drove out to their home, I was fascinated to discover that the author of the diary had been Sir Henry Loveday, my cousin's old friend, and that it covered some of the cruises in the *Contessina*.

The drawings were a disappointment. I couldn't see much market for 'Scene on the Meimbun River', 'Buludupi huts' or 'A street in Dobbo'. There were sketches of Sultans and Tungkus but none of them had names which made news. The diary was written in a style which I remember lantern-lecturers using at school: '. . . with the last rays the setting sun gilding the roofs of palace and pagoda, we bade farewell to ancient Nippon.'

This mockery is not a disloyalty to my host and hostess. I read passages aloud, and we all agreed it was no good.

There were many references to my cousin.

I took the diary to bed with me and was thumbing through it when a passage caught my eye.

Sir Henry and my cousin had landed on an island. Details of the birds they shot are recorded and then they started to make their way back to the beach. They came to an open space in the densely wooded country and in it was a dark lake with 'the last rays of the setting sun gilding the fronds of the nipas which fringed the water on every side'. Even through the turgid prose it was obvious that they had both been deeply moved by the beauty of the scene.

Absolute stillness. No breath of wind. Silence. Sir Henry records that the frogs had stopped croaking and for a moment not a cicada chirruped in the tree-ferns overhead.

'Suddenly from the towering wall of dense foliage on our right there burst like a meteor on our astonished gaze the most spectacularly beautiful member of the avian tribe that it has ever been my privilege to observe: the King Bird of Paradise, worthy monarch of its most gorgeous clan.'

My cousin shot it and, as it fell, with the crack of the shot still reverberating from the hill behind, 'it emitted a sound such as I have never heard before and which, I most earnestly hope, I shall never have the misfortune to hear again. My poor pen is powerless to describe the pathos of that piercing shriek, that almost human scream. Turning, I observed that Destrel had been as much affected as I by this unearthly sound. His face, normally ruddy, was of an alarming pallor, and his hands —nay his whole frame — shook as if he were in the grip of a violent ague.

'I laid a hand on his shoulder.

' "Ah Loveday," he cried, "would to heaven that I could restore its life.".'

They then went back to the yacht, and my cousin went below to his cabin where he remained for three days.

I showed the passage to my hostess next morning and told her of the incident at the funeral thirty-four years before. The Harry Loveday whom I had last seen when he was raising the bird into the air, had been her uncle. He had been dead for some years, she had not known him well and he had never mentioned the incident to her.

When I got home I went to the London Library and took out my cousin's book, *The Cruise of the Contessina*. It is well indexed and I soon found these two passages:

'Soon after our arrival at Ansus, on the south shore of Jobi island, we made friends with a pleasant-faced nose-barred savage who, by the size and finish of his mop and the character of his ornaments, was evidently something of a dandy. He was named Paperipi. To our enquiries about the habitat of the King Bird of Paradise he at first returned evasive answers, and it soon became apparent that his reluctance to furnish us with the information we required was due not to ignorance but to a superstitious belief in the supposed sanctity of the genus Paradiseidae.

'I will not weary my readers with details of the subsequent transaction but I can assure them that after the production of a set of Chinese buttons and two silver dollars (which are in great request for the making of bangles) Paperipi was prepared to "talk business". He indicated the island of Kaiari, saying that there we should be certain of finding a good specimen. On one point however he remained firm. On no account whatever would he accompany us if we decided to land on the island. Kaiari was within easy reach of our anchorage and we decided to make our excursion on the morrow.

'The natives tried rather eagerly to dissuade us from doing so, saying it was staked in every direction with sharp pointed bamboos in case of raids by the Alfuros. We did not believe the story and afterwards discovered that they buried, or rather exposed, their dead upon the island, which was possibly the cause of their unwillingness to let us shoot there.'

The book describes the expedition and brings us to the edge of the lake. There is no reference to the emotive overtones of stillness and silence.

'Here for the first time and only time in my life I saw the King Bird, streaming through the trees like a golden comet. This is the bird which Mr Wallace has described as "one of the most perfectly lovely of the many lovely products of Nature", "a gem of the first water": and indeed when writing of this bird – perhaps the most exquisitely beautiful of all living creatures – it is difficult to find words to express the admiration it arouses.

'With a blend of excitement and emotion I raised my gun to my shoulder and fired.

'When this long-coveted specimen lay lifeless at my feet I realised the inadequacy of superlatives. I could only feel that this creature was perfect and without fault; so perfect indeed that, in spite of the rarity of my prize, I could not help wishing that it lay within my power to give it back its life.'

I know the facts I have assembled do not make a complete

story, but it does seem possible to make an intelligent guess in explanation of that weird incident in an Oxfordshire church-yard forty years ago.

I discount altogether the possibility that my cousin intended the bird (unfortunately called 'of Paradise') rising from his grave to be a symbol of resurrection. It is totally untypical of the man as I remember him.

I believe he was haunted by that bird. Not in the sense that he thought he actually heard the ghostly flutter of its wings and its dying screech (though these phenomena would have made a nasty nightmare) but in the sense that he felt guilty and always regretted what he had done.

Putting myself in his place I think that is how I should have felt. I have never shot a top-sacred bird – 'perhaps the most beautiful of all living creatures' – on an island reserved for the dead after the locals had tried rather eagerly to dissuade me; but I've done various other rather reprehensible little things and I know how they hit me if I wake at two in the morning and remember them. And very nasty it is.

By the time my cousin wrote those 'very odd directions' for his funeral and left them in the deed-box for his lawyers to carry out, he must have come to realise that this thing which plagued him was with him for life. Only by a symbolic gesture after his death could he – literally – get it off his chest.

A Different Party

JOHN HAYLOCK

'WE want the party to be different, darling,' said Rosemary Harding to her great friend.

'What can we do to make it different, dearest? We can't have them all to a couscous meal – that wouldn't exactly be different in Morocco, anyway; besides, it'd be too much of a business. We'd have to borrow plates.'

'I hadn't thought of couscous – vile muck! But I refuse to give just a bloody boring cocktail party like the many we've been to in Tangier. Our party must be different, Vera.'

'But how, Bill?' asked the more conventional of the two, using her friend's pet name. It had been Rosemary who had suggested their letting their house in Rottingdean and spending six months in Morocco, and she again who had chosen the small fishing port forty kilometres down the coast from Tangier. Vera would have preferred to stay in the city, but Rosemary wanted to 'Get away and paint' and her wishes usually prevailed over Vera's.

'Also,' observed Rosemary, 'we're dragging the wretches all the way from Tangier. We must provide something to make the journey worthwhile . . .' she paused and rubbed the side of her long and slightly aquiline nose. 'Something that'll make the party go and be remembered, but what?'

'We could have those Arabs who play Moroccan music and that boy who dances –'

'Unoriginal. Besides, the Watsons had them and all sorts of things were missing from the house afterwards.'

'We could ask people to come dressed as the opposite sex.

Vera giggled. 'Can you imagine the Rear-Admiral as –'

'God no! Barbara did that. We can hardly copy her.'

'What about telling each guest to wear something that represents a famous book and –'

'Christ girl, you do have brilliant ideas! In Tangier where no one reads?'

Vera Adams gazed out of the window at the moonlit sea; there was a wind and the breakers were phosphorescent and just a little menacing. 'Darling,' she exclaimed, suddenly, 'I've an idea!'

'What?' Rosemary's sigh showed she expected another futile suggestion.

'Keef canapés!'

'Keef what?'

'We could serve them meat balls stuffed with keef. That ought to make the party go.'

'D'you know, girlie,' Rosemary said in the gruff voice she put on when she was pleased with her friend, 'I think you may have got something there.'

'Alice B. Toklas!' cried Vera, getting up.

'But the recipe in her book is for hashish fudge. No one would want fudge at a cocktail party, duckie.'

'We could follow the recipe substituting minced meat for sugar.'

'I'll leave it to you, darling. Now let's play the game.'

'Not now, Bill. There's the washing-up.'

'Hell to the washing-up! Come on!'

'Must we wear our "game" clothes?'

'Of course,' replied "Bill", sternly. 'Now, get to it, woman!' she added already entering into her part.

There was a series of 'games' which the two friends played. Their latest was called 'Clinic' and involved Rosemary dressing up as Dr Bill Harding, the specialist, and Vera acting the part of the patient for which she squeezed her dumpy figure into a tight grey *jellabah*, the usual outer garment worn by Moroccan town women. Rosemary, tall, angular with cropped pepper-and-salt hair very much looked the role of the irascible consultant in a tie, white jacket and spectacles. Vera had mixed feelings about the games — in another she was an out-of-work actress seeking employment from Bill Harding, the 'impresario' — but she agreed to play them because they put Rosemary into a good mood. Refusal caused disharmony and basically Vera feared her friend. Vera could not wholeheartedly share in these fantasies as she found them childish. It was a constant surprise to her that they amused Rosemary, who was more intelligent and more intellectual than she. Perhaps a predilection for the fatuous was a sign of genius, a necessary outlet, for her friend did paint extremely well. 'Can't we cut out the preliminary game?' Vera had once asked. 'It's more than half the fun,' Rosemary had replied, putting on a striped apron to play the part of a butcher to Vera's timorous housewife. The two friends had lived successfully together for over five years, that is as successfully as most people live together; there had been rows and twice Vera had run home to her mother, but the quarrels had subsided and the fugitive had returned. 'The skinny one has the talent, the fat one the money,' neighbours in Rottingdean said. Rosemary was admired; Vera was liked. The former had the prickly temperament of the artist striving for perfection; the latter was good-natured, sweet, and when it came to people she possessed what her friend called 'the curse of toleration'.

'Must I put on my yashmak too?' asked Vera when she had struggled into her *jellabah*.

'Yes,' answered Rosemary, fiercely.

'And go outside in the street and knock?' Vera didn't like going into the street in her Moroccan garb, for once she had been seen knocking at her own door by Ali, the friend of Charles, a neighbour; she had had to explain that she had tried on the maid's *jellabah* for fun. Ali had laughed.

'Yes.'

'Oh, not tonight. There's all that washing-up.'

'I said leave the bleeding washing-up, didn't I? Go on!'

'Bill!'

'Go on!'

'Bill, not the hypodermic this time.'

'We'll see if you need it. Get outside!'

In the game Vera pretended to be a Moroccan woman visiting a European doctor without her husband's permission. She would knock frantically on the door to be let in by Dr Bill Harding, smoking a pipe. 'It's after hours. Have you an appointment?'

'No, doctor. But I must see you.'

'I can only see people by appointment.'

'I must see you, doctor. Please!'

'All right, but it may cost you dear.'

Inside, the 'doctor' would carry out a thorough inspection, which ended in Vera, naked, being threatened with a hypodermic syringe.

'An injection is the only thing,' said the 'doctor' filling the syringe from a small bottle of water.

'No, doctor, no!' Vera resisted for a while and then the 'game' changed into 'love'. Vera felt as ambiguous about the 'love' side of her relationship with Rosemary as she did about the 'games'. She loved Rosemary, yes, but more than she loved 'Bill', and sometimes she wondered what it would be like to live with a man.

'I shall have to see about getting the keef,' Vera said the next morning at breakfast.

'You're not to get it from Charles. You hadn't thought of getting it from Charles, had you?'

'No,' Vera replied, although it was the source she had

thought of.

Charles lived a few doors away in a similar cottage that was also part of the sea wall. Rosemary disliked him, finding this bibulous, white-haired remittance-man a crashing bore, and his friend Ali, nineteen, pert and lustful, possessed all the masculine characteristics she loathed. Vera according to her nature was charitable about their neighbours; if it hadn't been for Rosemary she would have seen much more of them; as it was she met Charles shopping nearly every day and felt embarrassed that he had only once been inside the house.

'Where will you get the keef, then?' challenged Rosemary.

'From the Petit Socco in Tangier. That's where the hippies get it.'

'I'll leave it to you.' Rosemary usually left the irksome housekeeping chores to Vera. 'But you're bloody well not going to get the stuff in this town. Everyone would know. We'd have the police round asking for a rake-off.'

When Vera met Charles later that morning, she asked him about keef. 'One cigarette is no stronger than a whisky,' he boomed out in the voice of an Edwardian landowner. 'It's effect is sharper if it's eaten; it enters the bloodstream more quickly.' Vera had thought about this information and when she met Charles again she asked him what the effect of eating a keef cake would have. 'It would make everything seem more interesting: colours become more defined; music seems to have another dimension.'

'And what about people?' Vera asked. 'What's one's reaction to people?'

'One loves more, one hates more, inhibitions are released and so on. Why all these questions about keef, Vera? You and Rosemary are not getting hooked, are you?'

'No, of course not. So many people smoke it here that I wondered about it.'

'Ali smokes it every evening.'

'Does he eat it with his food?'

Charles let out his haw-haw laugh. 'No.'

'Do you?'

'God no! I prefer whisky. It's dangerous to mix the two, by the way.'

Keef canapés seemed just the thing for a different party and Vera was glad she had suggested them to Rosemary. The two friends did not quite see eye to eye about the guests for their party, however. Vera wanted to invite the three other British residents of the town but Rosemary was dead against having Charles.

'The drunken sot will insist on bringing Ali,' she complained.

'That wouldn't matter,' said Vera. 'Ali could help hand round the –'

'Keefed-up meat balls?'

'Yes.'

'He'd wolf the lot more likely. I've never known him lift a finger. Charles waits on him hand and foot. No, Vera, not Ali.'

'Then Charles won't come.'

'That suits me. He's no asset to a party, getting maudlin after two drinks. And Ali? I'm not having Ali in this house. Sexy little brute! High on keef, he's likely to start raping people. You remember Dorothy telling us how he wrecked her party by getting drunk and frightening poor old Mrs Cartwright? No, ducks, not Ali. Why, he's been in and out of gaol at least three times in the five months we've been here.'

'But Bill, they're our nearest neighbours –'

'You will clutter up your life with bores. I won't. You can have them to tea when I'm out.'

More of Vera's suggestions were vetoed by Rosemary.

'We're not having the Crosby-Johnstons.'

'But we've been to two of their cocktail parties,' protested

Vera.

'Our purpose in coming to Morocco was to avoid meeting people like the Crosby-Johnstons. We'll have plenty of opportunity to renew our acquaintance with people like them when we get back to Sussex.'

'You went to their parties.'

'Only because you were so mad on going.'

'Oh Bill, how can you! It was you who wanted to go.' Vera thought for a moment. 'What about Evelyn Parker?'

'What about her?'

'If we're not having Charles, then why should we have Evelyn Parker?'

'I don't see the connection.'

Evelyn was a successful writer of children's stories and also a neighbour. Rosemary liked her because she was one of the few foreigners who worked and therefore was 'interesting and had something to say'; Vera found her formidable and felt ill at ease in her company.

'The connection is,' explained Vera, 'that Charles'll be less envious if he hears that Evelyn hasn't been invited.'

'Nonsense.'

'All right. I'll agree to Evelyn if you let me put the Crosby–Johnstons on the list.'

'But there are the Tupper–Martins,' said Rosemary. 'I must invite them as he knows my brother and the Crosby–Johnstons and the Tupper–Martins aren't on speaking terms.'

'Let's mix them for once and see what happens.'

Rosemary laughed and said, 'Kinky girl,' and Vera gleefully added the two double-barrelled surnames to her list. It was the prankish side of Vera's character that had prompted her to think of keef canapés that now made her suggest inviting the Crosby-Johnstons and the Tupper-Martins. Few Tangier hostesses would have been so tactless. No one quite knew why the two couples were at daggers drawn: some said it was simply social envy between the wives – the Tupper–Martins were better connected; others maintained that Colonel Crosby–Johnston had got hold of the very house which Rear-Admiral Tupper–Martin had coveted on the New Mountain outside Tangier by a trick perpetrated through a shady agent, whom the Colonel had bribed. Whatever the cause there was no doubt that the two couples harboured considerable animosity towards one another. It was said that when an absent-minded hostess had introduced the Colonel and his wife to someone as Commander and Mrs Crosby–Martin the pair had taken umbrage and stormed out of the house; but probably this was not true, for most of the stories about parties in Tangier were invented by those who had not been to them.

Rosemary's suggestion that Dorothy Meade should be invited together with her Moroccan companion, Mustapha, provoked Vera into raising the question of Charles and Ali again by pointing out that if Dorothy could bring her Mustapha then Charles must be allowed to come with his Ali. But Rosemary was adamant.

'It's unfair,' complained Vera. 'When Charles hears that Dorothy Meade and Mustapha have been invited and he and Ali haven't, Charles'll be terribly offended. Mustapha and Ali are friends, don't forget.'

'Colleagues in the same profession of gigolo would be more accurate, dear. Mustapha can behave. He's nice. Ali can't. It's as simple as that. And what's more, I like Dorothy.'

'I like Charles.'

'How can you like that bloated bag of alcohol? You're only being contrary, darling, aren't you?' Rosemary gave her friend a rather patronising smile.

'Charles'll be hurt.'

'At his age? Life began for him a good while ago, as it did for us. He's not one to care about a silly cocktail party.'

'He is,' insisted Vera.

'Then he's even a stupider person than I took him to be. No, dear, I'm sorry, but Charles is absolutely out.'

Try as Vera did during the next few days, even refusing to play 'Clinic', she could not persuade Rosemary to change her mind about Charles and Ali. Not to invite the two friends was to Vera's way of thinking unkind. Vera had none of Rosemary's detachment and indifference; she hated snubbing people and appearing inhospitable.

Vera went to the shops every day while Rosemary, who was doing a series of pictures of waves breaking, stood at her easel in the sitting-room window. Vera felt herself to be deceptive and mean when she met Charles on his way back from the market with his shopping basket. As usual when a foreigner walked in the town a band of pestering brats was on his heels. 'Sir, sir,' the urchins cried, their faces screwed into expressions of acute pain, 'gimme one dirham! Plis, plis, one dirham, sir, plis!'

'Oh go away! *Yallah!*' Charles said, irritably.

Vera saw that her neighbour was worried. It could not be the children that were upsetting him for they were a daily nuisance to which one became as inured as one did to the winds of the blustery Atlantic coast. The reiterated 'Plis, plis, one dirham' meant no more than the sound of the waves.

'Good morning,' said Vera cheerfully, hoping that her tone would disguise the fact that she had noticed his troubled features.

'Not a good morning for me, Vera. A bloody awful one. Ali's in gaol again.'

'Oh, I am sorry.'

The children changed 'Plis, plis, sir' to their version of Vera's name. 'Hello, Veradams,' they cried. 'Hello, Veradams! How are you?'

Charles's bloodshot eyes flashed. 'It's the blasted police,' he said. 'Meddlesome swine! Little men with too much power! Look at the way they make poor old Pedro give them free drinks! They arrested Ali for brawling. He was only playing about, actually. It's just a way of getting at me. Xenophobia.' The corpulent Englishman seemed short of breath and there was sweat on his brow, although the April sun was tempered by a breeze. 'It's such a bloody bore,' he went on. 'I have to take him cooked meals. The prison food consists of some frightful gruel that not even Ali will eat. I feel such a bloody fool carrying dishes to the police station along with the mothers and sisters of the other prisoners.'

'Poor you,' sympathised Vera. 'How long will they keep Ali locked up?' If Ali were to be inside for five days she calculated, he wouldn't be able to come to the party and Charles could safely be invited.

'Only for a day or two I suppose, now I've paid the bribe.'

'That's not too bad,' said Vera, hoping that she didn't show her disappointment.

'All the same it's utterly monstrous. You going into Tangier?'

'Yes. Want a lift?' She guessed he didn't.

'No thanks. Have to roast a chicken for Ali's lunch.'

'Will you put a file inside it?'

Charles smiled grimly. 'See you,' he said and went on his way down the passage by the sea wall.

'Hello, Veradams! Hello, Veradams!' The children attached themselves to Vera and followed her closely, past the courtyard of the old palace, through the tunnel of the fortified entrance gate to the garage next to Evelyn Parker's renovated cottage with the yellow shutters. Vera and Rosemary rented the garage from Evelyn, who had no car. 'Veradams! Gimme one dirham!' Vera never said 'Go away!' or '*Yallah*!' to the children. She greeted their rude demands with a smile and a pat on the head, having a theory that they would respond to kindness; so far they hadn't, but perhaps they were less cheeky to her than they were to Charles. For some reason they rarely bothered Rosemary, who ignored them. Vera put this down to their fear of her friend and flattered herself that they liked her. She would rather be liked than feared. 'Veradams, *donne-moi dix francs!*' Should Vera invite Evelyn now? Would she tell Charles? With a certain amount of trepidation Vera rapped Evelyn's knocker. How absurd she was to mind! No answer. Vera opened the garage doors feeling relieved. She'd invite Evelyn another day. 'Veradams, one dirham!' 'You should not ask like that, you know.' An imp, called Mohammed, said with a devastating smile in an urgent whisper right into her ear, 'Veradams, I love you. For me, just one dirham.' The seductive, persuasive tone was irresistible. Vera squeezed herself into her Mini and when she had backed out of the garage she stretched her arm out of the window and put a dirham piece into Mohammed's grubby hand.

To the sound of shrill protests and violent scuffles Vera drove off down the now slightly wider passage by the sea wall, turned right by the school, passed the remains of the Portuguese castle and entered the modern part of the town. She stopped at Pedro's Café, the haunt of the tiny British community, and ordered drink for the party. No one else was in the bar at this hour of the morning. It was too soon for Sir Henry's regular call. The baronet was never at Pedro's before eleven. It was true that the British community of five boasted a real baronet, the fifteenth in fact, and it did not matter that Henry de Painville was seventy-two, twice divorced, childless and not at all well-off. Rosemary had raised no objections about inviting Sir Henry in spite of her latest fad of being anti-snobbish, for both friends loved 'old Sir Henry', who flirted with any 'gal' under sixty, pinching her bottom and nudging her breasts. The Tupper–Martins liked the harmless old reprobate; the Crosby-Johnstons on the other hand disapproved of him complaining that he let the side down, which was rather unfair since Sir Henry did absolutely nothing except tipple at Pedro's and totter home to his little house on the beach, where he fried himself eggs and chips on a primus stove.

Vera loved the drive into Tangier: the open stretch of weather-beaten brushwood by the sea; the rollers with spray blowing off them like lace; the shepherd boys in their coarse brown *jellabahs*, armed with rough staves. She would return the boys' peremptory signals to stop with a wave, but sometimes she drew up and gave the little shepherd who came panting up to her car a cigarette or a coin. Vera could not pass through the eucalyptus forest, known quaintly as the Forêt Diplomatique, without having a spasm of fear and excitement, for a few years ago a European woman had been raped amidst the trees by three lascivious louts. The culprits had been quickly caught, summarily tried and hanged. For a reason she could not explain Vera always found herself contemplating this ugly incident when she drove through the forest. How near the road had the rape occurred? Had the boy to whom she had just waved known the ravishers? What was it like to be raped by three men in succession? She had heard it said that it was better not to resist. What would she have done? If she stopped now, would satyrs appear and entice her into a sylvan cleft?

Once past the Forêt Diplomatique Vera turned her thoughts upon the purchase of keef; she would go to the Petit Socco where she was unlikely to meet any foreign residents as now only tourists and hippies patronised the cafés there. Soon the bare hills of the environs of Tangier were upon her. The fields were green and the roadside was bright with flowers – the mimosa was in bloom and tall irises reigned over daisies, buttercups and marigolds. Tangier appeared for a moment, white and gleaming, and then the city slipped behind a verdant hill topped by a new mosque which seemed to be standing impressively alone until one rounded the corner and saw the sprawl of a suburb on the other side. Farther on was an open space where Arab countrymen in chestnut *jellabahs* congregated, shouted and argued, and Arab women in enveloping white *haiks* and black yashmaks fluttered hen-like; where tough Berber crones in basket hats unloaded vegetables from donkeys; where there were buses, a petrol station, motor-tyre shops and the muddle of used spare parts and the oily grime of garages for repairs in which worked boys with greasy faces and unshaven mechanics in stained overalls. Vera did not like these squalid outskirts of the city. She was relieved when she had passed through them and had parked her car by the market in the Rue de Fez.

The Marché de Fez was a favourite shopping centre for foreign residents. Near the artistically displayed vegetables, by a mound of imported cheese, next to a dangling carcase friends would run into each other and gossip about other friends, while greengrocers, grocers and butchers waited with scales in the balance and knives poised. Vera went straight to her butcher, a pallid young man with rich brown curls, brown eyes and a well-shaped mouth. His English was good, but she went to him because his anaemic face appealed to her and when he smiled he looked so charming, fawn-like and in need of protection. 'A kilo of minced beef, please Ahmed.' Would one kilo be enough? While the butcher was mincing the meat in his machine, Vera looked round and saw the Coopers buying carrots at the stall opposite. The Coopers were on the agreed list for the party. Mr C. had planted tea in Ceylon, and his wife, who was still very striking, was supposed to have been a ballerina – some Tangier tongues said she had never got further than the chorus in a touring musical comedy company. With the Coopers was a large, grey-haired, blue-eyed Englishman in a dark suit; he had an ecclesiastical air about him and could have passed for a bishop. Mr Cooper introduced him as Nigel Banning. 'Banning's the name,' the man repeated in clearly enunciated tones that would have resounded in the largest of cathedrals.

'What are you doing so far from home, Vera?' asked Christopher Cooper in his habitual facetious manner, which could be irritating.

'Shopping,' replied Vera, bluntly. 'By the way,' she went on hoping to mitigate the effect of her almost discourteous reply, 'Rosemary and I are giving a small party on Saturday and we'd love you to come.'

'We'd love to come,' said Mrs Cooper. 'May we bring Nigel? He's just arrived and knows no one.'

'Of course.' Vera excused herself and went back to the butcher, who had put her meat into a polythene bag. 'Ahmed,' she heard herself saying, 'my friend and I are giving a small party on Saturday and we'd love you to come.'

Ahmed fiddled with a knife for a moment and then looking up at Vera across a lump of beef sang out a nonchalant 'O.K.!', as if there was nothing extraordinary about her inviting him.

Vera explained where the house was and exultant went on to her grocer. What would Rosemary say? Later, she drove to the Grand Socco, the large square on the edge of the Casbah, where she left the car, after carefully locking it, in the charge of a venerable-looking attendant with a white beard and a turban, who smiled ingratiatingly in reply to her Arabic greeting. When alone, Vera gave him twice the customary tip. She walked under the archway of the old Fez gate and into the narrow street that led down to the Petit Socco. Out of his camera and radio shop that also sold silk ties came Mr Domalpaz to greet her.

'And how is Miss Adams this morning?' intoned the Indian merchant.

'Very well thank you, Mr Domalpaz.'

'I am very pleased to hear it indeed, Miss Adams.'

'And how's business?'

The Indian shook his grey head sadly. 'Not good, Miss Adams, I am afraid to inform you. Not good at all.' He glanced through his heavy spectacles at the passing Moroccans, who, in their *jellabahs* and slippers, their cotton shirts, roughly-made trousers and cheap shoes, looked far from prosperous. 'The great trouble with these people, Miss Adams, is that they do not have any purchasing power.'

'No, poor things, I'm sure they don't.' Vera laughed.

'In the good old days when Tangier was an international city how different it was! Everybody had a great deal of money to spend. In Tangier there were three hundred and sixty banks. Nearly one for each day of the year.' Mr Domalpaz let out a high-pitched girlish laugh, then, lowering his voice to a conspiratorial level he said, 'Would Miss Adams be requiring any accommodation this morning?'

'No, thank you, Mr Domalpaz. Not this morning.'

The Indian hung his head. Clearly he would have liked to cash one of Vera's cheques on her English bank. 'Another day, perhaps, I can assist you in your financial problems.'

'Yes.' Vera felt sorry for Mr Domalpaz in his ill-fitting gaberdine suit, his new gaudy tie that accentuated his frayed shirt and his cracked black shoes. Because of his pretentions to respectability, his claims to be superior, he seemed more pitiable than the motley crowd of Moroccans who ambled past his shop. This expatriate Hindu, Vera conjectured, must be lonely, for who would befriend him in this city of penurious Moslems and comfortably-off Europeans? The former he despised and the latter would only have time for him when 'accommodation' was required. Vera said, 'My friend and I are giving a small party on Saturday and we would be very pleased if you and Mrs Domalpaz could come.'

'Oh, Miss Adams, how kind and considerate you are! Mrs Domalpaz and I will be more than delighted. I am not presuming am I if I ask about the other good ladies and gentlemen we shall have the pleasure of meeting at your house?'

Vera was puzzled. 'Who else will be there, do you mean?'

'That is what I had the intention of saying.'

'Well, Evelyn Parker, the authoress; Rear-Admiral and Mrs Tupper-Martin –'

'Yes, yes.' The Indian seemed pleased and eager to hear more illustrious names.

'And then there'll be Mr and Mrs Cooper and a friend of theirs who has just arrived.'

'Good. Very good.'

'And Mrs Meade.'

'Yes, yes,' said the rotund gentleman from Bombay delightedly.

Vera remembered Mustapha, Dorothy Meade's lover, and the butcher, but advisedly omitted them. She finished her list by saying triumphantly, 'And, of course, Sir Henry de Painville.' At the mention of the baronet's name, however, the dark lips parted over the very white teeth retracted a little, so Vera hastily said, 'Colonel and Mrs Crosby-Johnston' and all was sunshine again on the face of Mr Domalpaz. 'I am indeed honoured, Miss Adams. It is with the utmost pleasure I look forward to joining your happy gathering on Saturday. It will be a propitious day for us all I am sure indeed.'

Vera walked on down towards the Petit Socco. The satisfaction which inviting the Indian had given her was impaired by his obvious disapproval of Sir Henry. How dare Mr Domalpaz be even faintly censorious of one of her guests? She wished she hadn't asked the Indian and by the time she reached the little square she regretted having invited the butcher too. What had come over her? What would her friend say? But hadn't Rosemary often preached the importance of being truly democratic, quoting Jesus and Marx?

Vera sat at a table on the pavement of the café watching a young, dark Moroccan with African features pace madly up and down in the middle of the little square. She wondered if it were the keef that made the man act so strangely and where he had bought the stuff. The waiter tapped his head and then circled a forefinger in the air after he had placed a glass of mint tea in front of the Englishwoman. 'Keef?' she inquired, indicating the pacing man, who had just done an about-turn with military precision.

'*Oui. Il est fou,*' observed the waiter. '*Le keef l'a rendu fou.*'

The thought that a keef canapé or two would turn Colonel Crosby-Johnston or Rear-Admiral Tupper-Martin into a frenziedly pacing tiger amused Vera, but she was too shy to ask the waiter about buying the drug. There was only one hippie in evidence and he was slumped over a table in the café opposite with his abundant blond locks smothering the hands on which his head rested. Had he passed out? Would the stuff have the same effect on the talkative, busybody Christopher Cooper? How much should she buy? Half a kilo? A quarter? Probably a hundred and fifty grams would be enough. She ordered another mint tea but merely muttered '*Merci*' when the waiter brought it. She knew she was absurd; she knew that keef was marketed almost as easily as tomatoes in this land and that no Moroccan thought badly of anyone who used the drug. She must ask the waiter; there was no one else to ask. She signalled. At once he came to the table.

'*Un autre thé à la menthe, madame?*'

'*Non, merci. Cent cinquante grammes de keef,*' she said as if ordering an orange juice.

'*Il faut attendre. Abdelsalam n'est pas là encore.*'

'*Bien.*' It was easier to do it in French. Vera just had to wait. She had nothing to read and not being a tourist she felt conspicuous sitting outside this café that was now only frequented by foreign visitors and 'locals'. She prayed that a resident would not see her, but, as if the Almighty wished to punish her for making such a frivolous and selfish prayer, into the square came Hubert Pierce. He spotted her at once and approached. Almost the last person Vera wanted to see was this bothersome little journalist who liked to know everyone's business. The waiter might tell him about her errand. Damn!

Hubert usually had in his employ a 'secretary', but few believed that Aziz, a michievous lad of fifteen, could do anything with a typewriter except tap out his own name with one finger. 'Old enough to be the boy's grandfather,' said some carping tongues about Hubert. Nevertheless, this little man with his button nose, his blue, soup-plate eyes did not look like a grandfather; he more resembled a boy who had put on a grey wig. With tiny hands and dainty feet, Hubert possessed some of the childishness of a dwarf.

'Fancy seein' you 'ere, Vera. Mind if I join you?'

Vera's shudder of hostility might have warned off someone less thick-skinned, but Hubert ignored it and sat beside her.

'And what in the world are you doing 'ere, Vera? 'Ad a row with friend Rosemary? Now, if you were to ask me what I'm doing I'd tell you. I'm looking for my secretary. 'E ran off with some bloody tourist last night. You 'aven't seen Aziz 'ave you?'

'I don't think I'd know him if –'

'Everybody knows Aziz – little bastard!' Hubert ordered a beer from the waiter and then said, his large blue eyes all innocent and artless, 'So you and your mate are giving a party?

Vera caught her breath. 'Yes,' she admitted. Who could have told him?

'And you're not inviting your best chum?'

'Our house is so small,' explained Vera, feebly. 'We can't have all our friends at once.'

'Only special people like Domalpaz?'

She might have guessed that the babbling Indian would talk about the party to every European resident who passed his shop. 'There's a reason for inviting Mr Domalpaz.'

'I bet there is.' Hubert narrowed his eyes; almost a gesture seemed the movement of the lids towards each other. 'No one invites old Domalpaz without there being a bloody good reason.'

'I thought he was lonely.'

'Hindu merchants aren't lonely, provided they've enough money to count.'

All the time Vera was worrying about what she should do when Abdelsalam appeared. How would she set about buying the drug? She prayed the waiter wouldn't send the seller to her table.

'That chap's properly keefed up, isn't 'e?' remarked Hubert, jerking his head at the Moroccan who was still energetically pacing backwards and forwards in the square. He had a wild expression and seemed oblivious to his surroundings.

'Is he?' said Vera.

'Now look who's coming! See?'

A young Moroccan in a brown window-pattern suit loped into the Petit Socco. As he approached one became aware that the suit had been made, almost certainly in London, for someone twice the lad's girth. The slim body inside the voluminous jacket was as loose as a swizzle stick in an empty tumbler and the turned-up trouser ends billowed round the boy's bare heels and then covered the points of his yellow slippers. Hubert waved to Abdelsalam and turning to Vera said, 'D'you know what 'e told me the other day? 'E said that the ladies usually paid better than the gentlemen. Surprisin', isn't it?'

Abdelsalam returned Hubert's wave with a half-smile and went into the café. Vera looked round and noted that the waiter was in conversation with the young man. What should she do? She must act now. Vera rose. 'Excuse me, I must –'

'Spend a penny?'

'Yes.'

Vera entered the café and worked her way to the back past tables of men playing cards, talking or just sitting. 'Keef?' she said anxiously to the waiter. She knew Hubert was watching.

'*Oui. Combien, madame?*'

'*Pas beaucoup.*'

'*Bien.*' The waiter spoke to Abdelsalam in Arabic and the young man produced a flat cigarette tin. 'Sixty dirhams.'

Was the practical joke she was going to play worth five pounds? She hesitated and then said, '*D'accord*. But I go in there first.' She pointed to the lavatory. 'When I come out give me the box. *Compris?*' With her feet carefully placed on either side of the deep, malodorous hole, Vera extracted six ten dirham notes from her handbag and folded them into a wad. Breathing in gasps she counted up to a hundred and then left the little room. Outside the waiter dropped the cigarette tin into her open handbag and she pressed the money into his palm. The operation was done so deftly that it might have been rehearsed. She went through the café again to the table at which Abdelsalam was now sitting. 'Hubert,' she said, 'I must go. Here's the money for my two mint teas. D'you mind paying the waiter? I can't find him.'

'All right luv.'

Disregarding Abdelsalam, Vera hastened away, but not so fast as to miss Hubert's horrible laugh. Without much confidence she hoped her lie about the waiter had put Hubert off the scent, but Abdelsalam had probably told him about her purchase of keef already, for in the city of Tangier discretion was an unknown virtue and gossip a major occupation.

'Sixty dirhams!' cried Rosemary in dismay. 'Over five pounds for your joke? It can bloody well be your contribution. I'm not having it put in the housekeeping book. I'll do the flowers and I won't put them down.'

'All right,' agreed Vera meekly. She had not told her friend of her invitations and she knew she had to. Her agreeing to pay for the keef placed her in a position of advantage; all the same it was not until Vera had made several abortive attempts that she managed to blurt out, 'Oh, by the way, Rosemary, I've asked some other people.'

'Who, darling?' It was at the end of lunch, a time when a bottle of heavy Moroccan wine had usually made the two friends mellow and affectionate.

Vera mentioned the Coopers' friend, Ahmed the butcher and Mr Domalpaz and instead of flying into a diatribe of objection Rosemary laughed heartily. 'Oh, Vera you are the absolute end! A man who looks like a bishop, a butcher and an Indian merchant! What a cocktail! How will the Tupper-Martins and the Crosby-Johnstons take Mr Domalpaz? A brilliant idea!'

'And what about Charles and Ali, Bill? Don't you think that —. I forgot to tell you: Ali's locked up again but I don't know for how long. Charles thought he'd be out by Saturday.'

'You didn't —'

'No, I didn't mention the party, but don't you think we might just this once —?'

'No, Vera, no!' Sometimes the wine had the power of swiftly changing the mood.

'Just Charles then.'

'You know he'll insist on bringing Ali.'

'But Ali's in goal.'

'You said he'd be out by Saturday.'

'Dorothy's bringing Mustapha.'

'Mustapha knows how to behave.'

'Charles'll be hurt.'

'God! Must we go through all this again? I do not want that nasty little Ali at our party. At his age, Charles must realise that one can't invite everyone one knows to every party one gives.'

'But this is our first party. He'll be hurt, Bill.'

'Then let the great fat, swollen baby be hurt!'

*

'Try one, dear, before they come.' Vera offered her friend a plate of meat balls.

'No.' Like a wary dog sensing a trick Rosemary turned her head away. 'How many of these have you treated?'

'All of them.'

'What about these sausage rolls?'

'There's some in the sausages.'

'And the anchovy eggs?'

'They're free.'

Rosemary put an anchovy egg into her mouth and said, 'I hope you haven't gone too far.'

'We'll see, dear. It's a kind of experiment, isn't it? Bill, do let's go upstairs and see if the rooms are all right.'

The two friends' cottage in the sea-wall consisted of three rooms 'up' and three 'down'. Upstairs were the sitting-room, a bedroom and the bathroom, and downstairs the kitchen, the hall and another bedroom, the bed of which was in an alcove and screened off by curtains like a Moroccan bridal couch. The party was to be held upstairs in the sitting-room and in the bedroom, whose bed Rosemary had converted into a divan by pushing it against the wall and strewing cushions all over it. She had draped a beautiful blue silk kaftan over the long looking-glass and the chest of drawers had become the 'bar' by being covered with a sheet, bottles and glasses. Vases of mimosa and irises had been posted about the rooms and on the window ledge half way up the steep tiled staircase; in the hall Rosemary had filled a giant black and white striped pot with young eucalyptus branches.

'Pity it's too windy to use the terrace.'

'Just as well as I've put all the terrace cushions on the bed.'

'People could stand out there.'

'They might sit on the balustrade and topple off on to the rocks after they've —'

'What have you done with your latest picture, Bill?'

'It's on its easel in the bathroom.'

'Why not put it in here?'

'Because the bloody thing isn't finished.'

'It would go behind the sofa. Let's try.'

When the painting of the breaking wave, which showed some influence by Hokusai, had been put into place, Rosemary said, 'It looks damned good with the lamp on it, doesn't it?'

'I like it.' Since Vera had given in over not inviting Charles and Ali, Rosemary had been sweet to her; nevertheless, Vera still regretted the omission. She had felt very uncomfortable when she and Rosemary had chatted quite ordinarily to Charles in Pedro's café the other evening, uncomfortable and sly. It was too much to hope that Charles had not learnt about the party. In the unlikely contingency that he hadn't, then Ali in his foxy way would have smelt out the information, possibly while still incarcerated in the police station, certainly now he was free.

'You'll do the drinks, won't you Vera? I'll start off down-stairs and send people up to you. Don't let them pour out drinks for themselves, will you?'

'No, I won't,' replied Vera a little petulantly.

'Let's play Clinic,' said Rosemary.

'Now?'

'Yes.'

'But Bill, it's nearly half-past five. People'll be arriving in half an hour, and we haven't changed.'

'No one arrives punctually at a Tangier cocktail party. There won't be a soul here before six-thirty or seven. Get dressed, woman!'

'You want me to put on my *jellabah*?'

'Yes.'

'Oh, Bill!'

'Get to it.'

'And go outside and knock? People might see and –'

'Get downstairs, put on your *jellabah* and shout up to me from the hall. Pretend you've walked into the house without knocking. That'll make me more severe.'

'All right,' replied Vera. She did not at all want to play the game at that moment and only agreed to do so to humour her friend. When she had put on her Moroccan garment, its cowl over her head and the black yashmak round her face, she took hold of her handbag and called out timidly, 'Doctor! Doctor!'

'Who's there?' Rosemary, dressed in her white jacket, came half way down the stairs. 'What on earth d'you mean by breaking into my house? Visiting hours are over. Clear off!'

'Please doctor –'

At that moment the brass knocker made in the shape of a fist banged the front door. The knocks were accompanied by the familiar cries of, 'Veradams! Veradams!'

'Someone's come,' said Vera, stepping out of her part of Moroccan housewife.

'It's only those silly brats you will encourage.'

'They never knock without reason.'

'Go and see who it is then, Vera,' said Rosemary, no longer Dr Harding. 'It can't be a guest yet.' She retreated up the stairs. Vera heard the bedroom door slam to.

Forgetting she was in *jellabah* and yashmak, Vera opened the front door to Mr and Mrs Domalpaz, Mohammed and his band.

'Miss Adams?' inquired the Indian.

'Veradams! Veradams!' The children at once recognised Vera and roared with laughter.

'Go away! No, not you, Mr Domalpaz. Please come in. Mohammed, off with you! *Allez-vous-en!*'

'Miss Adams, please?'

'Give me one dirham.'

'I show your house, Veradams.'

'You give me two dirham and I stop these bad boys,' said Mohammed.

'Here you are,' said Vera, taking some coins out of her handbag.

Somewhat nonplussed, Mr Domalpaz again said, 'Miss Adams?'

Vera pushed back her cowl and unfastened her yashmak. 'I am so sorry, Mr Domalpaz. I was just – I find this garment so useful for working in.'

'Yes?' said the Indian, vaguely. He drew a breath and began, 'It is indeed a great and genuine honour to visit your homely abode. Please accept this small token –' he handed Vera a large box of chocolates.

'Oh, how kind!'

'It's just a small trifle. Allow me to present Mrs Domalpaz.'

Perhaps it was the Indian woman's sari, the red dot between her eyebrows or her putting her hands together in the position of prayer that intimidated Vera into doing a sort of curtsey, but Mrs Domalpaz did by any standards look formidable. She was immense. A roll of brown flesh bulged out of the gap between the upper and lower parts of her exotic dress, and scarlet toenails stuck out of her golden sandals.

Vera led the Indian couple up the stairs to the sitting-room, which Rosemary had stripped for action by putting the chairs on the terrace. 'No one wants to sit at a party,' she had declared. The only seat left in the room was the sofa, and Mr and Mrs Domalpaz filled it completely. Mrs Domalpaz inspected Vera with amazed dark eyes and spoke to her husband rapidly. After emitting an apologetic laugh, the Indian said, 'My wife is not understanding why you are wearing the street apparel of a Moroccan Moslem lady. I tell her of course that you use this type of dress for your housework, but then she asks why you have the yashmak too in the house. I say to her the yashmak is for the dust, but still she is not understanding.

She is very silly.'

'Tell her, I wear the *jellabah* over my dress to keep it clean.'
Because of the 'game' Vera had only her underclothes on
beneath the long outer garment. 'I find it a very useful house-
coat.'

'Yes of course. How wise and practical western ladies are!
I will tell my wife –'

'Before you do that Mr Domalpaz, tell me what you would
like to drink. Gin? Whisky?'

'Well, the whole truth of the matter is, Miss Adams, that
neither Mrs Domalpaz nor I partake of any alcoholic beverages
at all, but we would be very grateful indeed to have a cup of
your excellent English tea which –' Mr Domalpaz let out a
girlish shriek – 'comes from India.'

Cursing inwardly at the thought of having to make tea,
Vera went into the bedroom to summon Rosemary. She was
lying in the bath with the water up to her neck and squeezing
the soapy liquid in her large sponge on to her breasts, which
just broke the surface.

'Oh, Bill!' said Vera in a deprecating tone. 'Do hurry! The
Domalpazes have come.'

'Damn the Domalpazes!' Rosemary replied in Dr Harding's voice. 'They've no right to come early. Coming early to
a party is bloody bad manners. What are you doing in that
ridiculous garment? You still want to play Clinic, do you,
ducks?' Rosemary sat up in the water. 'Get undressed, woman!
What you need is a good enema. A deep one.' She stretched a
dripping arm out of the water and took hold of Vera's *jellabah*.
'Come on, girl, off with it!'

'Oh, do be serious, Bill! I must look after the Domalpazes.
They want tea.'

'God! Let them wait. Send them away and tell them to
come at the right time.'

'Oh, Bill!' uttered Vera peevishly and returned to the sitting-room. 'Excuse me,' she said to the Indians, who were sitting on the sofa with their hands folded on their laps looking like an enthroned Maharajah and Maharanee about to receive homage from their slave subjects. Downstairs, Vera put on the kettle and rushed in her bedroom to change, but no sooner had she begun to wriggle out of her *jellabah* than the knocker banged again. She pulled the garment down over her body and went to the front door. Outside were Evelyn Parker, Mohammed and his gang. The cry 'Veradams!' was as loud as if no previous danegeld had been paid.

'Hello Evelyn!'

'Veradams! Veradams!'

The authoress looked Vera up and down. 'You didn't say it was a fancy-dress party. But not all that original, dear, to wear a *jellabah*. I know well the attraction of native dress, but it should be resisted for *they* don't like being made fun of.' She laughed indulgently and started up the stairs.

'Veradams! Veradams!'

'Oh Mohammed, and I gave you —'

'These boys very bad. Gimme two dirham and I —'

'Here you are! Now, go!'

Vera shut the door. Upstairs she found the writer of children's stories with her hand on her chin gazing pensively at Mr and Mrs Domalpaz. 'Very clever,' said Evelyn. 'Now, don't tell me. I'd say you looked like an Indian merchant and his wife, but who are you really?'

'Have a drink, Evelyn,' said Vera after she had introduced the Indians.

The bedroom door flew open and out of it burst Rosemary in black raw silk trousers and a white Russian blouse with a red sash.

'Nureyev,' said Evelyn.

'Look after the drinks, Vera. I'll go to the door.' After greeting the authoress and the Indian couple, who only had time to raise their wide behinds a few inches, Rosemary dashed down the stairs with all the élan of the dancer.

'What'll you have Evelyn?' asked Vera, putting a pile of green paperbacks on the floor to keep open the bedroom door.

'What have you got?'

'The usual things.' Vera went into the bedroom and stood behind the 'bar'.

'Isn't it rather a cumbersome garment, Vera, for indoors?' asked Evelyn. 'Moroccan women take it off as soon as they get into a house.'

'I find it good for housework.'

The whistling kettle in the kitchen below started to shriek, Rosemary shouted, 'Vera, the kettle!' the knocker banged and cries of 'Veradams! Veradams!' revived outside in the lane.

'I must go down and make the tea,' Vera said. 'Do help yourself.'

'Tea?' asked Evelyn.

'Tea for the Indians. Indian tea for the Indians.' Vera giggled.

In the hall Rosemary was greeting Rear-Admiral and Mrs Tupper-Martin and Colonel and Mrs Crosby-Johnston.

'Now, you know each other, don't you? Do go upstairs and Vera will give you a – here is Vera. Vera, the General and the Air Vice-Marshal have arrived.'

The two retired officers looked sour, as if they had been told a very stale joke.

'So good of you to come,' said Vera.

The kettle was screaming itself hoarse.

'Veradams! Veradams!'

'Do those children always behave like that?' asked Colonel Crosby-Johnston.

'More often than not,' admitted Rosemary.

'We couldn't get near the house until we'd bribed them to let us by,' said Rear-Admiral Tupper-Martin, who seemed because of the little footpads to have formed a truce with the Colonel.

'Veradams!'

'Now that's the last time, Mohammed,' said Vera handing the boy a coin. She shut the door and hurried into the kitchen to put the kettle out of its agony.

While she was looking for the tin of Indian tea the knocker banged several times and she heard Rosemary first greeting Mr and Mrs Cooper and their friend Mr Nigel Banning and then Dorothy Meade and her friend Mustapha. When at last she had found the misplaced tin and was putting three teaspoons into the pot old Sir Henry's sonorous voice rang out with an apologetic, 'I'm not late, am I?'

'No,' said Rosemary.

'I was afraid I was. Where's Vera?'

'Upstairs.'

'I'm not,' cried Vera from the kitchen. 'I'm here making tea for the Indians.'

'Vera,' said Rosemary in a shocked tone, 'd'you mean to say no one's looking after our guests?'

'Oh, I expect they're managing.'

'But we agreed that you should do the drinks.'

'I can't do two things at once, can I? I can't make tea for the Indians and at the same time –'

'Tea for the Indians!' said Rosemary contemptuously. 'You shouldn't have invited those Indians.'

'Got some Indians here, have you?' asked Sir Henry with interest. 'I like Indians.'

'For God's sake hurry up with that blasted tea – tea at a cocktail party! – and come upstairs, Vera.' Rosemary went up to the sitting-room followed by the baronet.

Vera took the largest of the three laminated Swedish trays and loaded it with the tea things for the Indians, one plate of sausage rolls and another of meat balls. 'Here goes,' she said to herself as she mounted the stairs.

There were only fourteen people dispersed about the two rooms but the buzz of chatter was considerable. As soon as Vera appeared with her tray, Rosemary swooped upon her and seized the sausage rolls and the meat balls. 'Where have you been?' she asked angrily. 'There's nothing to eat up here.' Vera went over to the Indians, who were still sitting in state on the sofa like high caste orthodox Brahmins with a space between them and their untouchable subjects. No one was speaking to them.

'Here's your tea,' said Vera sweetly, pulling up a small table and placing the tray on it. 'Do you take milk and sugar? Please help yourselves.'

'We are so much enjoying this delectable gathering, Miss Adams. It is indeed a great honour –'

Rosemary appeared. 'Have a meat ball,' she said, pushing a plate under the Indians' noses.

'No, thank you. You are indeed kind.'

'Oh, go on!' Rosemary jerked the plates further under the dark twitching noses. 'Just to finish them up.'

Wearing an expression of revulsion, while his wife recoiled, Mr Domalpaz picked a meat ball off the plate and said, 'This indeed looks most delicious.' Then, as if dealing with a turd, the Indian put the meat ball in the saucer of one of the tea cups. Impatiently, Rosemary turned to her friend. 'Vera, do go and look after the bar. Evelyn's making such a mess of it. She's got through a whole bottle of gin already. I'll replenish these.' She put the remaining meat ball into her mouth and descended to the kitchen with her plates.

Vera made her way through the talking guests. As she passed she heard the Rear-Admiral say to Nigel Banning, 'Extraordinary taste those meat balls had, did you notice? Rather subtle.' Mrs Cooper was talking to Colonel Crosby-Johnston. 'I can't think why they were asked,' she said. 'Perhaps they do a turn,' the Colonel suggested. 'The rope trick or something.'

'Have to be a pretty strong rope.'

Wreathed in a halo of smoke Evelyn's tidy, closely-cropped head was bobbing about behind the chest of drawers, which was uncomfortably high for a bar. The authoress was efficiently putting empty soda and tonic water bottles into their appropriate cases. 'It's so easy to get these muddled up,' she remarked.

'Do let me take over,' said Vera.

'Willingly.' Evelyn straightened her back and took a glass off the bar. She gulped her drink and said, 'This is the most peculiar party.'

'Is it?'

'And I feel peculiar too. It must be that stooping over those bottles.'

'Do go to the Indians, Evelyn. People aren't talking to them. Please, Evelyn. You might be able to use them as copy, as oriental ogres or something.'

'That's what I mean when I said peculiar. You in that *jellabah*, those Indians sitting over there like that and those couples retired from the Services, who aren't on speaking terms.'

'Just for five minutes, Evelyn.'

'All right.'

Vera looked round and saw Sir Henry, Dorothy Meade and Mustapha huddled behind the bedroom door out of sight of the rest of the party.

'You look as if you're hiding,' said Vera.

'I am,' confirmed the old man.

'From whom? The Tupper-Martins or the Crosby·Johnstons?'

'From Domalpaz.'

'Why on earth?'

'A matter of a cheque,' explained Sir Henry.

'I see,' said Vera sympathetically. 'You too, Dorothy?'

'No,' she replied with indignation. 'It's just that Mustapha doesn't speak English and he feels rather out of it if I abandon him.'

Mustapha looked full of self-confidence and not at all the sort of person who would ever be shy in company. Tall and well-built, like many Moroccans Mustapha had frizzy hair which he tried unsuccessfully to part; his eyes were brown and they twinkled when his thick lips revealed a fine set of teeth that some might say was marred by a gap between the two top ones in front – Dorothy Meade, however, found this gap fascinating. The gap in his teeth, his African hair, his splendid physique or his gentle, pleasant manner may have been the reasons for his popularity, no one knew for sure, but everyone took to Mustapha, a fact that caused Dorothy a good deal of worry and made her behave like a jealous mother with a delicate only son. When Vera suggested that the young Moroccan might go into the sitting-room and meet the other guests, Dorothy objected. 'He can't speak English,' she protested.

Vera became unusually forceful. 'Mrs Cooper's French is passable. *Venez*, Mustapha.'

The Moroccan eagerly responded and Vera led him up to the beautiful Mrs Cooper. The ex-ballerina immediately broke off her conversation with Colonel Crosby-Johnston, put on her Swan-Lake smile, switched her glass from her right hand to her left and taking hold of Mustapha's long, elegant fingers, said delightedly, '*Je suis enchantée de vous revoir. Vraiment.*' She held on to his hand for several moments.

After relieving Nigel Banning and the Rear-Admiral of their empty glasses, Vera was just about to return to the bar when Rosemary appeared at the top of the stairs with Ahmed the butcher. Both bore plates of canapés. Vera hastened across the room. Worried that Ahmed might think he was being used as a servant, she put the glasses she was holding on the Indians' tea tray and took the plates from him. 'It's kind of you to help,' she said. Rosemary started to offer round more plates of meat balls and sausage rolls.

'What would you like to drink?' Vera asked the butcher.

'Coca-Cola.' Ahmed looked smart in a blue suit, but older and less pathetic than he always seemed in his blood-stained apron at the market.

'I'm afraid there isn't any. You must have whisky or gin.'

'Alcohol I never drink.'

'Have a meat ball, then; it was made with your meat.'

Ahmed hesitated and took a canapé.

'Have another.'

With his other hand Ahmed took a second meat ball.

Colonel Crosby-Johnston was in that embarrassing solitary state in which cocktail-party-goers sometimes find themselves. He was glaring at his wife, who was talking to Mr Cooper. On the way to the lone Colonel with Ahmed, Vera made a mental note to do something about the Indians as soon as she was free, for Evelyn, who had somehow managed to wedge herself between them, was no longer talking to them and all three were just sitting and smiling. Occasionally the authoress absent-mindedly helped herself to a canapé from the plates on the table in front of her.

'This is Ahmed,' said Vera to the Colonel. 'You may know him. He works in the Fez market.'

'Oh really? What do you do there?'

'I am a butcher.'

'Oh really?'

Vera escaped to the bar. Dorothy Meade and Sir Henry were still behind the bedroom door. The baronet was holding a plate of meat balls and he and Dorothy were popping them into their mouths as they talked.

'Not so fast,' warned Vera, seizing the plate from Sir Henry.

'Sorry. I become a compulsive eater at these functions. By the way, Vera, it's none of my business but why didn't you invite Charles? He was rather hurt.'

Vera was loyal to her friend. 'We,' she said, 'didn't want Ali because he behaves so badly.' Sir Henry's eyebrows shot towards his hairless scalp. 'Well, Henry, you know what he did at the Watsons?'

'He only gave old Mrs Cartwright a smacking French kiss – the first she'd had for years, probably.'

'He did more than that. She was quite shaken. Anyway one can't ask everyone one knows to every party one gives,' said Vera. 'Can one?' She appealed to Dorothy, who shrugged. 'Well it's done now. It'll soon be forgotten.' Vera frowned and went back to the bar.

'Same again, please Fatima,' joked Rear-Admiral Tupper-Martin, addressing Vera by the commonest Moslem girl's name by which foreigners invariably called their female servants in Tangier.

'I didn't have time to change.'

'It suits you. I say, who's that fellow Banning?'

'I don't know. He's new here. The Coopers brought him.'

'He seems absolutely bats. He told me he was the head of a counter-spy organisation sent here to search out Viet Cong spies. "Viet Cong spies in Morocco?" I said. "They're every-where," he replied. He must be off his rocker.'

Smiling, Vera poured out a liberal measure of gin and offered her guest a plate of meat balls. 'Try one of these!'

'Thanks. They're very tasty these titbits of yours. Hello, Henry!' The Rear-Admiral wandered over to the baronet and Dorothy Meade, who were still behind the door.

Vera went about her task of replenishing drinks. The guests were becoming animated. Mrs Cooper and Mustapha were sitting on the floor and looking into each other's eyes; Evelyn, still between the Indians, was rocking with laughter; Ahmed

was regarding his feet and nodding at Colonel Crosby-Johnston's loud and tactless statements about Morocco; Rosemary
was urging Mrs Crosby-Johnston and Mr Cooper to take the
last two sausage rolls and Vera heard Nigel Banning say to Mrs
Tupper-Martin, 'Morocco is the centre of an international spy
ring. I'm here to break it up.' As she carried empty glasses to
the bar and full ones back to ready hands, Vera smiled to herself, for if one judged the success of a party by the pother
people made then this one was a triumph. What a blessing,
Vera thought, that the idea of making keef canapés had come
to her! She must go down to the kitchen and get some more
since Rosemary seemed anchored to Mrs Crosby-Johnston and
Mr Cooper. At the top of the stairs Vera paused and glanced
at the sitting-room: Colonel Crosby-Johnston was still shouting
at Ahmed about the inefficiency of the public services, but the
Rear-Admiral had joined them; Dorothy Meade had come out
from behind the bedroom door and was looking askance at Mrs
Cooper, who was examining Mustapha's hands as if telling his
fortune; Nigel Banning had begun to emphasise the remarks
he was making to Mrs Tupper-Martin by punching his left
palm with his right fist, but the Rear-Admiral's wife had her
eyes fixed on Ahmed and was not listening. Evelyn's hysterical
laughter had begun to infect Mr and Mrs Domalpaz, who
were tittering gently in sympathy, and Rosemary had evidently
started to speak about her painting for she was pointing at her
'wave' picture and talking intently to Mrs Crosby-Johnston
and Mr Cooper. Sir Henry emerged from his hiding-place and
strode towards the inanely giggling Mr Domalpaz. Vera hurried down to the kitchen.

While she was putting some left-over meat balls on to
another dish and waiting for some more sausage rolls to get
warm, she listened with feelings of self-congratulation to the
sounds of the party. Suddenly her eyes were covered by hands.
She gave a little scream and jumped. One of the hands smelt

of tobacco. 'Who is it?' she asked, nervously. The hands moved from her eyes, touched lightly her breasts and then tightened round her ample waist; the body pressed against her back. She jerked her head round and saw brown curls out of the corner of her eye. 'Ahmed!' she said, reprovingly. His butcher's hands spun Vera round and lips smelling of garlic crushed against her mouth. 'Ahmed, no!' she spluttered. She caught sight of the eucalyptus branches in the hall and thought of the Forêt Diplomatique. 'No, Ahmed!' She tried to push the young butcher from her but he did not release his strong hold until he had given her a long deep kiss. 'Why not?' he asked. 'That is what you want, isn't it?' 'Yes. No. Not now.' 'Later?' 'Yes, later.' 'O.K.!' sang Ahmed and left the kitchen. Vera took a breath and uttered 'God!' as she exhaled. What would Rosemary think? With quivering hands she rearranged the canapés.

The din coming from upstairs rivalled that of riotous games at a children's party. No one could say that the guests were having a dull time, and nor could one of the hostesses. Concern about whether the neighbours were being disturbed made Vera think of Charles and Ali and a pang of regret passed through her. Perhaps they had gone into Tangier for the evening. She opened the front door.

'Veradams! Veradams!'

'Oh, please go away!' She looked down the passage to see if Charles's lights were on. They were, but they might have been left on to deter burglars. 'Mister Charles,' she asked Mohammed, 'is he there?'

'He there. Ali there. Police there.'

'Police?'

'Yes. Gimme one dirham.'

Vera obliged. 'That's six you've had tonight. Now, please be gone!' She shut the door.

While dishing up the sausage rolls she thought about the

police being at Charles's and presumed that Ali must again be in trouble. 'A good thing,' she said to herself,' that they weren't invited. Bill was right.' The noise from the party was now very loud indeed, unusually loud even for a Tangier cocktail party. 'The keef is working,' said Vera, mischievously, mounting the stairs with a plate of sausage rolls in one hand and a dish of meat balls in the other. Just as she had paused to regard with satisfaction the scene of the party in progress at the top of the stairs before descending to the kitchen, now on the same spot sheer amazement brought her to an involuntary halt.

With her hands holding Sir Henry's jacket, Mrs Domalpaz was trying to pull the old man away from her husband, for the baronet was shaking the Indian's shoulders and thundering repeatedly, 'Domalpaz, you're a bounder! A damned good hiding is what you need.' Evelyn had risen from the sofa and was sobbing in Rosemary's arms. 'If only you knew how I loathed writing about Little John and Little Joan,' she was saying. To comfort her Rosemary said, 'No one appreciates my painting.' 'I do,' insisted Evelyn. 'You're a genius. No one likes my serious novels. I write them under another name and usually they're turned down, so I have to go on churning out this nauseating muck for infants. I hate it.' Evelyn, normally so composed and superior had to Vera's surprise become a little girl in need of consolation, which Rosemary seemed willing to give. Nigel Banning had abandoned his benevolent, ecclesiastical air and was standing in front of Mr Cooper and Mrs Crosby-Johnston in a menacing attitude. He looked as if he was about to strike bossy little Mr Cooper, who was cowering. Ahmed had discovered the cushion-strewn couch in the bedroom and was lying on it by himself, but watching over him like a panther was Mrs Tupper-Martin, whose husband had an arm round Colonel Crosby-Johnston and was talking to him most amicably.

'I never wanted your house,' the Rear-Admiral assured the

Colonel.

'You can have it, if you like. I'll move out tomorrow.'

All of a sudden Nigel Banning whipped out a revolver and pointed it at the terrified Mr Cooper. Mrs Crosby-Johnston appeared to be in a daze and not to notice the weapon.

'Take off your clothes!' demanded Banning.

'I'll do no such thing,' said Mr Cooper.

'Cooper, undress!'

Meekly, Mr Cooper began to comply with the command.

Banning flourished his revolver at Mrs Crosby-Johnston. 'You too, lady, or you'll get it in the guts.' All the culture had gone from his accent, which was now quite rough at the edges. Mrs. Crosby-Johnston just smiled vacantly. 'Arthur, this ridiculous man wants me to strip,' she called in the tone of a mother amused at her child's prank, but her husband had gone into the bedroom with the Rear-Admiral and was out of ear-shot.

'No yelling now, or you'll have it. Off with 'em.'

'Certainly not.' Mrs Crosby-Johnston leant against the wall and watched with an amused expression the disrobing Mr Cooper. Having had his bluff called, Mr Banning ignored her and concentrated on his other victim.

In the bedroom Vera found the Rear-Admiral putting on the kaftan that had been draped over the looking-glass; the Colonel was rummaging through Rosemary's wardrobe – 'She's got nothing decent to wear,' he complained. Mrs Tupper-Martin sprang on to the couch and with a roar began a pillow fight with Ahmed. Her husband, the Rear-Admiral, was too busy admiring himself in the mirror to notice.

There was a series of crashes on the front door. It sounded as if people were kicking it. On her way through the sitting-room Vera passed Mr Banning and Mr Cooper; the latter was in his underpants and feebly protesting the command to take them off; Dorothy Meade was shouting 'Tell me who you

love' to Mustapha, whose right arm was embracing Mrs
Cooper, and Mrs Domalpaz was screaming while Sir Henry
went on shaking her husband. Evelyn had collapsed on to the
floor and was moaning and Rosemary was nowhere to be
seen. Some inexplicable inner compulsion made Vera put her
cowl over her head and her yashmak over her face before going
to the front door, which she opened not to the familiar cry of
'Veradams!', but to five policemen. The boys had fled, but she
now saw Ali standing in the lane watching. The officer in
charge of the posse of police spoke to her in Arabic. Ali said
something. The large, swarthy police officer with a revolver
in his belt, barked out a command and strong arms bundled
Vera out into the lane. The door slammed to. The policemen
were inside the house.

Upstairs, Sir Henry's hands were round Mr Domalpaz's
throat, 'If you had waited ten days the money would have
been paid in,' bawled the baronet; Mrs Domalpaz's screams
had not abated and Evelyn was still moaning on the floor;
Dorothy Meade had run out to the terrace and was shouting,
'I want to dive in and swim to Las Palmas. I *know* I could.
I want to get right away.' Mustapha and Mrs Cooper were
lying side by side on the floor, gazing admiringly at each other.
Mr Cooper was completely nude. 'What are you trying to do to
me?' he wailed. 'Look at my wife on the floor with that
Moroccan! You should turn your gun on him.' 'Shut up,'
snapped Banning. Mrs Crosby-Johnston, still leaning against
the wall, held a glass in her hand. Munching her third meat
ball she said, 'Make him put his hands on his head, Mr
Banning. You never know.'

'He is a Viet Cong spy,' said Banning.

'Naturally,' agreed Mrs Crosby-Johnston.

'I must hand him over to the police.'

'Here are the police,' said the Colonel's wife, sipping her

drink in an unconcerned manner.

Whereupon Banning looked round, dropped his gun and put his head in his hands. 'They've found out!' he sobbed. Mrs Crosby-Johnston at once picked up the weapon. 'Didn't you realise it was a toy, Mr Cooper? My son has one just like it. Don't they make them well nowadays!' She laughed.

In the bedroom, the Colonel, dressed in one of Rosemary's few skirts and a blouse, was waltzing with the Rear-Admiral in the kaftan. Ahmed was in a position of conqueror on top of Mrs Tupper-Martin.

Because the guests, preoccupied in their different ways, ignored his commands to be silent, the police officer began to shout. 'All of you are under arrest,' he said again and again. His men moved into the room and started to round up the revellers: Mrs Crosby-Johnston was roughly relieved of the toy revolver and handcuffed; Mr Banning pleaded to have hand-cuffs too, putting his wrists together and pushing his arms up. 'I am a dangerous man,' he insisted. Dorothy was just pre-vented from leaping off the terrace and was dragged into the sitting-room screaming about her love for Mustapha and her desire to swim to the Canaries; Sir Henry let go of the Indian and said to a policeman, 'Quite right of you to come. Arrest this man! He is a swindler, a currency cheat.' The Rear-Admiral and the Colonel, talking in the voices of schoolgirls, tried unsuccessfully to humour the law – 'We're only playing, officer,' lisped the Rear-Admiral; 'Just a little game,' minced the Colonel.

Ahmed leapt out of Mrs Tupper-Martin's arms into those of a policeman, and the Rear-Admiral's wife, her clothes awry, her hair dishevelled was hauled unceremoniously to her feet, as was the semi-conscious Evelyn from the floor of the sitting-room. One of the policemen sniffed a meat ball and poured the contents of the dish into a polythene bag. Soon all the guests, except Evelyn, who had to be carried, were being marched down the lane to waiting police cars. Those like the Rear-Admiral, the Colonel and Sir Henry, who were still elated by the keef, hilariously roared their way towards the cars but Mr Cooper, who had hastily redressed, had regained his aplomb. 'Look here,' he said, 'I'm perfectly willing to come to the police station and give evidence against this maniac Banning, but to arrest *me* is absurd.' The Domalpazes, who had not even sipped their tea, tried in vain to get the officer to release them. 'My wife and I,' said Mr Domalpaz, 'have nothing to do with these people, and as a matter of fact I was assaulted and caused most grievous bodily harm.' The officer brushed aside the plea. 'Everyone to the police station,' was his reply. Sir Henry bawled, 'That's right. And I shall be the first to put in an official complaint against this Indian rogue.' He did not seem to realise that he too had been arrested.

Horrified, Vera watched the procession down the lane from a downstairs window in Charles's house to which Ali had brought her. After they had all disappeared, the Moroccan explained that he had recognised her when she had opened the door and told them she was the maid and therefore she had been allowed to go free.

'Why did you save me?' asked Vera.

'Because you are good,' replied Ali.

'Thank you, but what about my friend? What about Rosemary?'

'I no see her.'

'God! Has she jumped into the sea? Where's Charles?'

'He in bed. You want see him?'

'Please.'

'O.K. You wait.'

Ali went upstairs. Vera heard voices, more than two people's she was sure. As in her cottage, Charles's sitting-room and main bedroom were on the first floor. Five minutes passed before Charles came clattering down the tiled staircase. 'Oh hullo, Vera,' he said. 'I'd gone to bed.' He was wearing a brown *jellabah* over his pyjamas and resembled a fallen friar who regularly committed most of the deadly sins.

'Is Rosemary with you?' asked Vera, anxiously.

'No.'

'Where can she be? You know what's happened?'

Charles was hesitant. 'Er, only vaguely. Come upstairs.'

Ali was not in the sitting-room so Vera felt free to confess to Charles about the keef canapés and their effect. Though, overwrought, she could not stop herself from laughing, if somewhat hysterically, at her description of the antics her guests had got up to. 'The keef made people sort of do their own thing, just like you said.'

'So that's why you asked me about keef?'

Vera nodded guiltily, and after a pause she asked, 'Why did the police come, d'you think?'

'God knows!'

'Someone must have tipped them off. Did Ali, d'you suppose? The police were here in your house. The kids told me that. Why did they come to you?'

Charles said, 'They'd had a complaint about the noise and thought it was coming from my place. A neighbour, I imagine.'

'But Moroccans don't complain about noise! And the keef? They knew about the keef. Did Ali know about it?'

Charles glanced at the bedroom door, which was ajar, and after giving Vera a shifty look, cast down his eyes to examine his left thumb as if it suddenly required close attention. 'How could he have done?' Charles murmured. He began to suck his thumb.

'Hubert Pierce could have told him,' said Vera.

The thumb made a succulent plop as it was withdrawn from the mouth. 'Hubert Pierce!' exclaimed Charles in an astonished tone which suggested that the most unlikely person in the world had been mentioned.

'I think he saw me buy the keef.'

'So what?' Charles bit the side of his thumb.

'Well, never mind. What's to happen now?'

Charles smirked. 'I suppose you'll have to go along to the police station tomorrow with supplies of food. I can't see the Crosby-Johnstons or the Tupper-Martins enjoying prison fare.' He guffawed. 'How many are there?'

Vera made a rapid calculation on her fingers. 'Fourteen. Without Rosemary thirteen.'

'They'll make quite a catering problem. You'd better make a large stew.' He started to laugh.

'It's not funny.'

'It is. It's hellishly funny. There hasn't been anything so funny happen here since that film star drew a revolver and shot at the lights in a night club. He was gaoled, much to the embarrassment of his hostess, who had arranged a luncheon party in his honour for the next day to which "tout Tanger" had been invited.'

'It's dreadful, Charles. What'll happen? What shall I do?'

'Better go and see the Consul in the morning. There's nothing you can do tonight, my dear.' Charles laughed.

'Oh, don't laugh,' said Vera crossly. She left Charles, put out by his amusement at her plight and returned disconsolately to her house. The appallingness of the situation, and she was to blame for it, was overwhelming. With plans about how she would cope with the problem in the morning and speculation on the fate of Rosemary racing through her mind, sleep was impossible; so leaving the front door open in case her friend had only gone out for some fresh air, she grimly set about the disagreeable after-party chore of clearing away the debris and washing up the glasses. She cried a bit over the sink; then while she was putting a plate in the rack there were footsteps outside. 'Bill!' Vera hurried to the door and saw Hubert

Pierce waddling down the lane in the direction of the town. 'So there was a plot!' Vera exclaimed. 'Damn them! If only Bill had let me invite Charles and Ali! Damn Bill! Oh, where is Bill?' Vera returned to the kitchen sink. Suddenly an idea came to her. 'Of course,' she said aloud, and placing a tumbler with the dishcloth still in it on the table she ran to the ground-floor bedroom and pulled apart the curtains that screened the bed: there lay her friend, asleep and serene. 'Oh Bill darling!' cried Vera in relief. She kissed her friend, who did not wake. 'How clever you are!' Vera went back to her uncompleted tumbler. Rosemary's safe presence in the house altered the situation and fresh plans started to form themselves in Vera's head. Why not run away? Their lease would expire in about six weeks; Ahmed obviously didn't care for anyone in partic-ular, anyone would do for him – fancy letting himself go with the Rear-Admiral's scraggy wife! Flight was the answer. To get away from corrupting Morocco and the dreary foreign community was the wise thing to do. Vera finished polishing the tumbler and then, after holding it up to the light, she put it down on the kitchen table and went into the bedroom. Rose-mary needed a lot of shaking to be aroused from her comatose slumber, and when at last she opened her eyes all she said was, 'For Christ's sake leave me alone!' But Vera persisted and made Rosemary sit up and listen. 'They were all arrested; they're in the police station; I was mistaken for the maid. How did you get there?'

'I don't know. I suddenly felt dizzy. I must have decided to go and lie on your bed. You say the police came and –'

'Yes, and took everyone off and the rest of the canapés. Hubert, Charles and Ali must have told the police in revenge for not being invited. But Bill, don't you see we may get into terrible trouble and we'll never be able to face any of those people again? We must pack and go to Ceuta. Tonight. It'll only take two hours to get there. It's just after one now. We could be ready in two hours, couldn't we? Once in Ceuta we'd be safe, and anyway we could catch the morning boat to Algeciras.'

'It may be an extraditable offence feeding friends keef canapés. Interpol might be asked to send us back.'

'Rubbish. Anyway we must take the chance. Let's go, shall we?'

'All right, but my God I feel foul. How about you, Vera, don't you feel like death?'

'No, just a little tired. You see, Bill, I didn't eat any of those things and I only drank half a glass of wine.'

'Vera, one day someone will murder you.'

The two friends only exchanged brief, practical words of suggestion and decision while they were packing, and it was not until half the journey to Ceuta was over that the tension of their flit subsided. When the lights of Tetouan appeared in the distance Rosemary broke the silence and said, 'D'you know, Vera, I don't think there's anyone I shall miss.'

'Not even old Sir Henry?'

'God no! What a vengeful old imperialist he turned out to be, attacking poor Domalpaz like that. Why should that wretched Indian cash his dud cheques?'

'Why should he,' agreed Vera.

'What about your butcher?' asked Rosemary. 'He was pretty bestial, wasn't he, throwing himself on to Mrs Tupper-Martin like that?'

Vera could not help defending Ahmed. 'It was she who threw herself at him.'

'Was it?' Rosemary yawned. 'D'you think that horror Hubert will send a piece to his London paper?'

'Bound to.'

' "British spinsters' keef party broken up by police," ' suggested Rosemary.

' "Retired senior officers don drag at party," ' said Vera.

' "Rear-Admiral's wife molested by Moroccan butcher," ' returned Rosemary.

' "Indian shopkeeper attacked by baronet." '

The interior of the little car resounded with the laughter of the two friends, and in a light-hearted, end-of-term mood they motored on through the silent streets of Tetouan to the frontier, where their gaiety puzzled the sleepy Moroccan and Spanish officials. The next morning, however, when they awoke in their Ceuta hotel, Rosemary and Vera felt ashamed at having run away, but not sufficiently so to run back and face the music. They crossed the Straits in the *Virgen de' Africa* and then set out towards Seville and the north. Not once did they mention the party.

The Custodian

SUSAN HILL

AT five minutes to three he climbed up the ladder into the loft.
He went cautiously, he was always cautious now, moving his
limbs warily, and never going out in bad weather without
enough warm clothes. For the truth was that he had not
expected to survive this winter, he was old, he had been ill
for one week, and then the fear had come over him again that
he was going to die. He did not care for his own part, but
what would become of the boy? It was only the boy he worried
about now, only he who mattered. Therefore he was careful
with himself, for he had lived out this bad winter, it was
March, he could look forward to the spring and summer,
could cease to worry for a little longer. All the same he had to
be careful not to have accidents, though he was steady enough
on his feet. He was seventy-one. He knew how easy it would
be, for example, to miss his footing on the narrow ladder, to
break a limb and lie there, while all the time the child waited,
panic welling up inside him, left last at the school. And when
the fear of his own dying did not grip him, he was haunted
by ideas of some long illness, or incapacitation, and if he had
to be taken into hospital, what would happen to the child,
then? *What would happen?*

But now it was almost three o'clock, almost time for him
to leave the house, his favourite part of the day, now he
climbed on hands and knees into the dim, cool loft and felt
about among the apples, holding this one and that one up to
the beam of light coming through the slats in the roof, wanting
the fruit he finally chose to be perfect, ripe and smooth.

The loft smelled sweetly of the apples and pears laid up there since the previous autumn. Above his head, he heard the scrabbling noises of the birds, house martins nesting in the eaves, his heart lurched with joy at the fresh realisation that it was almost April, almost spring.

He went carefully down the ladder, holding the chosen apple. It took him twenty minutes to walk to the school but he liked to arrive early, to have the pleasure of watching and waiting, outside the gates.

The sky was brittle blue and the sun shone, but it was very cold, the air smelled of winter. Until a fortnight ago there had been snow, he and the boy had trudged back and forwards every morning and afternoon over the frost-hard paths which led across the marshes, and the stream running alongside of them had been iced over, the reeds were stiff and white as blades.

It had thawed very gradually. Today, the air smelled thin and sharp in his nostrils. Nothing moved. As he climbed the grass bank on to the higher path, he looked across the great stretch of river, and it gleamed like a flat metal plate under the winter sun, still as the sky. Everything was pale, white and silver, a gull came over slowly, and its belly and the undersides of its wings were pebble grey. There were no sounds here except the sudden chatter of dunlin swooping and dropping quickly down, and the tread of his own feet on the path, the brush of his legs against grass clumps.

He had not expected to live this winter.

In his hand, he felt the apple, hard and soothing to the touch, for the boy must have fruit, fruit every day, he saw to that, as well as milk and eggs which they fetched from Maldrun at the farm, a mile away. His limbs should grow, he should be perfect.

Maldrun's cattle were out on their green island in the middle

of the marshes, surrounded by the moat of steely water, he
led them across a narrow path like a causeway, from the farm.
They were like toy animals, or those in a picture, seen from
this distance away, they stood motionless, cut-out shapes of
black and white. Every so often, the boy was still afraid of
going past the island of cows, he gripped the old man's hand
and a tight expression came over his face.

'They can't get at you, don't you see? They don't cross
water, not cows. They're not bothered about you.'

'I know.'

And he did know – and was still afraid. Though there had
been days, recently, when he would go right up to the edge
of the strip of water and stare across at the animals, he would
even accompany Maldrun to the half-door of the milking parlour, and climb up and look over, would smell the thick, sour,
cow-smell, and hear the plash of dung on to the stone floor.
Then he was not afraid. The cows had great, bony haunches
and vacant eyes.

'Touch one,' Maldrun had said. The boy had gone inside
and put out a hand, though standing well back, stretched and
touched the rough pelt, the cow had twitched, feeling the
lightness of his hand as if it were an irritation, the prick of a
fly. He was afraid, but getting less so, of the cows. So many
things were changing, he was growing, he was seven years
old.

Occasionally the old man woke in the night and sweated
with fear that he might die before the boy was grown, and he
prayed, then, to live ten more years, just ten, until the boy
could look after himself. And some days it seemed possible,
seemed indeed most likely, some days he felt very young, felt
no age at all, his arms were strong and he could chop wood
and lift buckets, he was light-headed with the sense of his own
youth. He was no age. He was seventy-one. A tall, bony man
with thick white hair, and without any spread of spare flesh.

When he bathed, he looked down and saw every rib, every joint of his own thin body, he bent an arm and watched the flicker of muscle beneath the skin.

As the path curved round, the sun caught the surface of the water on his right, so that it shimmered and dazzled his eyes for a moment, and then he heard the familiar faint, high moan of the wind, as it blew off the estuary a mile and more away. The reeds rustled dryly together like sticks. He put up the collar of his coat. But he was happy, his own happiness sang inside his head, that he was here, walking along this path with the apple inside his hand inside his pocket, that he would wait and watch and then, that he would walk back this same way with the boy, that none of those things he dreaded would come about.

Looking back, he could still make out the shapes of the cows, and looking down, to where the water lay between the reed-banks, he saw a swan, its neck arched and its head below the surface of the dark, glistening stream, and it too was entirely still. He stopped for a moment, watching it and hearing the thin sound of the wind, and then, turning, saw the whole, pale stretch of marsh and water and sky, saw for miles, back to where the trees began, behind which was the cottage and then far ahead, to where the sand stretched out like a tongue into the mouth of the estuary.

He was amazed that he could be alive and moving, small as an insect, across this great, bright, cold space, amazed that he should count for as much as Maldrun's cows and the unmoving swan.

The wind was suddenly cold on his face. It was a quarter past three. He left the path, went towards the gate, and began to cross the rough, ploughed field which led to the lane, and then, on another mile to the village, the school.

Occasionally he came here not only in the morning, and

back again in the afternoon, but at other times when he was overcome with sudden anxiety and a desire to see the boy, to reassure himself that he was still there, was alive. Then he put down whatever he might be doing and came, almost running, stumbled and caught his breath, until he reached the railings and the closed, black gate. If he waited there long enough, if it was dinner or break time, he saw them all come streaming and tumbling out of the green painted doors, and he watched desperately until he saw him, and he could loosen the grip of his hands on the railings, the thumping of his heart eased inside his chest. Always, then, the boy would come straight down to him, running over the asphalt, and laughed and called and pressed himself up against the railings on the other side.

'Hello.'

'All right, are you?'

'What have you brought me? Have you got something?'

Though he knew there would be nothing, did not expect it, knew that there was only ever the fruit at home time, apple, pear or sometimes, in the summer, cherries or a peach.

'I was just passing through the village.'

'Were you doing the shopping?'

'Yes. I only came up to see ...'

'We've done reading. We had tapioca for pudding.'

'That's good for you. You should eat that. Always eat your dinner.'

'Is it home time yet?'

'Not yet.'

'You will be here, won't you? You won't forget to come back?'

'Have I ever?'

Then, he made himself straighten his coat, or shift the string shopping-bag over from one hand to the other, he said, 'You go back now then, go to the others, you play with them,' for he knew that this was right, he should not keep the child standing here, should not show him up in front of the rest. It was only for himself that he had come, he was eaten up with his own concern, and fear.

'You go back to your friends now.'

'You will be here? You will be here?'

'I'll be here.'

He turned away, they both turned, for they were separate, they should have their own ways, their own lives. He turned and walked off down the lane out of sight of the playground, not allowing himself to look back; perhaps he went and bought something from the shop, and he was calm again, no longer anxious. He walked back home slowly.

He did not mind all the walking, not even in the worst weather. He did not mind anything at all in this life he had chosen, and which was all-absorbing, the details of which were so important. He no longer thought anything of the past. Somewhere he had read that an old man has only his memories, and he had wondered at that, for he had none, or rather they did not concern him, they were like old letters which he had not troubled to keep. He had, simply, the present, the cottage, and the land around it, and the boy to look after. And he had to stay well, stay alive, he must not die yet. That was all.

But he did not often allow himself to go up to the school like that, at unnecessary times, he would force himself to stay and sweat out his anxiety and the need to reassure himself about the child, in some physical job, he would beat mats and plant vegetables in the garden, prune or pick from the fruit trees or walk over to see Maldrun at the farm, buy a chicken, and wait until the time came so slowly around to three o'clock, and he could go, with every reason, could allow himself the pleasure of arriving there a little early, and waiting beside the gates, which were now open, for the boy to come out.

'What have I got today?'

'You guess.'

'That's easy. Pear.'

'Wrong!' He opened his hand, revealing the apple.

'Well, I like apples best.'

'I know. I had a good look at those trees down the bottom this morning. There won't be so many this year. Mind, we've to wait for the blossom to be sure.'

'Last year there were hundreds of apples. *Thousands.*' He took the old man's hand as they reached the bottom of the lane. For some reason he always waited until just there, by the whitebeam tree, before doing so.

'There were *millions* of apples!'

'Get on!'

'Well, a lot anyway.'

'That's why there won't be so many this year. You don't get two crops like that in a row.'

'Why?'

'Trees wear themselves out, fruiting like that. They've to rest.'

'Will we have a lot of pears instead, then?'

'I dare say. What have you done at school?'

'Lots of things.'

'Have you done your reading? That's what's the important thing. To keep up with your reading.'

He had started the boy off himself, bought alphabet and word picture-books from the village, and, when they got beyond these, had made up his own cut-out pictures from magazines and written beside them in large clear letters on ruled sheets of paper. By the time the boy went to school, he had known more than any of the others, he was 'very forward', they said, though looking him up and down at the same time for he was small for his age.

It worried him that the boy was still small, he watched the others closely as they came out of the gates and they were all taller, thicker in body and stronger of limb. His face always looked old.

The old man concerned himself even more, then, with the fresh eggs and cheese, milk and fruit, watched over the boy while he ate. But he did eat.

'We had meat and cabbage for dinner.'

'Did you finish it?'

'I had a second helping. Then we had cake for pudding. Cake and custard. I don't like that.'

'You didn't leave it?'

'Oh no. I just don't like it, that's all.'

Now, as they came onto the marshes, the water and sky were even paler and the reeds beside the stream were bleached, like old wood left out for years in the sun. The wind was stronger, whipping at their legs from behind.

'There's the swan.'

'They've a nest somewhere about.'

'Have you seen it?'

'They don't let you see it. They go away from it if anybody walks by.'

'I drew a picture of a swan.'

'Today?'

'No. Once. It wasn't very good.'

'If a thing's not good you should do it again.'

'Why should I?'

'You'll get better then.'

'I won't get better at drawing.' He spoke very deliberately, as he so often did, knowing himself, and firm about the truth of things, so that the old man was silent, respecting it.

'He's sharp,' Maldrun's wife said. 'He's a clever one.'

But the old man would not have him spoiled, or too lightly praised.

'He's plenty to learn. He's only a child yet.'

'All the same, he'll do, won't he? He's sharp.'

But perhaps it was only the words he used, only the serious expression on his face, which came of so much reading and all that time spent alone with the old man. And if he was, as they said, so sharp, so forward, perhaps it would do him no good?

He worried about that, wanting the boy to find his place easily in the world, he tried hard not to shield him from things, made him go to the farm to see Maldrun, and over Harper's fen by himself, to play with the gamekeeper's boys, told him always to mix with the others in the school playground, to do what they did. Because he was most afraid, at times, of their very contentment together, of the self-contained life they led, for in truth they needed no one, each of them would be entirely happy never to go far beyond this house; they spoke of all things, or of nothing, the boy read and made careful lists of the names of birds and moths, and built elaborate structures, houses and castles and palaces out of old matchboxes, he helped with the garden, had his own corner down beside the shed, in which he grew what he chose. It had been like this from the beginning, from the day the old man had brought him here at nine months old and set him down on the floor and taught him to crawl, they had fallen naturally into their life together. Nobody else had wanted him. Nobody else would have taken such care.

Once, people had been suspicious, they had spoken to each other in the village, had disapproved.

'He needs a woman there. It's not right. He needs someone who knows,' Maldrun's wife had said. But now, even she had accepted that it was not true, so that, before strangers, she would have defended them more fiercely than anyone.

'He's a fine boy, that. He's all right. You look at him, look. Well, you can't tell what works out for the best. You can never tell.'

By the time they came across the track which led between the gorse bushes and down through the fir trees, it was as cold as it had been on any night in January, they brought in more wood for the fire and had toast and the last of the damson jam and mugs of hot milk.

'It's like winter. Only not so dark. I like it in winter.'

But it was the middle of March now, in the marshes the herons and redshanks were nesting, and the larks spiralled up, singing through the silence. It was almost spring.

So, they went on as they had always done, until the second of April. Then, the day after their walk out to Derenow, the day after they saw the kingfisher, it happened.

From the early morning, he had felt uneasy, though there was no reason he could give for his fear, it simply lay, hard and cold as a stone in his belly, and he was restless about the house from the time he got up.

The weather had changed. It was warm, and clammy, with low, dun-coloured clouds and, over the marshes, a thin mist. He felt the need to get out, to walk and walk; the cottage was dark and oddly quiet. When he went down between the fruit trees to the bottom of the garden, the first of the buds were breaking into green, but the grass was soaked with dew like a sweat, the heavy air smelled faintly rotten and sweet.

They set off in the early afternoon. The boy did not question, he was always happy to go anywhere at all, but when he was asked to choose their route, he set off at once, a few paces ahead, on the path which forked away east, in the opposite direction from the village and leading, over almost three miles of empty marsh, towards the sea. They followed the bank of the river, and the water was sluggish, with fronds of dark green weed lying below the surface. The boy bent, and put his hand cautiously down, breaking the skin of the water but when his fingers came up against the soft, fringed edges of the plants he pulled back.

'Slimy.'

'Yes. It's out of the current here. There's no freshness.'

'Will there be fish?'

'Maybe there will. Not so many.'

'I don't like it.' Though for some minutes he continued to peer between the reeds at the pebbles which were just visible on the bed of the stream.

'He asks questions,' they said. 'He takes an interest. It's his mind, isn't it – bright – you can see, alert, that's what. He's forever wanting to know.'

Though there were times when he said nothing at all, his small, old-young face was crumpled in thought, there were times when he looked and listened with care and asked nothing.

As they went on, the air around them seemed to close in further, it seemed harder to breathe, and they could not see clearly ahead to where the marshes and mist merged into the sky. Here and there, the stream led off into small, muddy pools and hollows, and the water in them was reddened by the rust seeping from some old can or metal crate thrown there and left for years, the stains which spread out looked like old blood. Gnats hovered in clusters over the water.

'Will we go on to the beach?'

'We could.'

'We might find something on the beach.'

Often they searched among the pebbles for pieces of amber or jet, for old buckles and buttons and sea-smooth coins washed up by the tides: the boy had a collection of them in a cardboard box in his room.

'You could die here. You could drown in the water and never, never be found.'

'That's not a thing to think about. What do you worry over that for?'

'But you could, you could.'

They were walking in single file, the boy in front. From all the secret nests down in the reed-beds, the birds made their own noises, chirring and whispering, or sending out sudden cries of warning and alarm. The high, sad call of a curlew came again and again, and then ceased abruptly. The boy whistled in imitation.

'Will it know it's me? Will it answer?'

He whistled again. They waited. Nothing. His face was shadowed with disappointment.

'You can't fool them, not birds.'

'You can make a blackbird answer you. You can easily.'

'Not the same.'

'Why isn't it?'

'Blackbirds are tame, blackbirds are garden birds.'

'Wouldn't a curlew come to the garden?'

'No.'

'Why wouldn't it?'

'It likes to be away from things. They keep to their own places.'

They walked on, and then, out of the thick silence which was all around them came the creaking of wings, nearer and nearer and sounding like two thin boards of wood beaten slowly together. A swan, huge as an eagle, came over their heads, flying very low, so that the boy looked up for a second in terror at the size and closeness of it, caught his breath. He said urgently, 'Swans go for people, swans can break your arm if they hit you, if they beat you with their wings. Can't they?'

'But they don't take any notice, so come on, you leave them be.'

'But they *can* can't they?'

'Oh, they might.' He watched the great, grey-white shape go awkwardly away from them, in the direction of the sea.

A hundred yards further on, at the junction of two paths across the marsh there was the ruin of a water-mill, blackened after a fire years before, and half broken down, a sail torn off.

Inside, under an arched doorway, it was dark and damp, the walls were coated with yellowish moss and water lay, brackish, in the mud hollows of the floor.

At high summer, on hot, shimmering blue days they had come across here on the way to the beach with a string bag full of food for their lunch, and then the water-mill had seemed like a sanctuary, cool and silent, the boy had gone inside and stood there, had called softly and listened to the echo of his own voice as it rang lightly round and round the walls.

Now, he stopped dead in the path, some distance away.

'I don't want to go.'

'We're walking to the beach.'

'I don't want to go past that.'

'The mill?'

'There are rats.'

'No.'

'And flying things. Things that are black and hang upside-down.'

'Bats? What's to be afraid of in bats? You've seen them, you've been in Maldrun's barn. They don't hurt.'

'I want to go back.'

'You don't have to go into the mill. Who said you did? We're going on to where the sea is.'

'*I want to go back now.*'

He was not often frightened. But standing there in the middle of the hushed stretch of fenland, the old man felt again disturbed himself, the fear that something would happen, here, where nothing moved and the birds lay hidden, only crying out their weird cries, where things lay under the unmoving water and the press of the air made him sweat down his back. Something would happen to them, something . . .

What could happen?

Then, not far ahead, they both saw him at the same moment, a man with a gun under his arm, tall and black and menacing as a crow against the dull horizon, and as they saw him, they also saw two mallard ducks rise in sudden panic from their nests in the reeds, and they heard the shots, three shots that cracked out and echoed for miles around, the air went on reverberating with the waves of terrible sound.

The ducks fell at once, hit in mid-flight so that they swerved, turned over, and plummeted down. The man with the shotgun started quickly forward and the grasses and reeds bent and stirred as a dog ran, burrowing, to retrieve.

'I want to go back, *I want to go back.*'

Without a word, the old man took his hand, and they turned, walked quickly back the way they had come, as though afraid that they, too, would be followed and struck down, not caring that they were out of breath and sticky with sweat, but only wanting to get away, to reach the shelter of the lane and the trees, to make for home.

Nothing was ever said about it, or about the feeling they had both had walking across the marshes, the boy did not mention the man with the gun or the ducks which had been alive and in flight and then so suddenly dead. All that evening, the old man watched him, as he stuck pictures in a book, and tore up dock leaves to feed to the rabbit, watched for signs of left-over fear. But he was only, perhaps, quieter than usual, his face more closed up; he was concerned with his own thoughts.

In the night, he woke, and got up, went to the boy and looked down through the darkness, for fear that he might have had bad dreams and woken, but there was only the sound of his breathing; he lay quite still, very long and straight in the bed.

He imagined the future, and his mind was filled with images of all the possible horrors to come, the things which could cause the boy shock and pain and misery, and from which he would not be able to save him, as he had been powerless to-day to protect him from the sight of the killing of two ducks.

He was in despair. Only the next morning, he was eased, as it came back to him again, the knowledge that he had, after all, lived out the winter, and ahead of them lay only light and warmth and greenness.

Nevertheless, he half-expected that something would still happen to them, to break into their peace. For more than a week, nothing did, his fears were quieted, and then the spring broke, the apple and pear blossom weighed down the branches in great, creamy clots, the grass in the orchard grew up as high as the boy's knees, and across the marshes the sun shone and shone, the water of the river was turquoise, and in the streams, as clear as glass; the wind blew warm and smelled faintly of salt and earth. Walking to and from the school every day, they saw more woodlarks than they had ever seen, quivering on the air high above their heads, and near the gorse bushes, the boy found a nest of leverets. In the apple loft, the house martins hatched out, and along the lanes, dandelions and buttercups shone golden out of the grass.

It was on the Friday that Maldrun gave the boy one of the farm kittens, and he carried it home close to his body beneath his coat. It was black and white, like Maldrun's cows. And it was the day after that, the end of the first week of spring, that Blaydon came, Gilbert Blaydon, the boy's father.

He was sitting outside the door watching a buzzard hover above the fir copse when he heard the footsteps. He thought it was Maldrun bringing over the eggs, or a chicken – Maldrun generally came one evening in the week, after the boy had gone to bed, they drank a glass of beer and talked for half an hour. He was an easy man, undemonstrative. They still called one another, formally 'Mr Bowry', 'Mr Maldrun'.

The buzzard roved backwards and forwards over its chosen patch of air, searching.

When the old man looked down again, he was there, standing in the path. He was carrying a canvas kitbag.

He knew, then, why he had been feeling uneasy, he had expected this, or something like it, to happen, though he had put the fears to the back of his mind with the coming of sunshine and the leaf-breaking. He felt no hostility as he looked at Blaydon, only extreme weariness, almost as though he were ill.

There was no question of who it was, yet above all he ought to have expected a feeling of complete disbelief, for if anyone had asked, he would have said that he would certainly never see the boy's father again. But now he was here, it did not seem surprising, it seemed, indeed, somehow inevitable. Things had to alter, things could never go on. Happiness did not go on.

'Will you be stopping?'

Blaydon walked slowly forward, hesitated, and then set the kitbag down at his feet. He looked much older.

'I don't know if it'd be convenient.'

'There's a room. There's always a room.'

The old man's head buzzed suddenly in confusion, he thought he should offer a drink or a chair, should see to a bed, should ask questions to which he did not want to know the answers, should say something about the boy.

The boy.

'You've come to take him . . .'

Blaydon sat down on the other chair, beside the outdoors-table. The boy looked like him, there was the same narrowness of forehead and chin, the same high-bridged nose. Only the mouth was different, though that might simply be because the boy's was still small and unformed.

'You've come to take him.'

'Where to?' He looked up. 'Where would I have, to take him to?'

But we don't want you here, the old man thought, we don't

want anyone: and he felt the intrusion of this younger man, with the broad hands and long legs sprawled under the table, like a violent disturbance of the careful pattern of their lives, he was alien. *We don't want you.*

But what right had he to say that? He did not say it. He was standing up helplessly, not knowing what should come next, he felt the bewilderment as some kind of irritation inside his own head. He felt old.

In the end, he managed to say, 'You'll not have eaten?'

Blaydon stared at him. 'Don't you want to know where I've come from?'

'No.'

'No?

'I've made a stew. You'll be better for a plate of food.'

'Where is he?'

'Asleep in bed; where else would he be? I look after him, I know what I'm about. It's half-past eight, gone, isn't it? What would he be doing but asleep in his bed, at half-past eight?'

He heard his own voice rising and quickening, as he defended himself, defended both of them, he could prove it to this father or to anyone at all, how he'd looked after the boy. He would have said, what about you? Where have you been? What did you do for him? But he was too afraid, for he knew nothing about what rights Blaydon might have – even though he had never been near, never bothered.

'You could have been dead.'

'Did you think?'

'What was I to think? I knew nothing. Heard nothing.'

'No.'

Out of the corner of his eye, the old man saw the buzzard drop down suddenly, straight as a stone, on to some creature in the undergrowth of the copse. The sky was mulberry coloured and the honeysuckle smelled ingratiatingly sweet.

'I wasn't dead.'

The old man realised that Blaydon looked both tired and rather dirty, his nails were broken, he needed a shave, and the wool at the neck of his blue sweater was unravelling. What was he to say to the boy then, when he had brought him up to be so clean and tidy and careful, had taken his clothes to be mended by a woman in the village, had always cut and washed his hair himself. What was he to tell him about this man?

'There's hot water. I'll get you linen, make you a bed. You'd best go up first, before I put out the stew. Have a wash.'

He went into the kitchen, took a mug and a bottle of beer and poured it out, and was calmed a little by the need to organise himself, by the simple physical activity.

When he took the beer out, Blaydon was still leaning back on the old chair. There were dark stains below his eyes.

'You'd best take it up with you.' The old man held out the beer.

It was almost dark now. After a long time, Blaydon reached out, took the mug and drank, emptying it in four or five long swallows, and then, as though all his muscles were stiff, rose slowly, took up the kitbag, went towards the house.

When the old man had set the table and dished out the food, he was trembling. He tried to turn his mind away from the one thought. That Blaydon had come to take the boy away.

He called and when there was no reply, went up the stairs. Blaydon was stretched out on his belly on top of the unmade bed, heavy and motionless in sleep.

While he slept, the old man worried about the morning. It was Saturday, there would not be the diversion of going to school, the boy must wake and come downstairs and confront Blaydon.

What he had originally said was, your mother died, your

father went away. And that was the truth. But he doubted if the boy so much as remembered; he had asked a question only once, and that more than two years ago.

They were content together, needing no one.

He sat on the straight-backed chair in the darkness, surrounded by hidden greenery and the fumes of honeysuckle, and tried to imagine what he might say.

'This is your father. Other boys have fathers. This is your father who came back, who will stay with us here. For some time, or perhaps not for more than a few days. His name is Gilbert Blaydon.

'Will you call him "father", will you? . . .

'This is . . .'

His mind broke down before the sheer cliff confronting it and he simply sat on, hands uselessly in front of him on the outdoors table, he thought of nothing, and on white plates in the kitchen the stew cooled and congealed and the new kitten from Maldrun's farm slept, coiled on an old green jumper. The cat, the boy, the boy's father, all slept. From the copse, the throaty call of the nightjars.

'You'll be ready for breakfast. You didn't eat the meal last night.'

'I slept.'

'You'll be hungry.' He had his back to Blaydon. He was busy with the frying-pan and plates over the stove. What had made him tired enough to sleep like that, from early evening until now, fully clothed on top of the bed! But he didn't want to know, would not ask questions.

The back door was open on to the path that led down between vegetable beds and the bean canes and currant bushes, towards the thicket. Blaydon went to the doorway.

'Two eggs, will you have?'

'If . . .'

'There's plenty.' He wanted to divert him, talk to him, he had to pave the way. The boy was there, somewhere at the bottom of the garden.

'We'd a hard winter.'

'Oh, yes?'

'Knee-deep, all January, all February, we'd to dig ourselves out of the door. And then it froze – the fens froze right over, ice as thick as your fist. I've never known anything like it.'

But now it was spring, now outside there was the bright, glorious green of new grass, new leaves, now the sun shone.

He began to set out knives and forks on the kitchen table. It would have to come, he would have to call the boy in, to bring them together. What would he say? His heart squeezed and then pumped hard, suddenly, in the thin bone-cage of his chest.

Blaydon's clothes were creased and crumpled. And they were not clean. Had he washed himself? The old man tried to get a glimpse of his hands.

'I thought I'd get a job,' Blaydon said.

The old man watched him.

'I thought I'd look for work.'

'Here?'

'Around here. Is there work?'

'Maybe. I've not had reason to find out. Maybe.'

'If I'm staying on, I'll need to work.'

'Yes.'

'It'd be a help, I dare say?'

'You've a right to do as you think fit. You make up your own mind.'

'I'll pay my way.'

'You've no need to worry about the boy, if it's that. He's all right, he's provided for. You've no need to find money for him.'

'All the same . . .'

After a minute, Blaydon walked over and sat down at the table.

The old man thought, he is young, young and strong and fit, he has come here to stay, he has every right, he's the father. He is . . .

But he did not want Blaydon in their lives, did not want the hands resting on the kitchen table, and the big feet beneath it.

He said, 'You could try at the farm. At Maldrun's. They've maybe got work there. You could try.'

'Maldrun's farm?'

'It'd be ordinary work. Labouring work.'

'I'm not choosy.'

The old man put out eggs and fried bread and bacon on to the plates, poured tea, filled the sugar basin. And then he had no more left to do, he had to call the boy.

But nothing happened as he had feared it, after all.

He came in. 'Wash your hands.' But he was already half way to the sink, he had been brought up so carefully, the order was not an order but a formula between them, regular, and of comfort.

'Wash your hands.'

'I've come to stay,' Blaydon said at once, 'for a bit. I got here last night.'

The boy hesitated in the middle of the kitchen, looked from one to the other of them, trying to assess this sudden change in the order of things.

'For a week or two,' the old man said. 'Eat your food.'

The boy got on to his chair. 'What's your name?'

'Gilbert Blaydon.'

'What have I to call you?'

'Either.'

'Gilbert, then.'

'What you like.'

After that, they got on with eating; the old man chewed his bread very slowly, filled, for the moment, with relief.

Maldrun took him on at the farm as a general labourer, and then their lives formed a new pattern, with the full upsurge of spring. Blaydon got up, and ate his breakfast with them and then left, there was a quarter of an hour which the old man had alone with the boy before setting off across the marsh path to school, and in the afternoon, an even longer time. Blaydon did not return, sometimes, until after six.

At the weekend, he went off somewhere alone, but occasionally, he took the boy for walks; they saw the heron's nest, and then the cygnets, and once a peregrine, flying over the estuary. The two of them were at ease together.

Alone, the old man tried to imagine what they might be saying to each other, he walked distractedly about the house, and almost wept, with anxiety and dread. They came down the path, and the boy was sitting up on Blaydon's shoulders, laughing and laughing.

'You've told him.'

Blaydon turned, surprised, and then sent the boy away. 'I've said nothing.'

The old man believed him. But there was still a fear for the future, the end of things.

The days lengthened. Easter went by, and the school holidays, during which the old man was happiest, because he had so much time with the boy to himself, and then it was May, in the early mornings there was a fine mist above the blossom trees.

'He's a good worker,' Maldrun said, coming over one evening with the eggs and finding the old man alone. 'I'm glad to have him.'

'Yes.'

'He takes a bit off your shoulders, I dare say.'

'He pays his way.'

'No. Work, I meant. Work and worries. All that.'

What did Maldrun know? But he only looked back at the old man, his face open and friendly, and drank his bottled beer.

He thought about it, and realised that it was true. He had grown used to having Blaydon about, to carry the heavy things and lock up at night, to clear out the fruit loft and lop off the overhanging branches and brambles at the entrance to the thicket. He had slipped into their life, and established himself. When he thought of the future without Blaydon, it was to worry. For the summer was always short and then came the run down through autumn into winter again. Into snow and ice and cold, and the north-east wind scything across the marshes. He dreaded all that, now that he was old. Last winter, he had been ill once, and for only a short time. This winter he was a year older, anything might happen. He thought of the mornings when he would have to take the boy to school before it was even light, thought of the frailty of his own flesh, the brittleness of his bones, he looked in the mirror at his own weak and rheumy eyes.

He had begun to count on Blaydon's being here to ease things, to help with the coal and wood and the breaking of ice on pails, to be in some way an insurance against his own possible illness, possible death.

Though now it was still only the beginning of summer, now he watched Blaydon build a rabbit hutch for the boy, hammering nails and sawing wood, uncoiling wire skilfully. He heard them laugh suddenly together. This was what he needed, after all, not a woman about the place, but a man, the strength and ease of a man who was not old, did not fear, did not say, 'Wash your hands', 'Drink up all your milk', 'Take care'.

The kitten grew, and spun about in quick, mad circles in the sun.

'He's a good worker,' Maldrun said.

After a while, the old man took to dozing in his chair outside, after supper, while Blaydon washed up, emptied the bins and then took out the shears, to clip the hedge or the grass borders, when the boy had gone to bed.

But everything that had to do with the boy, the business of rising and eating, going to school and returning, the routine of clothes and food and drink and bed, all that was still supervised by the old man. Blaydon did not interfere, scarcely seemed to notice what was done. His own part in the boy's life was quite different.

In June and early July, it was hotter than the old man could ever remember. The gnats droned in soft, grey clouds under the trees, and over the water of the marshes. The sun shone hard and bright and still, the light played tricks so that the estuary seemed now very near, now very far away. Maldrun's cows tossed their heads, against the flies which gathered stickily in the runnels below their great eyes.

He began to rely more and more upon Blaydon as the summer reached its height, left more jobs for him to do, because he was willing and strong, and because the old man succumbed easily to the temptation to rest himself in the sun. He still did most of the cooking, but he would let Blaydon go down to the shops, and the boy often went with him.

He was growing, his limbs were filling out and his skin was berry-brown. He lost the last of the pink-and-whiteness of babyhood. He had accepted Blaydon's presence without question and was entirely used to him, though he did not show any less affection for the old man, who continued to take care of him day by day. But he became less nervous and hesitant, more self-assured, he spoke of things in a casual, confident voice, learned much from his talks with Blaydon. He still did not know that this was his father. The old man thought there was no reason to tell him – not yet, not yet, they could go on as they were for the time being, just as they were.

He was comforted by the warmth of the sun on his face, by the scent of the roses and the tobacco-plants in the evening, the sight of the scarlet bean-flowers clambering higher and higher up their frame.

He had decided right at the beginning that he himself would ask no questions of Blaydon, would wait until he should be told. But he was not told. Blaydon's life might have begun only on the day he had arrived here. The old man wondered if he had been in prison, or else abroad, working on a ship, though he had no evidence for either. In the evenings they drank beer together and occasionally played a game of cards, though more often Blaydon worked at something in the garden, and the old man simply sat watching him, hearing the last cries of the birds from the marshes.

With the money Blaydon brought in they bought new clothes for the boy and better cuts of meat, and then, one afternoon, a television set arrived with two men in a green van to erect the aerial.

'For the winter,' Blaydon said. 'Maybe you won't bother with it now. But it's company in the winter.'

'I've never felt the lack.'

'All the same.'

'I don't need entertainment. We make our own. Always have made our own.'

'You'll be glad of it, once you've got the taste. I told you – it's for the winter.'

But the old man watched it sometimes very late in the evenings of August, and discovered things of interest to him, new horizons were opened, new worlds.

'I'd not have known that,' he said, 'I've never travelled. Look at what I'd never have known.'

Blaydon nodded. He himself seemed little interested in the

television set. He was mending the front fence, staking it all along with old wood given to him by Maldrun at the farm. Now the gate would fit closely and not swing and bang in the gales of winter.

It was on a Thursday night towards the end of August that Blaydon mentioned the visit to the seaside.

'He's never been,' he said, wiping the foam of beer from his top lip.

'He told me. I asked him. He's never been to the sea.'

'I've done all I can. There's never been the money. We've managed as best we could.'

'You're not being blamed.'

'I'd have taken him, I'd have seen to it in time. Sooner or later.'

'Yes.'

'Yes.'

'Well – I could take him.'

'To the sea?'

'To the coast, yes.'

'For a day? It's far enough.'

'A couple of days, I thought. For a weekend.'

The old man was silent. But it was true. The boy had never been anywhere and perhaps he suffered because of it, perhaps at school the others talked of where they had gone, what they had seen, shaming him. If that was so, he should be taken, should go everywhere, he must not miss anything, must not be left out.

'Just a couple of days. We'd leave first thing Saturday morning and come back Monday. I'd take a day off.'

He had been here three months now, and not missed a day off work.

'You do as you think best.'

'I'd not go without asking you.'

'It's only right. He's at the age for taking things in. He

needs enjoyment.'

'Yes.'

'You go. It's only right.'

'I haven't told him, not yet.'

'You tell him.'

When he did, the boy's face opened out with pleasure, he licked his lips nervously over and over again in his excitement, already counting until it should be time to go. The old man went upstairs and sorted out clothes for him, washed them carefully and hung them on the line, he began himself to anticipate it all. This was right. The boy should go.

But he dreaded it. They had not been separated before. He could not imagine how it would be, to sleep alone in the cottage, and then he began to imagine all the possible accidents. Blaydon had not asked him if he wanted to go with them. But he did not. He felt suddenly too tired to leave the house, too tired for any journeys or strangers, he wanted to sit on his chair in the sun and count the time until they should be back.

He had got used to the idea of Blaydon's continuing presence here, he no longer lived in dread of the coming winter. It seemed a long time since the days when he had been alone with the boy.

They set off very early on the Saturday morning, before the sun had broken through the thick mist that hung low over the marshes. Every sound was clear and separate as it came through the air, he heard their footsteps, the brush of their legs against the grasses long after they were out of sight. The boy had his own bag, bought new in the village, a canvas bag strapped across his shoulders. He had stood up very straight, eyes glistening, already his mind was filled with imaginary pictures of what he would see, what they would do.

The old man went back into the kitchen and put the kettle on again, refilled the teapot for himself and planned what he was going to do. He would work, he would clean out all the bedrooms of the house and sort the boy's clothes for any that needed mending; he would polish the knives and forks and wash the curtains and walk down to the village for groceries, he would bake a cake and pies, prepare a stew, ready for their return.

So that, on the first day, the Saturday he scarcely had time to think of them, to notice their absence and in the evening, his legs and back ached, he sat for only a short time outside, after his meal, drunk with tiredness, and slept later than usual on the Sunday morning.

It was then that he felt the silence and emptiness of the house. He walked about it uselessly, he woke up the kitten and teased it with a feather so that it would play with him, distract his attention from his own solitude. When it slept again, he went out, and walked for miles across the still, hot marshes. The water between the reed beds was very low and even dried up altogether in places, revealing the dark, green-ish-brown slime below. The faint, dry whistling sound that usually came through the rushes was absent. He felt parched as the countryside after this long, long summer, the sweat ran down his bent back.

He had walked in order to tire himself out again but this night he slept badly and woke out of clinging nightmares with a thudding heart, tossed from side to side, uncomfortable among the bedclothes. But tomorrow he could begin to count the strokes of the clock until their return.

He got up feeling as if he had never slept, his eyes were pouched and blurred. But he began the baking, the careful preparations to welcome them home. He scarcely stopped for food himself all day, though his head and his back ached, he moved stiffly about the kitchen.

When they had not returned by midnight on the Monday, he did not go down to the village, or across to Maldrun's farm to telephone the police and the hospitals. He did nothing. He knew.

But he sat up in the chair outside the back-door all night with the silence pressing in on his ears. Once or twice his head nodded down onto his chest, he almost slept, but then jerked awake again, shifted a little, and sat on in the darkness.

He thought, they have not taken everything, some clothes are left, clothes and toys and books, they must mean to come back. But he knew that they did not. Other toys, other clothes, could be bought anywhere.

A week passed, and the summer slid imperceptibly into autumn, like smooth cards shuffled together in a pack, the trees faded to yellow and crinkled at the edges.

He did not leave the house, and he ate almost nothing, only filled and refilled the teapot, and drank.

He did not blame Gilbert Blaydon, he blamed himself for having thought to keep the boy, having planned out their whole future. When the father had turned up, he should have known what he wanted at once, should have said, 'Take him away, take him now,' to save them this furtiveness, this deception. At night, though, he worried most about the effect it would have on the boy, who had been brought up so scrupulously, to be tidy and clean, to eat up his food, to learn. He wished there was an address to which he could write a list of details about the boy's everyday life, the routine he was used to following.

He waited for a letter. None came. The pear-trees sagged under their weight of ripe, dark fruit and after a time it fell with soft thuds into the long grass. He did not gather it up and take it to store in the loft, he left it there for the sweet pulp to be burrowed by hornets and grubs. But sometimes he took a pear and ate it himself, for he had always disapproved of waste.

He kept the boy's room exactly as it should be. His clothes

were laid out neatly in the drawers, his books lined on the single shelf, in case he should return. But he could not bother with the rest of the house, dirt began to linger in corners. Fluff accumulated greyly beneath beds. The damp patch in the bathroom wall was grown over with moss like a fungus when the first rain came in October.

Maldrun had twice been across from the farm and received no answer to his questions. In the village the women talked. October went out in fog and drizzle, and the next time Maldrun came the old man did not open the door. Maldrun waited, peering through the windows between cupped hands, and in the end left the eggs on the back step.

The old man got up later and later each day, and went to bed earlier, to sleep between the frowsty, unwashed sheets. For a short while he turned on the television set in the evenings and sat staring at whatever was offered to him, but in the end he did not bother, only stayed in the kitchen while it grew dark around him. Outside, the last of the fruit fell on to the sodden garden and lay there untouched. Winter came.

In the small town flat, Blaydon set out plates, cut bread and opened tins, filled the saucepan with milk.

'Wash your hands,' he said. But the boy was already there, moving his hands over and over the pink soap, obediently, wondering what was for tea.

ROY HOLLAND

IT was a Friday, and Monday was a lifetime away. In that time, you could grow up, die, make a million, become famous, go lame, save Iris Witchelow from kidnappers, or draw hundreds of machines for torturing Miss Turton. Dollop, that's my best friend, who's called Dollop because he likes horses and because it rhymes with Heslop, and me, always spend the weekend making up tortures for Miss Turton, whatever else we do. She's our teacher, or tries to be, and is about twenty-five, or tries to be. Her hair is coal-black, straight, with a fringe she measures out every morning with a school ruler. Her face is round and she looks as if she's blushing at her nose, which is sharper than a tooth-pick. She wears heels like stilts, skirts like gym-slips, and looks about the same size as Dollop's mother, who's at least a foot taller than his dad. But you never notice all that, not unless you look hard for it. What you see first are her tits. They are the best friends me and Dollop have got in all the school. Even just sitting there marking the register, they strain away through her red, blue, yellow and green jumpers, like overgrown mushrooms coming through the pavement, which makes wrinkles under her arms and round the back. During P.T. they just go mad, and Dollop and me have to stuff the beanbags into our mouths to keep from screaming. When she leans over and puts a cross on your sums, they make you feel funny. She can't help it, but that's why we torture her every weekend.

'Books away, boys and girls!' she trills, clapping hands, and just missing them. 'Stand. First row ready to Mr Robinson's.'

'What's in 'em?' hisses Dollop.

'Ginger beer! Because of the fizz.'

'P'raps she's got a bicycle pump.'

'No talking there!' she snaps. And they bounce.

And we all crocodile out, leaving Miss Turton to do some marking with our two friends.

Robbo's classroom is big, with a ceiling so high you can't reach it if you stand on top of the book cupboard and stretch up with the blackboard ruler. In winter it gets covered with frost, on account of the altitude, and Robbo, who's about eight-foot-nothing of bone, gristle and wind himself, stands craning up at it, and puffing, and putting his fingers up his bum, and smelling them, with big appreciative sniffs, really enjoying himself. And that's why we like Robbo. He never takes any notice of you, unless you belch, or 'make a beast of yourself', and then he throws chalk at you, or the duster, and you look like Iris Witchelow's Dad who works in a flour-mill. Most of the time he walks about the classroom, saying nothing, gazing through the windows at the conker trees, smelling his fingers, and waiting for home-time.

There are a lot of windows in Robbo's room and in those desks you can almost sit on the branches in the white candles and the pink candles, under the green umbrella-leaves where it's gloomy, and it feels like a holiday.

'The first four there, you in the mental defectives' row, get your books out of the cupboard,' booms Robbo, and he goes on twanging like a tuning fork, while Eamsy, Pongo Waring, and Cyril Handy, who's got pimples behind his knees and white stuff all round his socks at the top, go into a scrum behind the doors, trying to bags first pick.

'And no fighting,' booms Robbo staring through the window, not even looking, 'or I'll twist your arms off, you shower of cripples.'

Our weekly art lessons are always like this. Last week Dollop and me had a big green 'cyclopaedia of many lands and found out that black women are just like white women, except for the colour. Ever since the last box of crayons got pinched from Robbo's cupboard, we all read books. He never had anything else. We've been three years with Robbo, and not even a woolly ball to show for it. Only Eamsy's ever done any art in our class, and he brought his own paints, because it was his birthday. The girls have sewing.

When it's our turn, Dollop and me creep out, and climb on the shelves so Robbo can't see our feet, and pull faces at each other. You're lucky if you can stay there for a whole lesson. It makes your arms ache.

'Hey, look at this! It's old Robbo's brother.' I point to the picture of a walrus in the book on the desk before us.

'Tittering teacups, an elephant.'

'Belching buffaloes, it can't be.'

'Dithering dogfish, it is. Look at its beak!'

And we bugle in Napoleon's army, snooze in the doldrums with Captain Slocum, invent the telephone with Edison, snigger, chide, smirk and explode in utter silence in every corner of the world, until Robbo starts twanging and booming again with:

'You've got fifteen minutes left. Then we're all going into the hall.'

'Please, sir. What for?'

'You, Waring,' booms Robbo. 'You're going to be publicly whipped. School dinner-money missing again.'

Pongo looks a bit sick, but grins like a rabbit with tooth-ache and we all guffaw, as they say in the *Hotspur*.

'So get your hands out of your pockets, Waring, and stand up straight when you're talking to me, lad, and take your punishment like a man.'

'Yessir,' says Pongo sitting down, in a voice you couldn't

hear an inch away.

'What's that, Waring?' says Robbo, cupping his ear, and acting like an old-age-pensioner and looking round him. 'Where did I put that ear-trumpet?'

'I said "yessir".'

'Good for you, Waring. That's the spirit,' booms Robbo.

'Please sir. It wasn't Waring. It was Cyril Handy, and he spent it all on sweets.'

'Did he now? Did he now?' twangs Robbo. 'Stand up, Handy, and open your mouth. Wider boy. That's better. Mmmmm. Just as I thought. Your teeth are going rotten.'

We are all having hysterics and the door opens and in comes the Turton.

'What's all this noise –? Oh! I'm so sorry, Mr Robinson, I thought you'd gone out for a moment.' And she blushes more than ever.

Robbo bows like that gambler in the Saturday serial, and she goes out, joggling.

'All right,' says Robbo. 'Heads down. You've got ten minutes yet.'

And he goes back to his favourite hobby.

Dollop takes out his handkerchief, a pale black colour, and pretends to blow his nose.

'Who's coming?' He makes no more noise than a couple of snowflakes falling in water, and looks sidelong at Robbo's wrinkled herringbone a foot away thinking of odours.

'Jesus, of course –'

'Don't be barmy.'

'I seen him.'

'Where?'

'Down the road. At the corner.'

'What doing?'

'Selling matches, next to the Wall's Ice Cream man, and he had a beard tied round his waist with string.'

'Matches!' snorts Dollop, with a face as if he'd just sat on something nasty. 'Jesus selling matches.' Robbo joggles on his two feet for a moment, Dollop looks up startled, and then Robbo walks off to the other end of the classroom.

'Jesus wouldn't sell matches! You mean buttons.'

'Well, buttons, then. Anyway, that's who's coming. The bell will ring in a minute.'

Ever since I was five, just starting school, I'd known about today. In five minutes the bell would ring, and we'd all troop in, every class in the school, with all the teachers standing round the hall, and Mr Brooks the headmaster, who had a face like the Dally-Lama in one of Robbo's books, would introduce our visitor, and in would come Jesus from the corridor outside, and he'd say:

'Boys and girls, today is the end of the world. You all know about that don't you, from William the Corncurer, only he called it Doomsday. And from now on, there'll be no more school.' Jesus's voice would sound like a liquorice bootlace, about two miles long, covered in sherbet, and by the time you had come to the end of it, you'd be dead.

'He's coming to tell us about the end of the world,' I whispered to Dollop.

'It's the end of the world every Friday in our house. Because our Dad gets drunk then.'

'That's only pretend. This is really the end of the world.'

We leave Robbo's art lesson and go into the hall. All the classes are standing in rows across the hall. Our class stands at the back, because it's the top one. Robbo stands next to the Turton, peering down at her bulges below him, a letter 'l' and two 'o's, sniffing his fingers thoughtfully.

'Where's Jesus, then?' asks Dollop.

'P'raps he's drinking a spare bottle of milk before he comes in. There's always some over on Fridays, because of the Clinic.'

Any minute, the hairy visitor in the shredded army great-coat tied round the middle with string would come shuffling in, with a white fringe round his mouth and whiskers, prophesying.

'Where do you think he'll leave his matches?' I whisper.

'Buttons.'

'Buttons, then.'

The white yokel's face of the school clock twitches its big finger down to one minute to half-past three. How long until the end of the world? The piano stops playing 'In a Country Garden' and every eye turns to the double doors at the end of the hall. 'Ta-ra, ta-ra,' trumpets Dollop under his breath. No one comes. What is the Dally-Lama keeping Jesus out for? Silence. Except for somebody's stomach making a noise like two planks clapping together. Miss Turton is hanging on a window-cord as if she's anchorman in a tug-o'-war, while Robbo watches her thoughtfully, sniffing in the fug, and not lifting a finger, except to smell it. The window stays shut.

Then in comes old Brooksy, alias the Dally-Lama; he's followed by a frail, pigeon-toed lady, with grey hair and bunions, who nearly falls over them trying to get on the platform. Brooksy looks up and down the rows, trying to find the titterers, over the tops of his glasses. Four-eyes Brooksy starts off about some sort of Savings Campaign, and then hands over to Bunions.

Bunions goes on and on about saving for the future.

'She means Heaven,' whispers Dollop.

It turns out that Smith's Crisps have offered a prize for the best saver in the school. We ransack our pockets to see what we've got. Dollop pulls out a fag-card of Gordon Richards and an Irish farthing with a hole in. I show him a half-used gob-stopper and an old pawn-ticket that me Dad gave me one birthday. The date ran out last year. In the end we make up our minds we shan't win, so we switch off and begin an elbow digging contest.

After school, me and Dollop corner Iris Witchelow in the cloakroom and make her swing upside down on the pegs before we let her go. She always wears white ones with fancy edging, and they're ever so tight.

Next to the Wall's Ice-cream man, at the corner of the street, Jesus stands dribbling into his beard, staring at the matches (or buttons) he never sells.

'How can that be Jesus? He's got no halo.'

'P'raps it's under his cap.'

'No. I know. It's too big for his head. And it's slipped. Look at the ring round his neck.'

'Hey! Don't forget to come round after tea. We're going round to my Aunty's tonight.'

'O.K.' says Dollop. And we gallop off to tea.

All tea-time I keep worrying about the end of the world. Thursday would be best, in the middle of the weekly tests. Our Mom hasn't got back from her charring at the Dog and Partridge, so I scribble a note:

'Gone to Aunty Lily's with Dollop. P.S. Mrs Mabley says she's run out of faggots.'

'Will your Aunty ask us to stay again?'

'Dunno. Haven't got my night things anyway.'

'I have.'

'Where?'

'Here.' And he pulls out a *Beano* comic and a little torch.

'Yah! They're no good.'

'Whatchamean? It's this week's.'

'You can't sleep in them.'

'But we can read under the bedclothes, can't we?'

'What about the batteries?' I ask.

'Batteries?' Dollop unscrews the bottom from the torch. It's empty.

We have to walk all the way to the posh houses, up Hall

Green, and it's getting dark by the time we reach my Aunty's. Her house has got a bathroom, and a garden with real grass in it.

'Whose Aunty is she?' asks Dollop.

'Mine! What are you talking about?'

'I mean, your Mom's or your Dad's side?'

'Dad's.'

'How'd she get so rich?'

'Marrying Uncle Clifford. She used to work in a office.'

Outside one of the houses near my Aunty's, Dollop finds a couple of Corona pop bottles and picks them up.

'Hey, it's got some in!' He takes the stopper off and starts glugging it down.

'Miss Turton said you're not to.'

'Why not? Finders keepers.'

'You'll get hygiene.'

When we get to my Aunt Lily's, we have to go round the back and take our boots off before we go into the kitchen. One of my socks looks like a piece of fishing net, and Dollop's got a sock with no toe in it.

'Which end do you put your sock on?'

'Both. Anyway, t'aint a sock. It's one of our Dad's spare mittens. I lost the other in the cut.'

The kitchen door is open, but my Aunty's got two doors, and this one's made of a sort of wire-netting to keep the flies out. We ring the bell and wait. In a minute my Aunty Lily comes tappety-tapping in her high heels on the red tiles, across the kitchen. She opens the door for the flies and says, 'Come in, boys,' in a school visitor's voice. She looks down at our socks. Dollop's toes are the same colour as his father's mitten, which is a sort of navy-blue.

'Like some lemonade?'

I say, 'Yes, please,' and Dollop says, 'Thank you, Mrs Greaves.' He knows his manners when he likes. We get two glasses of Tizer and two socking big pieces of home-made cake.

'What a Aunty!' says Dollop.

She comes back in carrying two pairs of fluffy slippers and puts them beside the table. Then she takes a white tin bowl out of a cupboard and puts some water in from the tap.

'When you've finished, make yourselves comfy with the slippers, boys. There's soap and flannel on the draining board. I've got to go out for a moment. Back in a jiffy!'

'We've only got one tap and it's cold,' says Dollop with a long face.

'Wonder why dirty water can make you clean?' he says, standing in the bowl wearing two long socks of white soap.

'Whoa! Look at all the mess. You won't half cop it!'

'Where?' asks Dollop, mopping it up with the towel.

'Hurry up! Let's go and play bagatelle in the outhouse.'

'T'ain't the outhouse. It's the conservery.'

'These slippers are lovely for my chilblains.'

Dollop picks one up and sniffs. 'Smells a bit pansy to me. Robbo wouldn't like 'em.'

The bagatelle has got a lot of silver steel balls and you push them up the channel with a stick with a knob on, and it's all polished. We play four games and win two each.

Then my Aunty comes in and asks us to go into the draw-ing-room, as she calls it. It sounds like 'rum' the way she says it.

There's a little frail old lady with grey hair sitting by the fire. I look at Dollop. He's frowning and pressing his lips together. I look at her feet. Her shoes are like little girl's shoes, and they've got slits where the bunions are.

'This is Uncle Clifford's mother,' says Aunt Lily.

We sit on the sofa and she asks us how we like school and how much do we save every week.

'Nothing,' says Dollop, 'But I had a stamp album once.'

Uncle Clifford's mother smiles, and you think her face is going to crumble into little bits because of the wrinkles, and she nods her head all the time and you wait for it to roll off and get lost under the armchair, hidden by the frills.

We have a few toffees, and some shortbread, and listen to the wireless, and the flames go right up the chimney, and Uncle Clifford's mother says, 'When is Clifford coming, dear?' at least a hundred times, and Aunt Lily says, 'Soon, mother,' about two hundred times, and then she says:

'You two boys pop off now, there's dears, and have a nice warm bath before you go to bed. In the boxroom. I left the light on so's you can read a bit.'

'Whoa! It's hot!' shrieks Dollop, 'Put some cold in for me bunions.'

'I'm in Heaven now, – asleep on Savings Certificates.'

'You've won first prize. A packet of crisps and a bucket of salt for your bunions.'

There are so many shrieks, splashes and gurgles, I'm afraid our Aunty might come. When we've finished we creep down and listen. I can hear my Aunty and Grandma Bunions and Uncle Cliff all arguing.

'Hey, your Aunty's crying,' whispers Dollop.

'But why not dear? It's only a bit of fun.' That's my Uncle.

'That's not fun. It's nasty!' twitters Grandma. 'Especially with boys about.'

'This isn't the first time. It makes me run hot and cold to think of it.' My Aunty's really sobbing.

'When I was in the –' my Uncle's voice sounds high and queer.

'You should be ashamed to talk about it.' Grandma again.

'How much do you think *she's* saved up?' whispers Dollop.

All of a sudden it goes quiet. I hold my breath. Dollop's watching the door. Aunty's shouting.

'Take them off! Now! Or I won't stay in this terrible house

another minute.'

'C'mon, let's go back.'

We're only just in time. The stairs creak like Miss Turton's knees on a wet Sunday. Dollop is already in bed, wearing his scented slippers. I'm about half an inch later. It feels nice in bed.

'Hey, Dollop,' I whisper, 'Your feet want soling and heeling.'

No answer.

'Dollop!'

'Shut up. I'm fast asleep.'

'They're scraping my shins off.'

'Ssshh!' he hissed, 'Shsh! Somebody's on the landing.'

Clickety-click – clickety-click! High heels towards our door.

'She's going to tuck us in.'

'Listen, listen!'

She clicks away down the landing, past our door, and on to where their own bedroom is. But the footmarks sound too heavy for Aunty: she's no bigger than a brick on a threepenny-bit, even in high heels. She clears her throat and makes a sound like Uncle Cliff when he's feeling ember-assed and the hairs in his nose wiggle from side to side.

Dollop looks at me and I look at Dollop. His eyebrows dodge into his parting, shrugging and pulling his mouth down, asking questions. Then the penny drops and the packet comes out.

'Hey! It's him!'

'Who?'

'Your Uncle Cliff.'

'Don't be barmy!'

'Thass why she sounded so funny, all –'

'Maybe it's a joke,' I brazen it out. 'Maybe he's trying to – to – to make her laugh.'

'What's she crying for then?'

'How do I know? I'll punch your head if you say anything about my Uncle Cliff.'

But I know he's right. Because the bottom of my stomach falls into an icy pond, and I'm all alone, in December, on a black night, in a wet shirt, with all the stray dogs of Billesley howling.

'Hey, c'mon. Follow me!'

And Dollop goes across to the door in his pansy-smelling slippers before you can say Jack Robinson or Monica Turton. That is, if you want to say anything at all.

Dollop is outside their bedroom door, looking sideways through the crack, with his hand waving at his bum telling me to be quiet. I don't want to follow him, but I go. Now I know what a stickleback feels like on a bent pin with the cotton tight. Then I'm crouching too, puffing in Dollop's ear-hole, landed.

Uncle Cliff is standing on his high heels in front of a long mirror, posing. He is modelling a nice silk dress, with flowers on; and they smell like nasturtiums. He's wearing a wig that's got dandruff, and stockings with ladders in. The dress is just the right length, and in the fashion, which is more than you can say for his moth-eaten moustache, and the furry thing he keeps moving and patting affectionately.

'What's that thing for?' whispers Dollop.

There's a dead fox's head on one shoulder with a silver chain coming out of its mouth; and its tail is wrapped round him, fixed at one end by the chain. The dead fox-eyes are friendly and sad, and they keep staring.

'It's got the mange.'

'It likes you. Look how pleased it is.'

I was feeling better, and sniggered.

'You nearly burst my eardrum,' hisses Dollop, rubbing his laughed-in ear.

Uncle Cliff prances about like Iris Witchelow doing ballet

lessons and watches himself in the mirror. He takes his fancy-dress off, bit by bit. He keeps humming, 'Keep The Home Fires Burning'. He's got down as far as that elastic thing with the suspenders dangling, and he's wriggling his bottom, trying to get it down, but it won't go, and he starts to grunt.

Dollop digs me in the breadbasket with his elbow.

'Hey, Turton's got some like that!'

'How d'you know, Clever Dick?'

'Seen 'em.'

'Liar!'

Uncle Cliff has managed to get it half off, and he's hopping about on one leg, in his high heels, trying to get his leg through. He catches his heel in one of the dangling 'spenders and falls on his chin with a crash.

'C'mon! Let's go back to bed.'

'Don't be daft. Let's watch!' hisses Dollop.

'How would you like it? Somebody watching your Uncle like that?'

'I ain't got a Uncle like that.'

I punch him in his lights and he grunts. Uncle Cliff stops struggling, sits up, and he listens for about three hours, so's we nearly suffocate holding our breath. In the end he's satisfied. He throws the 'spender-thing on to a chair and sits there a minute, with his back towards us, looking at the floor between his knees. Then he takes off his brassiere and they're full of sorbo to fill them out.

'What a swizzle!' whispers Dollop.

We watch. Uncle Cliff sits where he is on the floor, looking between his knees. He's sitting still, except that one of his elbows keeps moving.

'C'mon, Dollop.' I grab his wrists and give him the Chinese Burn. 'If you don't come, I'll thump you.'

It's beginning to feel like December again, and the dogs are howling, and my legs and feet have got no blood in them, –

and my ears are burning with the shame of peeping into my Uncle's secrets.

We get into bed with the light on.

We don't say anything for a long time and I keep wishing that Jesus had really come this afternoon and when Dollop starts off being funny about Miss Turton I want to punch his face in, but it's not his fault so I don't, and Dollop starts reading his comic and I can't stop thinking about him dressing up as a woman, and my Aunty crying and Uncle's funny little mother with her face cracking in pieces like plaster and, as the bits drop off, hundreds of halfpennies and pennies and sixpences start falling out on the carpet and that's the way she cries, and in the end she's just a money box with nothing in at all and there's nothing left of her but the bunions.

And then Uncle Cliff and Robbo and Turton and Grandma Bunions and Aunt Lily and the old tramp who is Jesus and all go into the school hall for Assembly, and Four-eyes Brooksy is on his platform, teaching them. He tells them to take off all their clothes, and they do. And I can't tell who Jesus is, or who Brooksy is, or who Uncle Cliff, or who anybody is. And Robbo is pushing pieces of chalk into his bum instead of his fingers, and Turton joggles and takes them off and they're stuffed with Savings Certificates and she throws them over the blackboard and says, 'Children, copy exactly what I'm doing,' and she vanishes. And then, like snowflakes on a window-pane, they all disappear, slowly. When they come back, they're all wearing their right clothes and they all look the same but different. Brooksy booms out from the bottom of a long tunnel, 'Boy, stand up and tell us what you know.' And I have to go to the front and stand on the platform and try to tell them what I know, but what I know I cannot say in words and I feel as if I'm crying. Then the big bell starts to ring and it's the black-liquorice end of the world, disappearing into a big dark gullet that never ends.

In the morning we have a big breakfast in the kitchen. My Uncle Cliff is pottering in the garden in his old clothes, and Aunt Lily gives us each a bag of sugar almonds to go back with. My Uncle doesn't even look at us.

This morning things have changed and it feels like the end of something. Not like the end of the world with Jesus selling off buttons. But, sort of.

'What shall we do today?' asks Dollop.

'Dunno. What shall we do?'

'Let's go fishing with your sock.'

'O.K.'

We catch a few tiddlers and one or two sticklebacks and put them in an old cocoa tin we find by the pool.

'Dollop!'

'What?'

'Don't say anything about my Uncle Cliff, will you?'

'Why?'

'Promise!'

'All right.'

'Cut your throat and hope to die?'

'Cut me throat and hope to die.'

Then I remember it's still only Saturday and Monday's a lifetime away. Maybe by Monday, I'll have grown up, or found a hidden treasure, or invented a new torture for Turton. Or maybe not. Maybe I'll just keep remembering it all over again and not liking it all over again and wondering how many times it has to happen to you before you really grow up. Or maybe you don't grow up at all. Maybe you just get older and start forgetting things.

ANNE MARRIOTT

THEY thought I'd gone to sleep, only I hadn't taken the pills (I don't like drugs) so Mum said to Auntie Mabe quite loud out in the hall that I was stiffening up with rheumatism, and that was the reason why I couldn't get out before the man found me.

'*Couldn't*,' she said. But of course, even if Auntie Mabe has been her best friend for fifty years, Mum still wouldn't tell her the truth.

And I haven't really got rheumatism – not yet. I've always had these big joints, knees and ankles and knuckles, just one of the many things about myself I've never cared for.

'Just relax and let it sort itself out, Stella,' our old doctor said. And then, out in the hall too, muttered something to Mum about 'Progress'. Maybe he was saying progress was to blame for it all, though it wasn't, not really.

We've been pleased, taking it all around, about progress coming to our street at last – though it would take more than new water-pipes and sewers to bring us really up to date.

A terrace, Mum calls where we live. Workmen's houses, I expect they called them when they put them up in 1900. Two-storey houses with wooden curlicues over the porches, and all joined together into a solid block. You don't see many like that in Canada, I'm sure.

The owners are doing their bit, along with the City, re-painting all the outsides. White, with lime-green trim, instead of the purplish chocolate with yellowish cocoa it's always been.

The colours always made me feel like being sick. But when

my father came out here after the first war he wasn't interested in colours – just glad to have a house. He'd been gassed, and he had the idea the air on the Pacific coast would do his chest good. Also, there'd be lots of work in the shipyards. He was wrong about both things.

I thought my father would have liked the new colours, though – after all, it'd been him who'd started me on the bulbs.

The houses might look alike the rest of the year – but in the spring 1240 – that was ours – was always different. All the *little* bulbs, scillas, chionodoxa, snowdrops, crocuses, and those pretty white narcissus. Someone gave me a box of parrot tulips once, but I threw them away. Too flashy.

'Thirty years!' Mum had kept moaning, standing at the front window, after the machine had come along and dug the trench and buried all the bulbs under the great long mound of clay. 'Thirty years – and they've been the joy of your life, Stell –'

'Twenty-nine,' I'd corrected automatically. I'd started the bulbs the same year I'd started my job, and the two had been all I ever cared about. But this year – and Mum knew it, only she never faces up to things – this year I wasn't interested in the bulbs. Not even though the snowdrops were almost open-ing and the others shooting up, that green something like they've done the houses, and then they were all squashed down under two or three feet of mud and rubble, I didn't feel anything at all.

She'd been standing looking out of the window again and moaning a little, when I came down to breakfast on Tuesday morning, and that made me worse right away.

I was up extra early, wanting to get the 8.10 bus instead of the 8.20, so I'd have time to run up to *his* room before work – Not that I'd slept, really, feeling as long as I kept awake and planning and praying, he'd be all right and I'd still have time –

I'd sat down at the table and reached for the Golden Shred when Mum turned around from the window and started in.

'I wouldn't wear that to work today, Stell, do you think, dear?' Staring at my silver-grey knit which he'd once said he liked.

'What's wrong with it?'

'It – well, it's such a depressing colour, dear. Half-mourning, they used to call it when I was a girl.' Then, quickly, as if it struck her she was being tactless, 'I never liked it on you from the start. It makes you look more – more flat-chested.'

'Oh, my God!' I cried, standing up. 'As if – as if things like my figure ever entered into *my* relationship with *him*!'

I put a lot of meaning into it, and Mum's face, which is red and a bit puffy at the best of times, went purple. For a moment I thought she was going to have a stroke, and I was sorry I'd spoken. I always tell myself I'll never make hints like that again – but then she gets me wild and I do it.

I can't have been more than six when my father came back from the beer parlour, where he'd gone with some men from home who *had* got work at the dockyard. He came back late, and when Mum was telling him off he turned on her and shouted, 'You forced me into marrying you, you old slut! Now you have to put up with me.' Or something like that.

I've worked out since she must have been six months on the way when she got him to the registry office. She was years older than him, and never pretty. But her figure was all right, then. It makes you feel a bit sick. However –

'Sorry,' I said, Tuesday.

'I just meant,' Mum went on, trying to make it better and making it worse as always, 'If you see him today – and after all, it's only fitting you should. Who has more right –'

'Mum! Please!'

'– and if you do, I was only going to say, if you wore something more cheerful-looking, for his sake –'

'Oh, my God! I said again. I left my breakfast and slammed the dining-room door.

But another of the things I don't care for about myself is the way I can never make up my mind and stick to it. I'd had a good reason for wearing the grey – but then I began to think perhaps Mum was right. The rose would be better. Oh, why couldn't people ever leave me alone?

But I changed, and that meant I had to do my hair over. So instead of leaving 1240 early, I didn't even get away on the dot of 8.10 like I always did, it was past 8.12. And I don't like to hurry.

'Be careful crossing the plank –' Mum said, like she had every morning. Of course they'd dug the trench long before they were ready for it, like they always do, and Mum was scared every time anyone went over the bridge they'd made. She wouldn't go on it herself, being so overweight and top-heavy now.

'All right!'

But when I was across I stopped for a second to wave to her, hiding behind the ecru lace curtain, because if I didn't she'd cry – and then I thought I heard the 8.20 bus coming and tried to run.

But the long open trench beside me made me feel dizzy. I had my black low-heeled office pumps on, but I still felt I was going to lose my balance and topple over, so I slowed down.

It was like a grave, the length of the block, I thought. One of those mass graves Mum and I saw on the newsreels at the show at the end of World War Two. People have said one of my problems is I don't have enough imagination – if I'd had any I wouldn't have stayed in the same job for twenty-nine years. But for a moment I saw a greyish thing like a dead arm sticking up out of the mud, and realising it was only a bit of wood didn't make me stop trembling.

Near the corner, a man was chipping away at the front door of the end house. I remembered – the numbers. We'd thought the owners had done their share with the painting, but they were actually doing something extra – new numbers, the kind that glow in the dark. The old numbers were all rusty, and some of them gone altogether, so a new postman always had a hard time till he got used to it.

I really heard the bus then, and had to run for it, trench or no trench. That driver's usually a friendly fellow – been on our route for years and has a jolly word for me. But Tuesday he looked sour.

'What happened to you this morning?' he asked without a smile. 'Usually can set a clock by you.'

'You're ahead of time!' I meant it to come out brisk and snappy, but it wasn't true anyway and it trailed off. He started the bus with a jerk and I went lurching down the aisle and hit my knee on one of the seats. The twinge went all the way down into my ankle.

I didn't have time to get calmed down before we stopped again – and there was Auntie Mabe. *Early* this morning! She always got the 8.30. Oh, God, I thought. I crouched down in the seat, turning my head as far as I could toward the window, hoping she wouldn't notice me.

For a while I went off calling her Auntie Mabe, as she isn't, but Mum got upset with me. 'She's got so little, poor Mabe,' Mum said. 'Never had a little girl like lucky me.' I squirmed. 'Makes her happy to feel she's got some family. Never know when you might be in the same position, Stell, do you, and be glad of someone to make you feel you're wanted.'

That was long after my father died, of course. Before, Mum used to put on airs a bit with Auntie Mabe. Once when it was my birthday and Mum had said I could ask another girl home from school, and I had a hard time thinking of one who'd want to come, I asked Auntie Mabe to come too. She was jolly in those days and I thought she'd make it better. But Mum took me aside and told me not to ask Auntie Mabe with other company because she was working class – she's kept herself all these years out here by being 'daily help' to well-off ladies up on the hill.

Auntie Mabe hasn't been jolly for years. Now, she's always telling me I'm losing more weight and getting peaky. 'Not like your Mum in that way, Stell, though you take after her in others. Quiet as a girl, and never one to strike out for herself.'

At least Mum had struck out in one way farther than Auntie Mabe had. But I never said anything. I was used to it, and I suppose she still thought I might strike out for myself if she hinted around it enough.

Of course she saw me on the bus.

Thump. She sat down beside me, furry in her old black coat and smelling of mothballs, Devon Violet and deep-heat rub – she's got arthritis these last years, Auntie Mabe has.

'How is he, dear?' she asked. Just like that, no 'good morning' or leading up to it. 'How is he?' And when I didn't answer, 'Near the end, is he, from what your Mum said Sunday?'

Damn Mum, damn Mum!

'He's all right!' I said it so loudly a couple of people turned to look. 'He – he's just having more check-ups, that's all. After the treatments he had in the fall.'

'Does more harm than good, some of those rays they use,' Auntie Mabe shook her head. 'What beats me is why a person in his line of work – right there in the hospital for thirty years –'

'Twenty-nine!'

'– why he wouldn't have the sense to have it taken in time. Seeing all the ones dying under his very nose, as you might say, who left it too late, you'd think he –'

'Excuse me!'

If I got off at the next corner and walked as fast as I could, I might just get to work on time, cutting through back streets. And I'd planned to be early! But I couldn't stand any more of this. 'There's something I have to do on the way –' There I went again, feeling I had to give her a reason –

She wouldn't let me past, just sat staring up at me. I climbed over her stiff legs, her black bag with her overall and dusters in it. She gave a little grunt but I didn't care. None of them ever give me a chance.

The Acting Administrator was in the outer office. From the first day he came – and I bet you anything he only got the job through being related to some higher-up – he made me think of slugs. Long and pale and soft-looking, with eyes sticking out a bit, like something I've found in the garden in summer that made me feel sick.

I came in, panting, and he looked up at the clock. 'We can usually set that by you, Stella,' he said. 'However, we'll overlook it this time. Hang up your coat and come into the inner office right away.'

I hadn't meant to say anything, especially not to him, but though I pressed my lips together as tight as I could it seemed to come out on its own, 'Have – have you heard – how *he* is this morning?'

He lifted his head a little, just like a slug raising up to see where it's going. 'Surprisingly, he seems to have rallied slightly since last night. As you know, they told me yesterday they didn't think he could last more than twenty-four hours.'

'I know.' I bit my lower lip, pressing the teeth in so hard my dentures hurt the top of my mouth. I wasn't going to cry, not a tear, in front of this one –

'You've been a good servant,' the Acting Administrator said, surprising me. I suppose he was trying to be kind. 'I hope you'll be as useful to me.'

'You *are* getting the job!' It just came out, in that tone, before I could think.

He frowned. 'Naturally.' His voice was cold, with a slimy sound. 'After all – I've been carrying the load for some time.'

'For one day!' But I didn't have the courage to say it aloud. Just for one day. Right up until last Friday, *he* had been doing it. Until two weeks ago, from his own chair, across the desk from me now. And then, when he had to give in and go to bed, from his bed until Friday, *he* did it all!

'Shall we get to work?'

I began to take dictation.

The kids we get nowadays in the office (just get them trained so they're some good and they leave to get married) – the kids call *me* 'Auntie' behind my back. I'm not as dumb as I look and I've heard them. But Tuesday was the first time anyone came out with it to my face – Marla, the newest one, black hair and snapping eyes and the kind of figure Mum's must have been, and scared of nothing that walks – Marla said, 'Can I plug the kettle in for coffee now, Auntie Stell?' Daring me to put her down.

I glanced at the clock. I felt as if I'd been in the office for a fortnight since nine and here it was only twenty past ten, and coffee break isn't until half-past. (Being a small hospital, we don't have a cafeteria and make instant in the little file room.) Usually I wouldn't let one of them plug in a minute early, but today I didn't care. All I wanted was to get out, go upstairs, see *him* while he was still there to – 'All right.'

I saw Marla look at the others, pleased with herself, but I didn't care about that either. I grabbed up my purse and got out.

I started toward the Ladies – and then it didn't seem to matter whether I powdered my nose again or not. All that did matter was getting to him, not wasting one single second that I could still have with him alive. If only Auntie Mabe hadn't been early –

I started down the corridor, almost running though I didn't really mean to. I didn't even notice an orderly, helping along an old man in a blue-striped dressing-gown, until I was almost into them. I swerved so sharply it hurt my knee again. The orderly gave me a nasty look.

Both of the elevators were in use, of course! I waited a few seconds, and then I started up the stairs.

I went as fast as I could, my mind running ahead of me, wondering what he'd be like today. Better than Friday? I could see his face, just like a skull now, the skin all tight over the bones. His grey eyes, sunken in, but bright and interested and clever, like they'd always been.

On Friday, he'd put out his hand and laid it on my arm. I could feel his bones, chilly, through the skin. It was the first time he'd ever touched me, except for a handshake at Christmas, the first time in the twenty-nine years.

'You've been my right hand all these years, Stella,' he said.

I'd put my own hand over his, pressing it, trying to warm it, till he pulled it gently away and said, 'I'll see you next week.' When I'd picked up my notebook and papers and gone to the door I looked back, and he'd lifted a finger and given me a sort of salute – weak, but still full of spirit.

It was then that I'd had the idea, the idea that as I started up the third lot of steps now made me feel all hot and cold. The next time I saw him, I was going to kiss him. I'd dreamed of it, of course, thousands of times I suppose, but I'd never dared imagine actually – but I was going to! Just once, while there was still the chance.

All weekend I'd thought about it, while Mum was carrying on about the trench, imagining what it would be like, how his cheek would feel, what he'd say – I even let myself imagine him saying he'd always hoped I'd kiss him – though of course he wouldn't.

But on Monday, when I got in, I heard he was worse, and when I got upstairs there was a supervisor I've never liked on the floor.

'What do you mean, you have to see him?' she barked at me. 'For heaven's sake, woman, it's taking all the man's strength just to breathe. He can't be bothered with the office.' And, in case I was too stupid to take that in, she added, 'He's dying.'

There'd been nothing I could do but go away. They never gave me a chance.

I'd checked the list back in the office and found that supervisor was going off for two days, and the one coming on was easier to get along with. If he just didn't die Monday night – as I said, I tried not to sleep at all, feeling as if I could keep him alive just as long as I willed and prayed him to be. And he'd even rallied!

As I puffed up the last steps, the thought came to me, like a bed of my spring bulbs bursting into bloom in my mind – perhaps he was going to get better! It was arrested, a miracle cure – they've been heard of. I was smiling as I turned along the corridor, to the left where the private rooms are (he'd have gone in the terminal ward with the others, except that he had to carry on the office routine).

And then I just stopped dead. It wasn't fair, oh God it wasn't. And outside visiting hours, too! She had no business – His wife was there.

Beautiful, she is, really, and dresses so smartly too, like the black and white costume she had on right now, which with her looks and her shape seemed to me to be overdoing it.

She saw me too, of course. Usually she gives me that nice smile, that kind smile which always upsets me, as if she could afford to be nice to me like she couldn't to some secretaries. But this time her face was set.

'Stella –' she said. Her voice was funny and she didn't say anything more.

I made up my mind. She wasn't going to stop me. As Mum had said, who had a better right? 'Excuse me,' I said, politely but quite firmly, and moved past her to his door.

'No –' she said. She put out her hand but then it just dropped to her side. I saw her lips were moving, but 'No –' was all I could make out.

'*Yes!*' I said, my hand on the door-knob. Suddenly I felt bold and sure of myself. For once, nothing was going to stop me.

I opened the door. I came face to face with a big beefy orderly – one I've always detested.

'You can't come in here,' he said.

'I have to see him,' I said smartly. My God, I thought, I'll kiss him in front of the orderly if I have to, but I'm not going to be done out of it at the last minute – 'Please get out of my way!' I said, making it sharp. After all, office staff outranks someone like him.

He didn't move so I tried to get past but he blocked me. I could see the bed with the shape of *him* in it, but there was another chap bending over him, so I couldn't see his face. I wondered what treatment he was having.

'You forgot to put the "engaged" sign on the door,' I said, sharper than ever, 'I'll speak about that.'

Then I saw what the orderly by the bed was doing. He was coiling up a long tube, like a thin snake, the tube they'd put in him when he had to go to bed, coiling it up into a basin and –

'You'll have to go,' the big orderly said.

When I didn't move he took my arm and turned me around and took me back out into the hall.

I stayed on in the office after everyone else had left. I told the Acting Administrator that I was a bit behind – which was true enough too – and that I'd like to work late, and he said of course everything must be kept up to date, and it would be helpful if I came in early as well. I really laughed after he'd gone out. I'd be here early all right! From now on, I was going to be here all the time.

I'd have to phone Mum eventually of course, and tell her I wasn't coming home and to send my things, but I'd let her stew in her own juice for a while. If she hadn't said that about my dress in the morning I'd have got the early bus –

I was a bit worried about the cleaning staff, but when one of them came into the offices about nine-thirty I stood my ground and made it plain he wasn't coming in there or disturbing anything, I'd be looking after it myself, and after arguing for a bit he looked at me kind of funny and went off. So that was all right.

But there's where I made my mistake.

I thought I'd like a cup of tea. I've never cared for coffee and I always keep tea-bags in my desk. *He* liked it too! (It was a bond – Brooke Bond! And they say I've no sense of humour.) I made sure the catch was on the outer door – but I didn't do anything else. If I'd just moved one of the desks against it, under the handle, things would have been different – but I didn't. I went into the little file room with a tea-bag and plugged in the kettle.

It was almost boiling when I heard the sound and looked out.

One of the doctors was in the office. The cleaner who'd been in before was behind him with his keys but when the doctor saw me he told the cleaner it was okay now, and to get along with his work.

The doctor stood there looking for a minute, hands in his pockets. He's one of the young ones and been in trouble a time or two for carelessness, but I've always had a soft spot for him, he's so cheery. He didn't look cheery now.

'Well, what are you up to, Stella?' he said, and then, moving forward suddenly to the door of the inner office, and staring at *his* desk, 'Good picture of him, eh? Did you take it?'

'It was a snap I took at the garden party a few years ago,' I said, 'I had it enlarged.' And always kept it in my big desk drawer, and a copy in my bureau drawer at home, but I didn't add that.

'Well,' said the doctor, still staring.

I'd taped the enlargement on to the back of *his* chair, and I'd got his nameplate out of the drawer where the Acting Administrator had put it on Friday, and set it back on the desk. I'd got *his* pen set, and the other things the Acting Admin. had cleared away this afternoon, and laid them out as they'd always been, and dusted it all as I always did, and put all the slug's stuff back where it belonged. Then, just to make sure, I'd printed up a sign, not flashy but big enough so no one could miss it, 'RESERVED', and I'd put that on the front of the desk.

If I stayed there all the time, no one could move any of it, and things could go on properly just as they always had.

'Have you had any dinner?' the doctor asked me suddenly. He kept rubbing his ear and a little flake of skin drifted off it.

'I'm not hungry,' I said shortly.

'No,' he said, still rubbing, 'I guess not.' Then, 'Well, everything has to change, doesn't it, Stella? That's life.'

That's death, I nearly added, but stopped in time. I wasn't going to mention that, not ever, not out loud.

'Come on,' he said, brisk all of a sudden. 'You've had a bad day – we all have. But it's time to go home now.' He took my coat off the rack and held it for me, 'I'll give you something to make you sleep and you'll feel better tomorrow.'

'I don't want anything – I don't like drugs,' I said.

'Well, come on,' he said. 'There's a bus in ten minutes and you'll just get it. – I'd run you home, but I have to be on duty in a couple of minutes, and everyone is tied up in Emergency.'

'No,' I said.

'Stella! You have to go!' He was sharp now; he gave my coat a little shake.

'No,' I said.

There was a pause. Then he said in quite a different tone of voice, 'Would you like another picture of him? I've got one – a flash snap from the convention banquet. It's in my place down the hall – come and have a look at it.'

If I'd had my tea my wits might have been a bit sharper. As it was, we were out of the office before I realised it was a trick. I tried to nip back in but he'd closed the door. I saw he'd picked up my purse as well as my coat.

'Sorry, Stella,' he said, 'That was a dirty one, but I had to get you moving. I'll walk you to the bus. Come on.'

Before I got on the bus I made sure I had my keys. I'd be back before anyone – and then it struck me what they were up to. No wonder that young doctor'd wanted to get me out of there in a hurry. They were going to change the locks, so I couldn't get back in. It was the Acting Administrator's doing. He didn't want me there any more, not really, not anyone who knew the way things ought to be done, who'd remind him of *him*.

If it'd been any other disease, I thought, I wouldn't have put it past the slug to have had a hand in *him* getting it.

It was lucky the bus driver was one who knew me and shouted at me to get off. I was so upset I didn't notice where I was and would have gone on riding.

Along the sidewalk, I tripped over a piece of wood – that same piece of wood, I thought, like a dead arm, thrown up here now for a change. I took a glance over at the houses. The new numbers were on already, they can work fast when they want to. Really grand we were now, with those shiny ones. There was our number, 1240, shining through the dark.

I turned on to the plank in front of it – and then I knew. Of course, it wasn't my house. They're all alike, and in the dark you can't really tell the drapes and curtains; maybe it was the one next door, I didn't know, but I did know it wasn't my place. For a moment I thought I must be getting silly and then I remembered. They were changing all the numbers – the houses had all been numbered wrong for a start.

Which was my place, then?

I stood there, hanging on to one of the ropes with a red reflector on it they had around the trench, looking up and down and trying to think. They'd turned me out of my office. Now they'd changed the numbers on the houses so I couldn't go home.

Suddenly I wanted Mum. She'd tell me which was our place, and where I had to go. She'd tell me what to do about the office and them changing the locks so I couldn't get in. She'd say it was my right to be there, she always had. Besides, she was all I'd got now, wasn't she?

'Mum!' I called, 'Mum!' And over and over, 'Mum! Mum!'

But the television was loud in the house there – the 1240 that wasn't 1240 – and I knew no one could hear me. I kept on for quite a while though, 'Mum! Mum!'

Then I looked down into the trench. I could just see the bottom of it. It looked nice and smooth, I thought, and as far as I could tell quite dry. Like a grave. I wondered when they would put *him* in his grave – he hadn't wanted to be cremated, he'd made that clear. Not that it really made any difference, he was sure God didn't care if his body was ashes or dust, but he'd liked the thought of the ground better.

Well, I said to myself, I expect they want me there too. I
expect it's the only place left for me.

I got down on my hands and knees and edged in under the
rope. It rubbed on the back of my coat and I was afraid it
might have made a mark but then I thought it didn't matter.
I let myself down carefully into the trench.

It was more comfortable than I'd expected, really – the
ground wasn't too hard, and with my coat wrapped around
me and my purse under my head it was quite cosy.

I was like a bulb, I thought, a big bulb, and they'd cover me
with dirt with the machine in the morning, and perhaps next
spring I'd sprout up. That would surprise them! I even giggled
a bit.

I closed my eyes and began to feel quite sleepy. Everything
would be all right, I thought, if they'd just leave me alone.

FRANK TUOHY

SHE approached him with such a kind humorous sparkle in her eye that he thought for a moment that they had already met somewhere, that he knew and had forgotten her, and ought to be concerned about it.

Here he was in someone's house in the country: his sister, who had brought him here, had told him the name of his host and hostess, but it had escaped him. Those two fine children, owl-eyed and with bright fox-coloured hair, obviously belonged to them. There were about a dozen people in the drawing-room, which was pleasantly warm. Outside were bare trees, a glimpse of lawns blackened by winter, and cars parked down the drive.

One of the children came round with a plate of little things like owl-pellets to eat. He took one nervously. It was extremely good, minced meat, strongly spiced, rather Greek in taste. He tried to grab another, but the fox-child had already gone.

'Your sister told me who you were,' she said. 'I must introduce myself.'

Her eyes were grey, large, very bright. Everyone in the room seemed to know her, and to want to talk to her. She wanted to talk to him, and what could be better, on a winter Sunday morning, with cars parked in the drive, and rooks blown about the sky? He supposed her to be in the late thirties; not really attractive, but happy, unsubdued. Yes, attractive. She would be the one to bring him, however temporarily, into the tone of the gathering. (But in the long run this would be created by sherry and gin-and-tonic, and later you'd hear cars started with violence, brakes squealing, and there'd be the tenseness of wives trying hard not to offer to drive home. But not yet, not yet: the time was only half-past twelve.)

'I felt I simply had to talk to you,' she went on, 'because I know you know the Wickershams.'

'Yes, of course I do.'

He eased himself more comfortably against the chimney-piece. He felt that with this nice woman it would be easy to carry on conversation about acquaintances. He hadn't caught her name, either. He wondered, without really bothering, which of the large booming husbands on the other side of the room belonged to her.

'Do tell me, how are they?'

'Flourishing as always.'

When he thought about the Wickershams, who lived in London, he was reminded of the hymn that ends: 'There beside my Father's throne, I shall know as I am known.' The Wickershams were known, but they didn't know. People mentioned the Wickershams but they didn't, on the whole, mention people. They were a tall rather lank couple, distracted and elegant. When you were with them, they talked about you, because you were what they were dealing with then. And they always ended the conversation first, put down the telephone first; they never rang you, you rang them. They were remote and, since he had known them for some time, he knew that they had reasons for remoteness. It was strange that this nice friendly woman should know them as well.

'I haven't seen them for ages,' she went on.

And suddenly he lost most of his equanimity. He saw danger ahead, fences, water-jumps, elephant-traps.

She had lost touch with the Wickershams, she told him,

when her husband had been stationed abroad for five years. Abroad was a new subject, and he tried to deflect her on to it. However, it turned out to be some middle section of Africa he knew nothing about. In any case she was intent on getting back to the Wickershams.

'We all used to go to Positano, quite early, before everyone went there. We had marvellous times because John knows everything about Italy.'

'He's written two books about it.'

'We've got them at home somewhere.'

'You're lucky. There are extremely few copies around.'

She laughed at this. 'Patsy was a great, great friend. She was quite lovely. I expect she still is. The boy was the same age as our eldest.'

This was the first hurdle. John Wickersham's wife was called Victoria and had been for several years.

'Do they still live in Fulham?'

'It's Campden Hill Square now.'

She nodded, appreciating this as part of John Wickersham's merited progress. In fact, of course, it was his second wife's money.

He accepted another drink. By his silence, he had suppressed the truth, and he was not going to be able to go back on it. It had been an instinctive choice, timorous and wrong. Yet otherwise their conversation, all right according to the not very high standards of before lunch on Sundays, would have become awful. Everyone else was talking about central heating or rose-bushes. He had absolutely no luck.

'Does Patsy still paint?'

'Patsy?' he said, looking hard into his glass. 'I haven't heard.'

'You haven't heard?'

'I mean, not any exhibitions or anything.'

'She never used to exhibit. She always sold privately.'

She watched him intently and he could feel her beginning to have doubts about him.

Damn it, couldn't she accept that she was in a category of protected people? No shooting on Sundays, not in this part of the world, in commuting distance of London. It was not renaissance Florence, but in its own way it was not uncivilised: it could probably cope with much more human pain than one gave it credit for. But not before lunch on Sundays. After all, she probably had to go back and cook. Or at any rate go down on her nicely rounded hunkers and fish the food out of the Aga cooker.

'We have one of her early things at home. A small landscape.'

They had been in Africa when it happened, of course, and knew nothing. In any case, these things are easy to miss, and probably it hadn't even been in the newspapers. He wondered how she would react if he told her. There was the image of the dead child, the death of children being pretty much the absolute for human frightfulness.

'Ross-on-Wye,' he said aloud, not thinking.

'What was that?' She observed him with a marked detachment. Perhaps she thought he was drunk.

'Nothing. I was trying to remember something about John.'

'The Wickershams are a Suffolk family,' she told him in a precise, distant way. 'It was the Suffolk churches that started him off on Art History.'

'I didn't know.'

'He studied at the Courtauld Institute, of course.'

'I knew that.'

She relented. 'You know I'd really love to see them all again. Edmund must be eleven now. He is the same age as Amanda. Have they any more?'

'No more.'

She looked puzzled at this. She won't ask for their address, he thought. She realises it has been too long, far too long. She thinks of John and Patsy as continuing elsewhere, step by step, as she and her husband have been continuing. Whereas Patsy has come to the end. When all the business about Victoria started, Patsy took Edmund to a hotel in Ross-on-Wye, or perhaps it was Hereford, and killed him with sleeping pills, and tried to kill herself. Luckily she died in hospital. People said that she was mad. Absolutely nothing can be gained from anyone knowing this now.

'Please give my love to them when you see them.'

'Of course I will.'

'I know you probably think we're all suburban down here, and Patsy will not want to hear. But she will. So please tell her.'

'Of course.'

As she left him, she gave a funny little grimace. Either she didn't believe in him at all, or she thought he was being diffi-cult and pretentious.

Oh, nice Mrs Er – what was her name? – he addressed her retreating back, you will never realise how I have been protect-ing you from unhappiness. Because of me, you'll be able to eat a good lunch, with your nice booming husband, and the children too, if you haven't packed them off to boarding schools. I'm presenting you with this afternoon, for leafing through the *Sunday Express*, and tidying in the garden, and taking the spaniels for a run. All this has been in my gift, and I've bestowed it upon you with all the grace I could manage, which admittedly wasn't a great deal. Yet you're offended with me: you think I'm unfriendly and superior.

Then his sister came up and told him they were leaving.

He said good-bye to half the people in the room, the ones he had spoken to, and this involved saying 'hullo' to the other half, the ones he hadn't spoken to before. Nearly at the door, he caught up with her again. She was talking to his sister.

She frowned and said to him quite crossly: 'Now please don't forget, my best love to Patsy.'

'Yes, of course,' he said. 'Of course.'